The Only One My Love

Samanthya Wyatt

Love Endures

The Only One My Love

Also by

THE BROTHERS GREYSTOKE
The Daunting Greystoke (Book 1)
Greystoke Heir Apparent (Book 2)

ONE AND ONLY COLLECTION
The Right One For Me (Book 1)
My Angel The True One (Book 2)
The Only One My Love (Book 3)

Contents

Chapter 1	1
Chapter 2	9
Chapter 3	16
Chapter 4	21
Chapter 5	28
Chapter 6	39
Chapter 7	46
Chapter 8	58
Chapter 9	67
Chapter 10	76
Chapter 11	84
Chapter 12	90
Chapter 13	95
Chapter 14	108
Chapter 15	116
Chapter 16	122

Chapter 17   132

Chapter 18   146

Chapter 19   155

Chapter 20   163

Chapter 21   177

Chapter 22   188

Chapter 23   199

Chapter 24   213

Chapter 25   221

Chapter 26   231

Chapter 27   239

Chapter 28   248

Chapter 29   257

Chapter 30   267

Chapter 31   275

Thank You   288

The Daunting Greystoke   289

Acknowledgements   290

About the Author   291

Chapter 1

New Orleans, 1825

I t was a day to try a man's soul.

Giles Heathcliff Montague Litscomb, Duke of Nethersall, wondered for the hundredth time why he'd volunteered for this venture. He had visited the Americas before, so he'd been accepting of the unexpected trip, if not excited. Perhaps boredom prodded the root of his disquiet.

His life had grown considerably dull since his spying days; years of dangerous assignments, which brought him more than satisfaction. Hell, he had lived for the thrill and risk without a care for his own safety. He'd learned a set of critical skills, managing to deliver his comrades through hell and come out alive.

Although, days of adventure were not necessarily in his past. The familiar leap of exhilaration pumped through his veins from the mere thought of a precarious situation. Only months ago, he'd gone to India in search of a sea captain who barely made it home alive. 'Twould seem danger ran in their family. Remembering his latest endeavor brought a smile to tug at the corner of his mouth. The mission had involved danger and mystery in the rescue of his best friend's bride.

Giles' brow furrowed in thought. His friend had a spitfire on his hands, but the two were well suited. The couple deserved an extended bride month—which led to his agreement in taking care of the groom's New Orleans business.

Boredom.

After the last few months, he deserved a rest. And he had retired from dangerous missions. But he could not help the yearning in his soul.

Only by chance had he found out about Hudson's auction. The young clerk from the shipping office informed him of an event where owners came from all over, displaying horseflesh. The clerk had also hinted there would be a certain gentleman in attendance with an animal of special interest.

So, here he was.

Giles found himself amazed at the number of patrons attending the auction. By the size of the crowd, either a great number of horses were to be sold, or this event marked the highlight of the New Orleans Season. With an abundance of steeds, perhaps the day would turn out not to be a waste, after all.

The shipping clerk, Joe, suggested they ride horseback, and now Giles understood why. Carriages filled the meadow. Men waited in line for stable hands to help with their mounts. Numerous horses had been tethered, helter-skelter, to trees scattered about the field. Giles waited while Joe took care of their steeds.

"Told ya."

Giles turned to Joe as he stepped next to him. "Yes, I see what you mean. Quite a crowd."

"Anybody who is anybody, and then some."

A mass of men, seemingly from all cultures, attended the auction. Some were dressed in proper suits. Some of the dandy peacocks Joe had mentioned, strutted about. Even some of the lesser class who looked as if they could not afford their next meal, let alone a mare or stallion.

"You mentioned some of the best horseflesh. After seeing this crowd, I hope you were not exaggerating."

"Naw. You won't be disappointed. Come on." Joe led him around a building and over to a fenced-in meadow. Several hastily made structures—stables of sorts—sheltered stock.

A stallion captured his gaze. A shiny coat, like black silk, now *there* was a handsome creature. A lad stood beside the beast, his hand brushing the horse's mane. Farther down, two more steeds caught his notice. A big grey and an Arabian. He needed a closer look.

"This way," Joe said.

Giles jotted a mental note of the horses' location, then followed Joe in the opposite direction.

With only a few clouds in the sky, the sun blazed hot, making him glad he wore a wide brimmed hat. A slight breeze helped keep the day pleasant, even with the smell of horse and dung swimming in the air.

"Who is that gentleman?" Giles gestured to a large man in the center of a group. Important gent, if the others vying for his attention was anything to go by.

"That's Mr. Carmichael. Owns a spread two days' ride from here. Over a thousand acres just for his horses. Some say his plantation covers ten times that. Plenty of money. Has a family. Wife, three sons, and a daughter who's a hoyden."

"A thousand acres just for his horses? Does he have a breeding farm?"

"Has a sugarcane plantation, and breeding besides. He employs some of the best trainers, too. One imperative fella has his own way of training. Some new-fangled idea he conjured up himself."

Giles gave a low whistle through his teeth.

Wonder if the chap would want to share his ideas. Or better yet, if he would be interested in a job—on the other side of the ocean.

"Is he someone I should meet?"

"Yes, sir. The very one. You might be especially interested in his private stock."

"Private stock?"

"One in particular, if you like the white Mr. Morgan got."

It would appear many knew the story of how his friend gained a magnificent white stallion while on one of his business ventures to the colonies. Seeing an owner beating his horse, Morgan had trounced the man, then gallantly relieved the cur of his animal—paying

him good money, of course.

Giles' jaw tightened. "Do not tell me he is the previous owner of Pegasus."

"Nope. Morgan scared that man out of the county. Mr. Carmichael would have loved to get his hands on Pegasus. Come on, I'll introduce ya."

Filing the information away to mull over later, Giles followed Joe over to the crowd of impressively dressed men. Giles towered most men, but the largest man in the group was just about his height, and broader in width.

Joe called to him. "Are you buying or selling this day?"

The large man turned around. Bushy dark brows shot with a hint of silver, kind brown eyes. When his gaze landed on Joe, he gave a blinding smile.

"Joseph, you old son-of-a-gun. How are you?"

"Just fine, Mr. Carmichael." Joe shook the man's hand. "Just fine. And I hope your family is well."

One brow rose in reproach. "There's no 'mister.' My name is James as you well know it."

"Yes, sir." Joe flashed a set of white, even teeth.

"My family is fine as well. Around here somewhere." James glanced over the crowd, searching, then gave a slight wave of his hand.

"James, I'd like you to meet Giles Litscomb, the Duke of Nethersall."

"Mr. Carmichael, I would rather no one knew of my title." Giles frowned briefly at Joe as a gentle reminder. "Which, by the by, means little in this land."

"I'm James." He thrust out his hand. "What shall I call you? Nethersall? Litscomb?"

"Giles will do," he said as he grasped James' hand.

"So familiar? An aristocrat of noble birth?" James shrugged. "So, you prefer an image of mundane circumstance. But, one of wealth?"

"Enough to buy some blue-blood." Giles offered a crooked smile while assessing the man.

"Very well." James slapped him on the back. "Welcome to Hudson's horse auction. The best of the best. You will find your blue-bloods here."

"I am looking forward to it."

"Giles, here, is a friend of Morgan." Joe referenced Morgan with familiarity, and not as an established lord of nobility. He spoke as though the information he gave was important. 'Twas obvious Carmichael knew exactly who Joe meant.

"So, you're a friend of the man who owns Pegasus."

Another person obviously impressed with the story. "You know Morgan Langston?"

"Everyone has heard the tale concerning the man who saved the white stallion. Called him the *Dark Devil*. But a man who does not allow another to mistreat a horse is more than all right in my book."

"Glad to hear it," Giles said with a nod.

"Well now, Giles. Since this is your first visit, allow me to be your guide. I've even brought a few of my mares for the auction."

First impressions usually rang true, and Giles prided himself as a good judge of character. There were times when his life had depended on sizing up his opponent rather quickly. His assessment of Carmichael described him as profitable, educated, with a fondness for horses, a cared-for family, and by his group of associates, he possessed moral fiber.

Carmichael led him, talking non-stop, explaining everything he thought Giles should know about the gathering—the people, the horses. Giles followed the man with an air of indifference, a single question burning uppermost in his mind—why Joe seemed to think he would be interested in *one in particular* of James Carmichael's private stock.

Alexandria brushed her hand over the horse's mane. He was a beauty. Nothing caught an admirer's eye quicker than a shiny black coat of silk. She glanced down. *And white stockings.* Her lips turned up in a smile. Only a year old, and the most stunning horse she had ever seen.

She didn't like his name. *Blackie.* How unoriginal. And with four white feet? The owner could not have appreciated this fine animal, saddling him with such a name. She would change that at once. The black tossed his head as if he agreed. She stroked her fingers down his nose, determined he would be hers. Now she just needed to find her father.

Alex hurried around the building, searching the crowd. With so many heads towering above her, it was difficult to see She darted this way and that, seeking a broad back larger than most.

Her father, tall with wide shoulders, had dressed in dark blue today. As she scoured the lot looking for a blue coat, she encountered her father's good friend.

"Mr. Barnum."

"Why hello, Alex. Fancy seeing you here today." His smile conveyed affection, and a hint of teasing.

"You know me," she said with a shrug. "I couldn't stay away."

"Never seen a girl love horses as much as you. Has something caught your fancy?" His eyes twinkled.

"Sure has." She was bouncing with excitement. She wanted that black. "I'm looking for my father. Have you seen him?"

Mr. Barnum gave a nod over his shoulder. "Last I saw, he was over by the presenter stage. No doubt getting a look at the first lot."

"Thanks." She turned to go.

"Alex?"

She pivoted on her boot and gazed up at him.

"Be sure and ride over next week to show me your new mount."

"Yes, sir." Anticipation bubbled in her chest. Her father was here to buy horses, wasn't he? She would just add Blackie to his list. She cringed at the thought of naming such a glorious mount anything that ordinary. Instantly she pondered a list of new names. Midnight, Night Fire, Black Velvet, Night Dancer—of course she would need to see him run first. If he ran as fast as she hoped, maybe Lightning.

With names for the black occupying her thoughts, she nearly slammed into the back of a rather large body. She quickly side-stepped and jerked her head up. A man scowled, then suddenly his eyes widened. The apology died on her lips. Obviously, he had thought her a boy and just realized the blundering muttonhead who bumped into him was a girl. Her lips tightened as she felt heat flame her face.

Probably never seen a girl in trousers before.

With a toss of her braid, she stepped around him.

Eagerness overcame her embarrassment when she remembered her mission. Then she glimpsed her father just ahead. A tall man stood beside him. Black hair, the same shiny hue as the horse she wanted to buy. He turned just a bit . . .

Alex stared in shock as the breath left her lungs. She stood immobile, her feet frozen to the ground.

The sun silhouetted him in profile.

The duke.

He was back.

Chapter 2

Alex studied the man of her childhood whimsies. Wide shoulders filled out his tailored coat nicely. A slim torso and hips, with thighs encased in tight fitting breeches displaying his superb backside. Hair as black as ink gleamed under the sun. Beneath the shadow of long lashes, his dark eyes sparkled. The man had to be the most beautiful . . .

Of all days. Of all places; Hudson's stock auction.

She was wearing breeches, for heavens' sake.

Her family accepted her frequent attire—well, maybe not her mother so much. And if Aunt Cornelia saw her, she'd shake her head and tut. Aunt Cornelia was the most superbly dressed woman on the earth. And she would be ashamed if she could see her niece now.

Alex slipped behind the stage and peeked around the corner for another look. Drawing back, she let out a huge breath. He seemed so much bigger. She might only have been twelve at the time, but the moment she'd set her eyes on him, she had vowed she would marry him someday. Her child fantasy grew in her mind, larger than life. She had carried him in her head and in her heart, waiting for the day her prince—or rather duke—would return.

So determined the English aristocrat would be hers, she had actually outlined a strategy to get him, not once considering his title, or that he lived on another continent. Her family had always given her what she wanted. So, in her mind, the duke was no different than anything else she craved. The thought never entered her head that once he returned to his homeland, she would never see him again.

When that point became clear, she elected a new plan. She decided that once she grew up, she would simply get on a ship and follow him to England. After all, Aunt Cornelia lived there.

During her aunt's visits, she stressed the importance of the nobility—proper protocol, proper behavior, and proper dress. Alex had soaked up every word. She understood how her duke would require a proper bride. She prayed he would not marry anyone else until she had a chance to get his attention. Blinded by her fascination with the man she had set her sights on, she'd initiated a daring endeavor—especially for a young girl.

If she were to acquire the duke's attention, she needed to learn, and she needed to practice. Kissing was wicked, but what was a girl to do? She could not let the duke think of her as a child. She must behave as a woman. And the butcher's son had been most willing to aid her.

On her last birthday, she turned eighteen. A woman. How convenient for the duke to show up at the appropriate time. Soon, she would be able to use what she had learned. She glanced down at the clothes she wore.

Breeches.

On a normal day, her attire suited her actions. What else would she wear to a horse auction? Of course, there weren't many girls around. The few who attended wore dresses, with silly parasols for blocking the sun. Alex supposed she did rather resemble a boy. And mean old Mrs. Farsberry had called her a tomboy. Something about 'connotations of rudeness and impropriety.'

Papa set her straight. Said his daughter was a spirited girl, and he had no intention of clipping her wings. The shock on the old bat's face was enough to have Alex chuckling.

Aunt Cornelia had scolded Papa. Then she took Alex shopping, purchasing some of the most amazing dresses. She supposed they were all right for special occasions, but where did she ever go to wear such finery? She spent most of her time with horses. The animals would laugh if she wore such getups to the stables, not to mention the human inhabitants on the plantation.

But the duke, he would notice her in a dress. Perhaps give a compliment. She wanted to be pretty for him. With another quick glance in his direction, Alex wished she had one of those gowns on now.

The speaker announced the final auction of the day as the last horse, and noticeably the finest, was led to the block. A solid black with no markings, unlike the previous stallions shown earlier. A magnificent blue-black with a cresty neck and powerful legs, he would be a superb breeding animal. Perfect for re-establishing Morgan's stables. Giles kept his eye on the knowledgeable handler, suspecting this could be the man Joe mentioned. He wondered if the gent would be interested in accompanying the horse after the sale. An experienced trainer, and one with the patience this man obviously possessed, was worth his weight in gold.

With the first bid, Giles turned to see who made the offer. Another man spoke, and another. The price rose quickly. Giles waited until the bidding dwindled down between two people. Being a good judge of character, he studied each man. One dark, with a wide-brimmed hat shadowing his eyes. By the look of him, a coarse man. Hard taskmaster.

Giles glanced to the other man. An impeccably dressed gent with a beauty clinging to his side. He obviously wanted to impress the woman on his arm. Neither man deserved such a creature. *Time to put an end to this.*

"I will double the last offer," he called out in a deep voice.

All heads turned to him. Quiet slashed the crowd. Giles' eyes connected with the auctioneer, and never blinked. Finally, the man found his voice. "Going once! Twice! Sold!" Only when he slammed the hammer down on the podium, did Giles release his gaze.

Murmurs echoed through the mass of assembled bodies.

"Congratulations." James stepped closer. "Well done."

"Thank you. I'm sure Morgan will be pleased to have the stallion for his stables."

"More than pleased, I should say." His grin beamed from ear to ear as he shook Giles' hand.

Glancing over James' shoulder, the man with the wide brim hat gave a harsh glare. With an annoyed jerk, he pivoted and turned away. His angry strides assured Giles he'd done the right thing in securing the black stallion.

"You gave us some show," Joe said.

"Show?"

"We've had biddin' wars here, but the one stomping off over there is a mite sore. He's used to getting his way. He thought he won the highest bid 'till you entered the game. Threw him off, 'cause he doesn't know you."

"I merely purchased a horse." Giles shrugged. Nothing out of the ordinary had occurred.

Joe laughed. "Most people expected a high price for Abram's stallion. But the amount was already exorbitant before you added your voice."

"He's right," James added. "But then, you have bigger pockets."

Yes, he supposed he did go a bit high. But he cared not for dickering. If he wanted something, he got it. Morgan would approve.

Several more patrons offered congratulations and clapped Giles on the back as though he belonged in their group. They made him feel comfortable, but in the back of his mind, the harsh look from the dark man lingered. He shrugged it off as unnecessary awareness from his spying days.

"Pap." A young man with similar features and the same build strode up to James.

"Giles, this is my son, Ben."

"A pleasure to meet you, Ben."

"Thank you. Same to you, sir."

Giles appreciated a boy raised with manners.

"I see you added to your stock today." A gentleman spoke from the other side of James.

"Hello, Henry." The two men shook hands. "This is Giles." Then turning toward him, "And this is Henry Barnum."

"Mr. Barnum," Giles nodded.

"Just Henry. Glad to meet you, Giles. Did you bring any horses with you today?"

"No. I came here to buy."

"Well, you got the best of the lot. That stallion is a handful. Tore down Hudson's fence when they tried to put him in the paddock."

"I think I will go take a closer look at him." Giles glanced to the big black pawing the ground. "Do you know anything about the trainer?"

"Has a way with the horse. Only man who could get close enough to calm him down."

"Do you suppose the man would be interested in continuing their relationship?"

"Well, now." Henry rubbed the stubble on his jaw. "Think he just might entertain such an idea."

"Before you rush off, I'd like to invite you to my spread," James said. "Won't take no for an answer. Come to my home in a day or two, after you get your business settled. Sarah will appreciate a visit from an Englishman. My sister, Cornelia, lives in England and just happens to be visiting us." James hooked his thumbs on the lapels of his coat. "Needless to say, her visits aren't as frequent as we'd like. My daughter worships her. Cornelia fills her head with parties and balls and such. The girl will probably beleaguer your brain with questions." He paused and searched the surroundings. "She's around here somewhere."

"Where else would she be, Pap? More 'n likely she's latched on to the black with the white stocking feet you got her."

"Alex nearly ran me over looking for you before the auction. Knew one had caught her eye." Henry tilted his head as he gave a wink. "Also, knew you would get it for her."

"Spoiled. That's what she is," Ben said.

"He's not the only horse I bought today." James leveled a glower on his son.

"Right, Pap." Ben shuffled his feet. "I better go help Kit."

James laughed. "Boy spoils the girl as much as I do."

"Who's Kit?" Giles asked.

"My oldest, Christopher. Benjamin is the middle boy, and Samuel is the youngest. A number of years went by before Sarah gave me a girl. Alexandria has had her brothers wrapped around her little finger since the day she was born."

Ahh. Must be the hoyden Joe mentioned.

"Got something on my property that might interest you." James hooked his fingers in the top of his belt.

Ah, he wondered if this might be what Joe had been referring to. Intrigued, Giles gave Carmichael his full attention. "What, pray tell, would that be?"

"You do have an eye for horseflesh. I've got an animal I think you might want to see."

Chapter 3

An orange glow filtered in Alex's bedroom window as the sun topped the towering oaks. She threw back the covers and greeted the day with a smile. Mornings were the best. The beginning of a new day. And this morning, more special, because today she would confront the duke. A thrill warmed her throughout.

Her steps grew lighter as she skipped across the room. Happiness filled her heart. A slight twinge of nerves seeped in, but she ignored them. She had waited eons. Ever since she'd seen him six years ago. Plenty of time for her to build him up in her head. Seeing him at the auction, all she could do was gape. Her breath had caught at the sight of him. She could not believe her eyes. It was truly him. Bigger than life. Swooning was not in her nature, but her stomach had turned upside down.

The duke had grown more handsome. As if one could improve on perfection. Tall with dark hair and sparkling eyes. Kind eyes. Eyes that had captured her soul at the age of twelve.

He was back. She had not been able to face him at the auction. She had needed time to accept his presence. Now, there was no more time to waste.

Quickly, she changed her clothes. Since Mama and Aunt Cornelia would not be about this early, she donned her favorite breeches for her morning ride. On her new black.

With such spirit, he deserved a great name. She really must decide. Her feet took wings as she flew across the corridor, down the steps, and nearly ran into Cook.

"Slow down now, Missy." Phebe flapped her apron as Alex flew past.

"Can't. Papa bought me a new stallion." She heard the woman chuckle just before the door slammed behind her. Alex's feet barely touched the ground. She ran for the stables and saw Horace swing one door wide. The stable master normally rose before the sun.

"Mornin' to you, Alex."

"Morning, Horace. How's the black?"

"Right where I left him. Not settling too well to his new place. Maybe you can calm him a bit."

Alex grabbed a carrot from the barrel just inside the doorway, and stuck an apple in her pocket for later.

The black tossed his head, and his nostrils flared. Alex stepped closer. "Hey, Beauty. No one is going to hurt you. I'm your new owner." She kept her tone light and calm, hoping to soothe the beast. "I'm sure glad of that fact. And soon I hope you will be, too."

The black snorted.

"Guess what I've got." She slowly lifted the carrot into view.

He pawed one hoof in the dirt.

"None of that now. If you're good, I have a surprise in my pocket." Alex gave a slight wave of her hand, tempting the animal with the carrot.

Not too fast.

Not too sudden.

Come on, boy.

Blackie gave another nod of his head.

"I haven't picked a name yet. Got lots of possibilities. But you deserve something special. Why don't you come on over here ..."

She held her breath.

The horse took one step, shook his head and then plodded forward.

Happiness pierced her when he took the carrot between his teeth. She crossed her arms and leaned on the wooden gate. "Thatta boy. We are going to be good friends. I just know it."

She placed her hand out, palm up. He came closer, probably looking for another treat. She took a piece of sugar out of her pocket with her other hand and carefully held it under his nose. He eagerly slurped up the chunk. She patted him on the side of his snout.

"Well, I'll be." Horace stepped up behind her. "That's the quietest that animal's been since your pa brought him home."

"New surroundings."

"Yep. Your pa didn't want to put him in the pasture just yet. Figured he might jump the fence. Got to get him familiar with knowing this is his home now."

Alex caressed the black's nose, thrilled that he accepted her. "I'd be heartbroken if he took off."

"You got a name picked out for him, yet?"

"Working on it. It has to be special. Just like him."

"Black Devil comes to mind. That stallion is spirited, Miss Alex. And he's over sixteen hands. You best be careful."

"Now, Horace. You know there's not a horse I can't ride."

"Before now, I would have agreed. I'm just saying to watch yourself. He's still a baby."

"He's a year old. And perfect timing to be introduced into a new family."

"For the price your papa paid, I hope the animal proves he's worth every penny."

"He's worth it to me." She smiled with satisfaction, glad the horse belonged to her.

The sun rode high when Alex decided the black had accepted her for a friend. Yearlings were full of energy, quite unpredictable, and this one was no exception. It was obvious he'd already had some training, and Blacky took to her exceptionally well.

She really needed to decide on a name. Soon.

She led the black by the reins to the corral fence. He nudged her shoulder, looking for another sugar. She chuckled.

"Let's see how you take to the saddle. Then you will get your reward." But he was so darned endearing, the way his nose rubbed her shirt. She relented. "All right. Just one."

His big pink tongue lapped up the sugar.

"Sure is a beaut."

Turning, Alex saw her brother, Ben. Pride added a bounce to her step.

When he hoisted the saddle from the fence rail, the stallion reared back. Ben lowered the saddle to the ground.

"Mite skittish, ain't he?"

"He likes *me*," she said as she calmed the black.

"Guess he's not too smart."

She stuck out her tongue. "Smart enough to know he should be wary of you."

"Then saddle your own horse."

"I planned to."

Ben ignored her. "Easy fella," he said as he approached. "I'll bet she's been feeding you sugar. Can't have too much of that.

Now be a good boy, and come here." He lifted his hand, knuckle side up.

The stallion tossed his head at first. He lifted one foot and clomped once, twice. Ben held his arm still. The black wavered.

"There you go. Smell me. I'm one of the good guys."

"Quit trying to steal my horse."

Ben chuckled. "He's a tall one." Ben hefted the saddle again, slower this time. Alex rubbed the horse's shiny nose while Ben tossed the saddle onto his back. "You might want to mount from the rail."

"You just tighten the girth. I know how to get on a horse."

Once done, Ben held the bridle while Alex grabbed the saddle horn and leaped. With a smooth move she'd mastered a million times, she landed in the saddle. The black jerked loose from Ben and pranced, his feet stomping the ground. Before Ben could jump forward, Alex had the animal under control and allowed him to dance about.

Restless energy oozed from every pore of the stallion's proud lines. He danced, eager to be off. At her brother's anxious look, Alex called, "He needs to run, Ben."

She flicked the reins. Clods of turf flew about as the steed raced across the meadow. The wind in her hair, she gave the black free rein.

As soon as they cleared the trees, she leaned over the stallion's back. He needed no urging. Hooves thundered, moving in a blur of force. Strength fueled his power, energy and excitement oozed from the beast into her. A thrill like no other filled her soul.

Never had she felt so free.

Chapter 4

Giles whistled an English ballad as he cantered down the lane paralleling the river. Astride Gent, one of his recent purchases, he congratulated himself on finding such a fine animal and keeping this one for himself.

The steed's prior owner declared the horse behaved like a true gentleman, thus the animal's name, short for Gentlemen's Integrity. The horse was educated, well-mannered, powerful, yet well controlled. Those attributes won over Giles' decision to purchase the gelding for himself. He had accumulated a good number of stock for Morgan's breeding stables. After this visit to Carmichael's plantation, Giles should be ready to set sail for England.

Stepping lively, Gent seemed eager for a run. Giles decided to cut through a group of trees, and discern the golden beast's proficient speed.

A shiny black stallion bolted from the forest, catching Giles off guard. It took him only a second to recover his surprise and recognize Carmichael's black from the auction. A lad from the plantation must have taken the horse for a ride, and now the stallion raced out of control. Fearing for the boy's safety, Giles sent the huge thoroughbred thundering after him.

Being an excellent rider, Giles pressed forward, his body one with his new horse. The black demon raced like the wind. Giles kicked his heels into Gent's sides. Lying low, he swayed with his steed's pounding rhythm.

A cloud of dust trailed behind the horse and rider he chased. A wail echoed along the trees, sounding strangely like laughter. Giles dismissed the ludicrous idea. The boy must be scared half out of his mind. He could be killed. Giles urged Gent faster.

A phenomenal creature, the black's whizzing hooves blurred a hazy motion as if his feet never touched earth. The stallion dashed across the meadow, but Giles was gaining ground.

Almost.

Just a bit closer . . .

He held one arm in readiness. Coming abreast he snatched the boy from the stallion's back and plopped the squirming body onto his lap.

The lad fought him. *What the devil?*

"Calm down, you little rapscallion."

Giles brought his horse to a slow canter, then stopped. The lad continued to struggle. Suddenly he felt curves which did not belong on a lad.

"Let me go!"

The boy—or was it a *girl*—continued to squirm. Giles let go and the youngster landed on the ground. Her cap fell off and masses of hair tumbled down in long, brilliant, golden waves, catching the sun's glint just right.

His eyes examined the girl's furious face.

"What do you think you're doing?" A raging spitfire full of venom, yelled at him as she scrambled from the ground. "He'll run away!"

"You should not be on a horse you cannot control," he growled.

Her hands fisted and her cheeks reddened with anger. "I know how to ride a horse."

"It did not appear that way to me. The horse looked spooked. I thought you needed my help."

"*Help?* You let my horse get away."

Did the urchin work for Carmichael? Who in God's name would allow their daughter to run around dressed in boys' clothing, acting like a wild heathen?

"I rescued you." His voice rumbled with irritation.

"I did not need rescuing." She stepped closer and boldly stared into his eyes, clearly revealing her ire. Blue irises blazed, and he could not ever remember a female upset with him. "I will have you know I can ride a horse better than any man."

He couldn't help it. A bark of laughter burst from his throat. Then he shifted in the saddle and narrowed his eyes with an accusing glare. "Were you stealing that horse?"

"Of course not," she choked. "He belongs to me."

"You?" He used a knuckle to shove his hat a bit higher. "I beg your pardon, I believe Mr. Carmichael just bought that very horse at auction."

"And you may very well have just cost him a stallion." She turned to gaze at the retreating horse. "He's in unfamiliar surroundings. He doesn't yet know this is his home."

Home?

The sadness in her voice sent a ping to his gut. He would never disappoint a woman. Err, female. Just how old was this urchin?

Leaving the inn at sunup, Giles had proceeded to Carmichael's plantation. The directions were simple enough, and the notable landmark a mile or so back suggested he neared his destination.

"We are on Carmichael land?"

"Yes." She shielded her eyes as her gaze met his.

The girl seemed a bit uneasy. Whether she stole the horse or not, he would acquire her identity and gain the connection she claimed to Carmichael. If he were to acquire the answers he sought, some of his ducal charm might be called for.

He climbed down from his horse to be on equal footing. "Forgive me. Mr. Carmichael invited me to his plantation. My name is Giles Litscomb." He removed his hat and gave a slight bow. A female was a female, whatever the clothing, and his aristocratic heritage demanded he behave in a gentlemanly fashion.

The chit blushed. "I . . . I know who you are."

"You do?" he asked in a bored voice, but his curiosity prickled.

"I'm Alex. That is, Alexandria."

He waited, giving her the opportunity to explain her connection. When she offered no further clarification, he prodded.

"And?"

"James Carmichael is my father."

Well, well, well. That explains a lot.

So, this was the hoyden? He remembered Joe saying the youngest Carmichael *was* a girl. He had a devil of a time hiding his surprise. Alex? Short for Alexandria. A smile tugged at one corner of his mouth.

"Miss Carmichael. It is my pleasure to meet you. I must apologize for my earlier handling of your person. My honor as a gentleman demands I beg your forgiveness." Abruptly, he recalled firm young breasts. He cleared his throat. "Although, for the sake of uprightness, and clearing any misunderstanding in the urgent decision making of what appeared to be a critical situation, I thought you needed help. I was completely unaware of your . . . umm . . ."

Seeing her face flame anew, he had best steer clear of her female—or childlike—significance. "Your . . . riding capabilities."

"Oh." Air puffed from her cheeks. Her gaze fastened on Gent. "Where did you get this fella?"

"I acquired him at Hudson's auction." He watched as, palm up, she waited for the golden giant to draw near.

"Hey, fella. Haven't see you around here before." The horse nudged Alex's shirt pocket. A tinkling giggle floated on the light breeze. She shoved her hair over one shoulder, drawing Giles' attention to her female attributes. Definitely a woman. The greedy horse nuzzled one blossoming breast, which again, caused immediate speculation on the age of the girl.

Gentleman, my arse. Upon further deliberation, he conjectured his new steed's real name was most likely 'Knave.'

"What have you got tucked away in your pocket?" His voice came out a bit more gruff than intended.

"Sugar."

"His previous owner did not tell me Gent had an uncontrollable sweet tooth."

"I have an apple in my other pocket."

He quickly shifted his gaze to her other breast, expecting to see a huge bump on top of an already significant bosom. No apple there. Which damned pocket—?

She reached closer to her waist, procuring the red fruit.

"More to my liking." He gave a slight sigh.

"You want the apple?"

"No. I would rather Gent not have the sugar."

"Gent, huh?" She ran her hand over the horse's nose. "My brothers don't like me giving sugar to the horses, either."

"I take it you do so without their knowing."

"Blackie..." she began, then grimaced. "The black stallion. I wanted to make quick friends with him."

"That black does not need any added stimulus. He is spirited enough, and from what I have seen, needs nothing to exhort more speed."

"I'm surprised you caught me, though Gent's speed is remarkable." Her hand slid from the horse's nose and paused on his neck. "Will you help me find Blackie?" A distasteful *moue* turned down the corners of her mouth.

"For one who owns such a striking animal, you cringe when you say his name"

"I hate his name. He deserves one better."

Giles lifted his shoulder in a shrug. "Then give him one."

The delightful expression springing to her face speared his gut. An urchin, but a beautiful one.

"You agree? I've thought of several, but I haven't decided."

"You will find one which suits him just right. For now, I suppose I should take you home. If Bla . . . the black goes to the stables without you, your family will be concerned for your safety."

"Ben was in the paddock when I left. He expects me to take care of myself."

"An animal such as this stallion, new to your stables, should be enough to cause alarm. Even if your brother is completely aware of your riding skills, there is always a possibility of an accident."

"How do you know Ben is my brother?"

"I met your family at the auction. Your father and your brothers. I garnered an idea of your love for horses from them. And, I saw your father purchase the black."

"You bought the last sale of the day. Also, a black stallion. Why aren't you riding him?"

Giles wondered how she knew that. He tucked the thought away to ponder on later. "He needs a bit more gentling."

"If the stallion is too much for you, bring him to our plantation. I'll show you how to *gentle* a horse."

The cheeky minx. Too young to realize her taunt could be considered coquettish. Shrugging, he concluded her lightheartedness stemmed from her age. How old was the chit anyway? Not as young as he first expected. She was quite lovely. Filled out a pair of breeches rather nicely. But he was not here to dally. And certainly not with Carmichael's daughter.

While holding the reins to Gent, he put one foot in the stirrup and swung into the saddle. Staring at Alex from this height, a smile threatened. No sense asking if the girl rode astride. He held a hand out to her and she grabbed hold. He hefted her at the same time she jumped, and she landed smack in back of him.

With no urging, she snuggled against him and slid both arms around his middle.

So much for his earlier assessment.

It was going to be a long ride.

Chapter 5

Alex always looked forward to Aunt Cornelia's visits. Being a lady of English nobility, Cornelia accepted her brother's American ways, but the one thing she insisted on while residing in James' American home was her usual habit of afternoon tea. Mama, most happy to acquiesce her husband's sister's wishes, set forth a light repast of tea and crisp little cakes, which became a daily occurrence.

On this very afternoon, unaware of the duke's arrival, Cornelia and Mama settled in the parlor for their tea. While Papa greeted the duke, Alex hurried upstairs and dressed in a gown more becoming of a female. As she descended the stairs, she met a kitchen maid with a steaming pot and a tray of freshly baked biscuits.

Ahhh. Just in time.

Before she stepped through the doorway of the drawing room, she glanced inside. *Only mama and Aunt Cornelia.* Cornelia glanced up as Alex entered, her blue taffeta skirts rustling. She supposed the duke was most likely somewhere with her father.

"Alexandria," Aunt Cornelia cooed. "You look lovely, my dear."

Alex traipsed across the room and plopped in the chair directly across from her aunt.

"We will need to work on that."

"On what?"

"Harrumph. Every tongue in London would be wagging if you walked about like a man intent on—"

"Dearest, please," Mama interrupted. "I think Alex hears more than she should on the matter of society and English ways. She isn't familiar with certain . . . particulars."

It was bad enough Aunt Cornelia pointed out her lack of grace, but now mama added to her embarrassment by speaking as if she still belonged in the schoolroom.

Cornelia patted her strawberry blond tresses streaked with grey. Mama poured tea from the steaming pot, and then took one of the tiny cakes. Alex could pick up three or four with one hand. She grabbed a biscuit and stuffed the thing into her mouth.

Alex watched as Cornelia picked up a delicate China cup. Immediately her aunt's smallest finger lifted into the air as if aiming an arrow.

Guess all the ladies in London drink their tea with such gestures.

Being well versed in etiquette and proper decorum, Cornelia often regaled stories from England. Alex had hung on every word, seeing the glittering city of London and the fashionable aristocracy through her aunt's eyes. At the moment, Cornelia divulged a buzzing tale of a nobleman hosting a ball presenting his daughter into society.

"Of course, I gave her mama the name of my *modiste* to design the girl's coming out gowns. The poor chit had to tie her stays so tight; she had no bosom to speak of."

Not so of Aunt Cornelia. Her breasts were so big, Alex would be jealous if she weren't afraid she would tip over from the added weight.

"Even so," her aunt continued, "she had a lot of admirers. Dandies had their sights set on a prize. After all, her papa was a marquis."

Which must be someone very important, as on earlier visits her aunt had explained the lineage of the aristocracy. And Alex knew a duke was well up in the social standing on the elitist hierarchy. But how could she introduce a particular duke into their conversation?

"What's a dandy?" Alex asked.

"A gallant man who places particular importance upon his physical appearance, and considerable emphasis on his image. Giving airs, self-import. His demeanor suggests refined language, and leisurely hobbies, often imitating an aristocratic lifestyle despite coming from a middle-class background. Really, he is no more than a clothes-wearing man."

"Don't all men wear clothes?"

"Alex, dear girl." Cornelia placed her tea cup on the saucer with a dainty click. "Picture in your mind a peacock strutting about the yard with his colorful tail-feathers spread wide. That is a Dandy."

The men Alex knew only dressed in their Sunday finest when going to church or some special event. Even Papa wore what he called his work clothes every other day, mostly brown, and plenty dirty by suppertime. She couldn't imagine her brothers in anything resembling 'Dandy clothes.' As for strutting? Sam strode around in front of girls like a rooster sometimes.

Alex licked crumbs off her fingers. "Mama, Papa has a guest."

"A guest? Do you know who?"

"The man he met at Hudson's auction. He's here." Since no one mentioned his identity, Alex wouldn't let on like she knew he was a duke.

"Now?" Mama banged her cup in its saucer and jumped from her seat. "Why didn't you say so? I must make sure everything is in readiness." With a whirl of her skirts, she hurried from the room.

Alex grabbed the last two cakes. She tucked her feet beneath her on the sofa.

"Are you quite comfortable, dear?" Aunt Cornelia raised a brow and peered down her nose.

"Oh yes, very," she mumbled with her mouth full of the sugary morsels.

"Alexandria. A lady does not speak with food in her mouth. And where are your shoes? A lady does not prop her feet upon the sofa." Aunt Cornelia shook her head.

"Yes ma'am." Alex sat up straight and arranged the ruffles of her dress.

"That's better."

"Will you tell me more? You were speaking of dandies."

"Very well. Let's see, now. Two such men used a sonnet as they fought over who would win a certain debutante's heart. Each gentleman wrote an ode to pledge his eternal love."

"An ode?"

Cornelia spread one hand over her large bosom and held the other aloft. "Your eyes are like blue bonnets. Your lips like cherries." She waved her extended hand dismissively. "Some such drivel."

Alex giggled. "Who won?"

"They were still putting pen to paper when I sailed."

Alex rose from the settee, cradled her arms, and pretended the duke held her. Barefoot, she danced and twirled on the braided rug. "How do I look, Aunt Cornelia?"

"Pucker your lips like you have just eaten a sour lemon and you will look perfect, my dear."

Alex fell to the carpet in a peal of laughter.

"Oh my child, it would not do at all for a lady to crumple to the floor. Necklines are cut so low, a young maiden's bosom is in danger of toppling right out of the top of her gown."

An image popped into Alex's mind, causing her eyes to bulge. She glanced down at her own gown. With nothing to enhance her bosom, she supposed her breasts were adequate. But she refused to wear a contraption that squished the breath out of her. It was bad enough she had to give up her breeches. Still, she needed Aunt Cornelia's advice on how to dress if she were to win her duke.

"Fashion dictates what a lady should wear. And the *ton* adheres to fashion." Aunt Cornelia took a deep breath for emphasis. "It is a wonder any man could hold his gaze above a lady's neck with so much flesh exposed."

"I wish I could go to such parties and balls. See the elegant gowns, and watch the ladies dancing on a handsome man's arm."

"Well dear, you are all of eighteen now. I should think your papa would allow you to journey home with me." Cornelia clapped her hands as if confirming a decision. "Actually, I think that is a fine idea. I shall ask him."

How long would the duke visit America? Alex mentally calculated the length of her aunt's visit to compare.

"Alex." Her aunt's tone suggested she had called her name more than once.

"Yes, Aunt Cornelia?"

"I asked if you were sure." Aunt Cornelia looked down her long nose, staring into Alex's eyes. "You would be away from your mama and papa a long time."

Her brain fogged and her pulse sped up. She would have her duke, or follow him to England.

"Yes, I'm sure. You must convince Mama and Papa. But we have time, don't we? You only just arrived. You will be here for weeks yet."

Time enough for her to pursue the duke.

The Carmichael family observed many of the English customs, such as dressing for dinner. Whether due to James' sister visiting from England, Giles didn't know. Or perhaps this was a normal occurrence in the home. Thankful he'd packed a more formal suit of clothes, he gave a patrician smile and studied the group before him. Expecting a *'haute' dame,'* Cornelia had instead been surprisingly pleasant, and likable. Once she discovered his title, she demanded the others address him with proper respect. Discomforting, since he had hoped to present a lower profile.

But James had imparted the truth to his wife, and of course she passed the knowledge on to his British sister. If the woman acquainted herself with the upper crust of the *ton*, of course she recognized his name. So, he gave the appropriate nod and resumed the role expected in the drawing room. How quickly, and easily, he slipped in and out of character.

He never thought his life would change from the angry lad who rebelled against his father, to accepting the responsibilities that came with being a duke. It was expected. Had been drilled into him since birth, apprising him of his responsibilities, knowing no matter how much he hated his father, he would one day end up taking the man's place. Of course, he had rebelled. He fought being forced. Not his place in the aristocracy, but the cold, uncaring man who was his father. Sometimes he wondered if the man truly did have blue blood—for there was no way he had any warmth flowing in his veins.

For several years Giles had lived for thrill and risk, without a care for his own safety.

Yes, he'd done his job, with vengeful abandon. And made a lifelong friend in the bargain.

Morgan.

Another lost soul bent on destruction who was set for his own design of dark vengeance. Maybe they had saved each other. Who knew? When his good friend returned home to accept his title as an earl, Giles could do no less than accept the life that had been prearranged for him since birth.

No one would associate his past transgressions with the man he was today. Mrs. Cornelia Hargrave would develop apoplexy if she were to find the duke anything resembling a scandalous villain.

Giles redirected his thoughts, noting Carmichael's sons. The two younger brothers strolled in, Ben giving Sam a slap on the back as he laughed. The youngest boy's ears burned with indignation. A house filled with love. An experience unknown to him. The only member of the family missing was the urchin.

James pulled his fob out of his pocket. "Where is that girl?"

Cornelia lifted a gloved hand over her mouth and gave a lady-like, "Uh-hm."

"What is it, Cornelia?"

"A young lady needs time to make a respectable appearance."

"She's been at it long enough. While you're giving my daughter instruction on proper etiquette, you can educate the girl on how to tell time."

"James, please." Mrs. Carmichael twisted her hands in slight discomfort. "We have guests."

Giles was only an outsider. He did not want his bloody title to stress the woman, or designate ceremonial goings-on other than her normal evenings.

"Our guests are hungry, too." James' boots echoed as he stomped into the foyer. He went to the bottom of the stairs, glanced up and came to a sudden stop.

Lounging to the side of the entryway, Giles had a good view. Alex stood at the top of the stairs in a gown with all the alluring qualities of a woman. His eyes nearly popped out of their sockets.

What a transformation. The lovely vision was enough to put a hitch in his breathing.

As Alex descended the stairs, her gaze remained on her father. The man's face expressed surprise. Surely, he had seen his daughter in a dress before, had he not? When she reached the bottom of the staircase she turned, and locked her eyes with his. A coy smile curved her lips while that small chin of hers hinted to willfulness.

The chit had been handed everything on a silver platter, probably from the day she'd been born. One corner of his mouth lifted at the admirable change from the girl he'd caught wearing lad's breeches.

Giles studied her features. High cheekbones, full lips, and striking molasses eyes. Silver combs pinned strands of her hair, swirled high on the sides of her head, in an intricately coiled coiffure. Wisps clung softly along her temples with a few curls hanging in front of her delicate ears. A burnished gold chain around her throat held a chocolate jewel. Golden flecks glistened, matching the shimmering sparkles in her striking eyes.

She wore a light blue creation. The gown covered her shoulders, yet exposed a good amount of creamy skin. The lines of her slender, graceful neck drew his gaze lower to the jewel resting on a swell of cleavage . . .

Giles' fist covered his mouth as he cleared his throat.

Not only must he submit to Alex's beauty, but he had to keep in mind the girl was an adolescent.

"Lo and behold, Alex. Is that you?" Sam's eyes bulged and his mouth hung open.

"That's not Alex," Ben said. "That's a girl."

"Can't be her," Sam sputtered. "Alex is a child."

Fire flashed in her eyes and her cheeks burned red. If the girl's complexion was any indication of her thoughts, murdering her brothers topped the list.

"Open your eyes, Brother. Appears she is no longer a child." Kit leaned an elbow on the mantle and crossed a booted foot over the other.

"My God. The hoyden has gone and grown into a woman." Sam adopted an air of disbelief.

"When in hell did that happen?" Ben shouted.

"Boys, I will remind you of your manners, and curb your tongues in your mother's presence," James warned.

In unison, all three mumbled their apologies.

"You look lovely, Alexandria." Cornelia delivered a glare to the outspoken brothers.

"Why, just today she paraded around in boys' breeches," Sam blurted.

"I did not *parade*," Alex huffed. "Papa. Can't you do something?"

"Stop. You are embarrassing your sister." Mrs. Carmichael addressed her sons in a caring tone.

Alex stuck out her tongue.

A smile curled at the corner of Giles' lips. Nothing like this had captured his interest in months.

"After all, you boys have allowed her to hang on your coat-tails," her mother continued. Obviously, she had not seen the girl's rash gesture.

"Mama, surely you don't think I had a hand in Alex's untamed ways." Kit's comical expression displayed a poor attempt at appearing outraged.

James quickly interrupted. "Boys, I suggest you mind your conduct if you want to join us for dinner."

All three straightened as if they'd had a good kick in the arse.

Truly enjoying the scene, yet feeling the need to come to her rescue, Giles stepped forward. "Miss Carmichael." He took her hand and pressed his lips in the vicinity of her knuckles. "May I say you are exceedingly captivating this evening."

Which was an understatement. He was not sure what he had expected, but the young *lad* wearing a gown—a very form fitting one that had caused him to linger with a second look—was definitely not it.

Her mouth formed an 'O' as she stared at her hand. He had not yet let go. Her gaze lifted to his, and she must have noticed the glint in his stare, for her eyes widened and her brow furrowed in deliberation. Suddenly, she straightened her spine, which in turn thrust out her chest.

Giles appreciated a woman that was well endowed as much as any man. Glancing at those uplifted breasts, he had difficulty remembering this young woman—who obviously did not know how to flirt—was still in an early stage of her life.

"Thank you."

Good God. Was she about to curtsy?

She dipped and stumbled. He grabbed her hand, placing it on his arm, and steadied her.

A flush flamed her face.

He tilted his head slightly, leaning close for her ears alone. "It takes more than a dress to be a lady."

Her lips stretched tight as if she was about to hurl an oath.

Cornelia, as befitting as any matron of the *ton*, began issuing instructions as though she were in a grand English home. "Kit. You will escort Alexandria to the dining room. James, Sarah..."

Giles offered his arm. "Mrs. Hargrave. If you will allow me."

"Thank you, Your Grace." The matron beamed as if he had given her the moon. Giles wondered how long he would have to endure Cornelia's insistence on being addressed properly as his duke's entitlement. Two steps behind him, he heard Alex's brothers mumbling.

"Face the music, brothers," Kit said.

"What?"

"Thanks to the two of you, we are being served humble pie."

Chapter 6

Carmichael took the seat at the head of the elegantly set table while his wife sat at the other end. Kit, Sam, and Alex proceeded around to the opposite side.

"Please, Your Grace. You will sit here." Cornelia gestured with a nod.

Taking her hand from where it rested on his sleeve, Giles helped her to sit, then took the chair next to her, directly across from Alex.

He noticed James and Sarah Carmichael displayed a mutual respect for one another, a shared affection. In contrast and to the outside observer, Giles' parents were excessively handsome people gifted in commerce and conversation. Yet they never indulged in demonstrations of sentiment or warmth. Behind closed doors, the two shared no more than a dwelling. It was a wonder he had been born. But then, he supposed their cold co-existence had not always been that way. And a dukedom must have an heir.

"Our cook has excelled this evening in honor of your presence." Sarah beamed with pride. "She has prepared roast pigeon, a kettle of fish, mince pies, sweet potato pudding, and syllabub with cocoa beans in a frothy dessert."

"Sounds delicious. I shall be sure to thank her personally." Giles bestowed a smile to his hostess.

Through the first and second courses, Cornelia tried to keep generating interest on topics of England and his nobility. He had no desire to embellish on his private life, and steered her in other directions, all the while keeping up with the conversation and allowing his mind to drift to Alex. He darted short glances to better note her sparkling brown eyes, her high cheekbones, her sun-glistened hair.

When Alex smiled favorably at him, Giles let his gaze linger on her full lips. With his strength of mind in diplomatic affairs and daring escapades, it astounded him that this bit of fluff disturbed him.

He held her gaze for long moments before Ben's voice shook him free.

"Found something interesting today, Papa."

"I'd say," Sam added with a mouth full of food.

With a slight shake of her head, Sarah gave a look of reproach to her son.

"Pardon, Mama."

"Sam and I rode out on the north meadow." Ben leaned back in his chair, sending glances between Alex and his father.

"What was so interesting out there?" James stabbed a piece of meat with his fork.

"Well, we found something. Just wandering around on our land."

"Yeah, Pap. Just grazing in the grass." Sam attempted innocence, but his grin suggested tomfoolery. Same with Ben. The two were leading up to mischief. Being a curious sort, Giles' ears perked up with interest.

"An animal?" James asked.

"Yep. And this particular animal belonged to someone," Ben answered.

"Yeah," Sam chortled.

"Well, what was it?" James raised a brow as though he tired of the game.

"A stallion."

"Black."

"Alone."

"With no rider."

Back and forth, taking turns, one brother started a sentence and the other one finished it. Giles swallowed a chuckle.

"Had a saddle, though."

Of the three, Ben gave the impression of being the most outspoken. By his smug countenance and flamboyant gestures, he took great delight in teasing his sister. Alex shot him a spiteful look. Any moment Giles expected her to explode. With his long legs in close proximity, he only hoped he did not receive a kick meant for her brother.

Sam continued, "Can't imagine why anyone would let a shiny black wander off like that."

All eyes turned to Alex.

"What's this?" James asked, his brow furrowed. "Surely this is not the same horse I purchased for Alex from Hudson's."

"Papa, I can explain," Alex sputtered.

"We figure the black threw her," Sam said with glee.

"He did not!" Alex shrieked.

Sarah gasped. "Alex, are you all right?"

"Mama, I did not—"

"He's a big one, Pap. I think you should give him to me." Kit joined into the fray.

"Now just a minute. That's *my* horse."

"Which, evidently, you cannot handle."

Alex glared at her brother. Giles held back a chuckle.

"Young lady, I am waiting for an explanation." James' gruff voice rang with chastisement.

Alex jumped up and pointed a finger directly at Giles. "It's his fault!"

Silence filled the room.

Cornelia and Sarah looked like they were about to have apoplexy. Kit grinned in amusement. Sam's mouth hung open, and Ben looked incredulous.

"Alex," James said in a low voice with a hint of embarrassment. "Sit down."

Glances swung from Alex to Giles. After a gasp or two, silence hung heavy in the room. He might as well offer some sort of clarification. "I believe I should intervene." He folded his napkin and casually placed it beside his plate.

"Giles, please forgive my daughter."

"Papa . . ."

A glare from her father cut off anything else Alex wanted to say. She dropped her head and slowly slid back onto her chair.

"Allow me to enlighten you." He studied each face at the table before speaking. "I was having a leisurely ride on my new steed. Following your directions," he nodded to James, "at the appropriate landmark, I rode into a meadow bordered by a group of oaks. A black stallion bolted from the tree line. Immediately, I recognized the black you purchased from the auction. At first, I felt admiration. I was pleased to see such a fine animal race across the open field. But, then, it dawned on me the horse was out of control, and the lad might be in trouble."

He glanced at Alex. She fumed, tight-lipped and stiff-jawed. Angry eyes glared back at him.

"I had no idea your daughter was the rider on that horse. Fearing for the lad's safety, I set off after him—uh, her."

A choked laugh caught his attention. Kit's shoulders shook.

"Gor, Alex," Sam cried.

"Did you catch her?" Ben turned his sharp gaze on his sister.

"Of course." Giles couldn't keep his lips from turning up into a grin. "I rescued her."

"You did *not* rescue me!"

Receiving a fulminating glower from her father, her eyes lowered to her hands—which fisted before quickly hiding them in her lap.

"What happened?" Sam asked with excitement.

"I only recently purchased Gent. The steed's owner declared the horse powerful. Quite worth the purchase price. Not only did I catch up with Alex, I snatched her right out of the black's saddle."

All three brothers burst out in loud guffaws, and so did their father. However, Cornelia fanned herself, and Sarah hid a smile behind her fingers.

"That explains the missing rider." Ben leaned an arm on the back of his chair. "But not why the horse was alone when we found him."

"My guess, the black kept running." Kit turned his amused grin on Alex.

"You are correct. Your sister was afraid the stallion would run away." Giles turned to James. "I apologize earnestly for my rash actions, as I apologized to your daughter as soon as I found out the lad was a girl."

"Papa, there is nothing to be concerned about. I did not—" Alex began, only to be cut off by her father.

"Nothing to be concerned about? Not only did you lose your new horse, but a gentleman had to come to your rescue. And he thought you a boy."

"Not the first time," Sam piped in.

"Dear God. Sarah, do you have smelling salts?"

Kit frowned and leaned forward in his chair. "Aunt Cornelia, are you going to faint?"

"Cornelia is fine, dear." Sarah raised her crystal wine glass, and then gazed at him over the rim.

"It's easy to mistake Alex for a boy," Ben said. "Why, my own eyes nearly bugged out of my head when she walked in here in that dress."

This time the urchin did kick, and sure enough Giles felt the ramifications. He flinched and swallowed a grunt of pain.

"Alex. One cannot behave foolishly in front of others and not expect it to spread like wildfire," James scolded. "From this day forward, there will be a new set of rules put in place. Your mother and I, and Cornelia, will discuss the matter after dinner."

She practically wilted under the table.

"Perhaps what your father is trying to say, is that you are of an age now. A young lady is expected to behave a certain way." Cornelia tried to retain the ambience at the dinner table. Maybe even save Alex some embarrassment in the process.

"I find her spirited behavior quite amusing." Giles watched Alex's face as he spoke. Sure enough, signs of a temper flared. He discovered he liked baiting her as much as her brothers. He ground his lips together to capture the chuckle bursting inside.

"Spirited?" Ben grumbled. "She's a big pain in my—"

"Ben!" Sarah cautioned. "I remember a time when Alexandria worshiped the ground you walked on. She tagged along behind you like a shadow. You had no problem with her then."

Ben cleared his throat. "She was a baby."

"Your Grace, I apologize for my children's outspokenness."

"Please, Mrs. Carmichael. I would rather you not address me so formally. And I am not offended by the dinner conversation." He offered a heartfelt smile. "I find their quibble enjoyable, in fact. The dinners I normally attend have traces of pompousness about them. Thinking to put on airs, so to speak. I much prefer normalcy. A more relaxed gathering where one might breathe easy and not be subject to decorum."

"How kind of you to say so, Your Grace," Cornelia said from beside him.

"Please, Lady Hargrave. You call your brother James. Would it be so difficult for you to call me Giles?"

She gasped aloud, her expression one of horror. "I could not."

"Surely speaking my name is not as horrible as all that? How about, Nethersall?"

"Well, um, if you insist."

"I do." He softened his command with a smile.

The dear lady blushed. Giles relaxed his tense shoulders. This family welcomed him into their home, and he fit. How refreshing, their banter and their mirth. A long-awaited sense of home and contentment spread through his body.

He lifted his wine goblet and glanced across the table—straight into a pair of livid brown eyes.

Chapter 7

G iles normally rose each morning at the crack of dawn. This morning had been no different. He'd been closeted in James' office for the last hour, getting an idea of the man's sizable holdings.

Such a lordly plantation. Carmichael had acreage down to the river's level. His cane-field contained about five hundred acres, which just last year produced a crop of three hundred eighty-four tons of sugar. He housed a variety of stock. A numerous herd of cattle delivered fresh butter, cheese, and cream for all who lived on the land with enough left over to send to market. And then there were the thoroughbreds.

Good God, the plantation was a world of its own, filled with culture and all the refinements.

James had a special love of horses, one thousand acres set aside just for the creatures to roam. And he had promised a special surprise.

Giles inhaled the rich steam rising from his coffee cup. Tea may be the drink of his ancestors, but he preferred the rich, black brew. He'd developed the taste during his wild and free days, and lived on the stuff during the course of many missions.

"Good morning."

Giles lowered the paper he'd been reading and glanced at the girl. She took up entirely too much time in his head. As the night before, Alex had donned a gown. A twinge of regret darted through his thoughts, seeing she wore a skirt instead of the curve-revealing breeches.

"Good morning." Applying his gentlemanly manners, he stood, waiting for Alex to settle in the chair opposite him.

A sparkle in her eye, she gave him a huge smile. Then she smoothed her skirts and sat.

As he lowered his frame back to his own chair, he wondered what the minx was up to. The cook came in before he could dwell on the idea.

"Good morning, Missy."

At his raised eyebrow, Alex quickly explained. "She's always called me Missy." She turned to the cook. "Good morning, Phebe."

"Here you go." Phebe placed a plate of eggs and ham in front of Alex.

"Thank you, Phebe. Ummm. Looks delicious." Alex smiled at the older woman.

"More coffee, Mister Giles? The cream is fresh and rich."

"Yes, please." He held up his cup, with a smile and a nod. She poured black brew from a white, China pot, steam rising into the air. Good. Nice and hot.

"I'll have coffee too, Phebe."

The woman gave the girl a sharp look, and then ignored Alex as though she had not spoken.

Sitting back, he observed the exchange between the two women.

"Do you have everything you need, Mister Giles?"

"This is perfect, Phebe. Thank you." Giles shared a wink.

A beaming Phebe strolled back to the kitchen.

He was still grinning when his gaze returned to Alex. He took in her delicate features under the flaming blush on her cheeks. It had been quite a while since he'd paid much attention to a woman. How easy it would be to get lost in her natural beauty. He narrowed his gaze, drinking in every detail, including her pert, rounded nose and full lips. With a silent groan, he shook away the uninvited thoughts and concentrated on his paper.

"You seem to be occupied with the Louisiana Gazette."

"By that, if you mean am I reading current events, the answer is yes."

"Papa says there is very little space devoted to current events since news happenings are common knowledge long before the sheets come off the press. But he still takes the paper. Mama likes to look at the clippings, and there is poetry printed as well."

Beautiful *and* keen? An unusual combination in a lady, let alone one so young.

From the corner of his eye, he saw her lift her fork and then hesitate. "Have you already eaten?"

"I have been with your father in his study."

"Papa? Good, he's gone."

Giles lowered the paper enough to peer over the top. "Beg pardon?"

"You are here alone, so Papa must be gone."

"No. I am waiting while he deals with some private business. Then I shall accompany him on a tour about the plantation."

"Oh." Her smile disappeared and her shoulders dropped.

He raised the paper in hopes the man would be done soon.

"Maybe I can come with you."

If he ignored her, maybe she would go away. She was entirely too distracting. Her character and speech made her seem more mature than her years.

"I said, maybe Papa will allow me to go with you."

Evidently not.

Giles lowered the paper again. "Do you make a habit of join-ing your father when he is conducting business?"

Another flush. He almost felt guilty for his harsh tone. "No."

With a slight shake of hand, he snapped the paper, and tried to focus.

"Are you doing business with my father?"

Bloody hell.

"Yes." This time he answered through the words that were beginning to blur. Damned nuisance trying to read with bleating echoing in his ears.

"I need to take Blackie for a run."

Ignoring her was not working. Not at all.

"Thought you were going to change his name." Giles affected a bored response.

"I am. Would you put that paper down? It's annoying when I'm trying to have a conversation with you."

"Any other female would understand this as a hint."

"A what? Please, lower that thing."

"'Thing?' The Louisiana Gazette?" When he peered over the top, he saw that Alex had fisted her hands, one on each side of her plate.

He hid a grin and directed a pointed glare to her hands. She quickly lifted her napkin and toyed with it in her lap.

"A hint. An indirect, noticeable implication, suggesting perhaps I might not want to engage in conversation." His gaze bore into hers.

"Oh." Just as she took a lungful of air, about to spout more gibberish, her father entered with the force of a gale wind.

"There you are. Good morning, Alex." Even her father called her Alex.

"Good morning, Papa."

"Giles, I've finished. Now, ready to see the plantation?"

"Most assuredly." Giles folded the paper and stood, wondering if the chit would ask her father to come along. She did not.

"Tell your mother we'll try to be back in time for dinner." James turned to Giles. "We have a lot of ground to cover."

"I'm looking forward to it." He glanced to Alex and found her chewing on her bottom lip. "Good day, Alex."

Cunning eyes darted to him. Giles groaned under his breath, for surely a plan of some sort was forming in her mind.

Surrounded by splendid groves, the mansion sat sagaciously in the middle of a plantation laid out for beauty and productiveness. Massive oaks and graceful magnolias provided shade. The gardens occupied a large area, filled with brilliant roses and all manner of rarer blossoms that reflected the rays of the sun. Flowers of every description perfumed the air.

Fields stretched for miles toward a dark belt of timber. Extensive orange and cherry orchards produced fruit and more.

A group of white buildings were at intervals, rather than clumped together, within the back field. Sugar-houses and cottages occupied by the laborers, a kitchen where the fieldhands took their meals, and sheds where the carts and costly machinery were housed.

Giles had been observing for hours, but time passed quickly for there was much to see. James had not exaggerated when he described miles of acreage.

"This section may, without the least exaggeration, be the best land in the world." James shifted on his horse and beamed with pride. "It protects the Mississippi channel. The rivers and bayous furnish fish and oysters of the finest flavor. The soil here is sedimentary formation. As you can see, we grow fruit and vegetables in tropical abundance."

"Yes. Quite impressive," Giles admitted.

"The conditions of life are easy. But make no mistake, my friend, the laborers work hard. I am not cruel, but I am a demanding taskmaster. In addition, I make a very comfortable living."

A horn sounded from a steamboat on the river.

"Ah, the *Paragon*," James said, identifying the boat. "Three hundred and fifty-five tons. One of the finest boats on the river. Headed to Louisville, no doubt, with a full cargo."

"I have just invested in a new steamboat design." Giles thought he would share his venture and get James' estimation of the project. "A gentleman proposed to connect each side wheel to one engine only—thus one wheel would be able to go forward while the other went backward, and the boat could be turned in its own length."

"How big is he planning to make this boat? That would cut considerably on the cabin size and the amount of space for cargo."

"There has been a lot of controversy over flexibility of steering and roomier cabins. He has designed two more stories of cabins and the pilothouse would sit atop that."

James considered the idea. "Such a vessel would be top-heavy. More than likely turn over."

"The gentleman has proved, in theory of course, the boat would cut easily through the water. That it would steer as if by magic." Warming to the subject, Giles' voice grew in enthusiasm.

"Now that I would have to see."

"The merchant has my money. So, time will tell."

"Be sure to let me know when it is completed."

Giles agreed with a nod.

"Tomorrow we will visit the cane field. A profitable culture, sugar and rice. I have not forgotten I promised you a surprise," James stated.

"I must admit I have been eager to see what that surprise might be."

"Some men do not like surprises." The older man winked. "I think you will like this one."

Clicking the reins, he spurred his horse into a gallop. Giles followed.

"Well? What do you think?" Proud as a father boasting of his newborn son, James' face beamed with pleasure.

Giles wondered if he should trust his vision. There, in front of him, appeared to be a replica of Morgan's white stallion. Surely it could not be the same horse.

"Ha. Just the look I expected," James said excitedly. "And before you ask, his name is Chrysaor. Like his namesake, he is brother to Pegasus—the horse your friend owns."

"You were right." Gazing at the mystical beast, Giles spoke with awe. "This is a surprise I most assuredly like. I had no idea two such identical beings existed."

"You won't be able to get too close. Ben has staked his claim for now. He's the only one who can get within touching distance." James shifted in his saddle. "We let Chrysaor roam free. Ben makes sure he doesn't stray off our land."

"So how did you come by him?"

"Morgan created quite a stir when he took Pegasus. The story of how he faced down a cruel owner and saved a prized stallion—which resembled a mythical creature, no less—spread far and wide. Embellished as the story flourished from one town to the next. And beyond."

James removed his hat, thrust his fingers through his hair, and shoved the covering back on his head, all the while keeping a worshipful gaze on the animal. His tone might be matter-of-fact, but clearly he derived more than satisfaction from owning this particular stallion.

"Word came back of a man who owned such a horse. Jacobson, the man's name, declared he'd never mistreated any animal. That's how we found out there were two." James glanced to Giles briefly, then resumed his admiration of the beautiful stallion in the pasture.

"Turned out the original owner had an accident and lost the use of his legs. The man he hired to help out, stole the horses and disappeared. Evidently this thief sold one to Jacobson. Said he was down on his luck and needed money, but could only part with one horse. Jacobson tried to buy both, but the man refused to sell the second one, which he claimed was named Pegasus. We figure that is most likely the man Morgan took the whip from."

"How did you get this stallion?"

"Took some doing. I fancied that horse. Made Jacobson an offer no sane man could refuse." A smile engulfed James' face. "Look at him. Prances around as if he were a king. Have you ever seen anything so magical? He's like a spirit."

"That he is." Giles had to admit the animal looked exactly like the one in England. "And so is his brother."

"Before you ask, he's not for sale." James appeared as if in a trance, and stared at the stallion as though he marveled at a dream.

"Clearly, this animal is special to you," Giles stated.

"Uninhibited. Free. Beautiful. Spiritual. There are no words to describe what I feel when I look at that horse. Imagine two such creatures roaming that field."

Ah-ha. That's what this is about.

"I share your admiration, James. But I'm afraid you must be satisfied with only one. Whether or not Morgan's feelings run as deep as yours, he would not give up Pegasus."

From her upstairs window, Alex mulled over the last several days. The first time she saw him, she thought Giles had to be the most beautiful man in the world. Then her friend set her straight. Men were handsome—not beautiful. Didn't matter to her. Giles was beautiful. She made up her mind to marry him. Another wild idea from the imagination of a child.

Determination she learned from her father. There was nothing he could not do, could not have. So, she made up her mind to be just like him, and like her father, once she set her mind on what she wanted—that was that.

One would think she would have outgrown her infatuation. Even when she realized he was not coming back for her, there was a flicker in the back of her mind—secretly hoping—perhaps one day... Then, she thought she had conjured him up at Hudson's auction. He was larger than she remembered. When she realized the man she was looking at truly was Giles—

They're back.

Her fingers tightened on the curtain as Papa and Giles rode into view, and on to the stables.

She had grown up. She could talk to him now the way she could not before. She could have an adult conversation. He could accept her as a woman and not a child. Good grief, Betty

Sue got married and she was seventeen. Not only was Alex of age to marry, she was smarter and more educated than most girls her age. Just because she preferred riding in breeches did not make her a child.

She had carried his image for years, but the man she stared at was flesh and blood. His height towered over her. His eyes drew her. The sensations running through her body confused her. Robbed her of breath.

He was real.

Her infatuation never went away. In fact, she had fallen deeper into the pit of yearning. No other man stirred such feelings. Most males her age seemed like mere boys. They made fun of her. She could take the ridicule from her brothers—well almost—but she knew they were only teasing. The foolish boys she knew were much like the dandies her aunt described.

The duke was unlike any man she had met.

He had to see her as a woman.

He just had to.

She raced across the room, threw open the door and peeked left to right. No one to see her escape, she raced down the steps, hurried to the kitchen, and nearly collided with Phebe.

"Where you going in such a rush?"

"Uh, nowhere. Thought I might grab an apple for a snack."

"Um hum." Phebe crossed her arms under her big bosom. "You seem to be in a mighty fine hurry."

"I'm hungry." Alex snatched an apple from a basket.

"More 'n likely it's for that black beast."

Better Phebe assumes the treat was for the black than know the real reason for her urgency. "Isn't he a beauty?"

"Go on with ya." Phebe laughed and fluffed her apron. "Guess he's gotta eat, too."

Alex tried to slow her steps, hoping to make a smooth and graceful exit, but her feet were as anxious as her galloping heart. She put one foot in front of the other and sprinted out the back door. As soon as the door closed, she took off, trying not to jump for joy in her excitement.

The afternoon sun blazed down in all its glory, warming Alex before she entered the cool shade of the stables. The sight that met her eyes knocked her heart to a roaring halt.

Bare chested, Giles stood next to his golden steed. Slightly bent, a dark lock of hair—the same sable highlights of her stallion—fell forward to block the side of his face. Dark curls generously spread across a masculine chest. He had the body of an imaginary god that she'd only seen on statues in the books in Papa's library.

With a brush in his hand, Giles' husky voice soothed his horse. Alex nearly gaped at him while he brushed the silky golden coat. Bulging muscles, covering his back and arms, flexed with each stroke across the horse's flank. Warmth flowed through her center at how his muscles stiffened and released, only to stiffen and release again . . . and again.

Her eyes glued to his glistening, damp skin, Alex drank in the vision before her. She stood there, mouth agape, filling her eyes, amazed at how seeing a man's body could thrill her so. Every shift of muscle across his bare shoulders made her throat close a little more. Powerful emotions swamped her, making it impossible to look away.

Quietly, barely breathing, unable to move, she stared. One of his hands held the curry brush and stroked the steed, while the other smoothed along behind as if to caress. The smooth movement almost hypnotizing. The softly spoken words Giles issued to Gent were having an enchanting effect on her. She felt warm all over. Heat spread through her chest and on to settle low in her belly.

She must have made a noise, for his head jerked up and his eyes bore into hers. Heat flooded her cheeks. His fixed stare unsettled her. His lids shuttered, then he went back to the task at hand.

"Do you need something, Alex?" Putting the brush away, he lifted his shirt from the post.

The simple act caused her stomach to flutter. Where had her wits gone? She'd seen her brothers bare backed before. Watching Giles aroused sensations she'd never encountered. His naked flesh, springy black curls over an impressive chest, made her lose any coherent thought she might have had.

Buttoning his shirt, he stepped next to her with an expectant expression, as though he waited for an answer.

"Uh. No. Nothing."

Giles turned, grabbed the leather lead of his horse, and settled Gent in a stall. He closed the gate and glanced at her once more. She couldn't move. Without another word, he left.

Alex sucked air into her lungs.

Fearing the floor would come up to meet her, she leaned against the wood of the next stall, completely undone. Infatuation had just taken a dangerous leap.

She was besotted in the extreme.

![Chapter 8]

Chapter 8

F our days of trying to secure the duke's attention, and he avoided her at every possibility. Alex had a heart to heart with her feelings. She'd been chasing an idea for so long, she was acting without completely understanding how a relationship might be between them. After seeing him half naked, she had to come to terms with reality. Once she sorted out her reaction, she realized she needed a different approach.

Oh, she still wanted the duke.

She was more determined than ever.

Remembering what happened the last time the two of them were together, her reaction appalled her. Oh, not the part of seeing him almost naked, and ogling him, and her mouth going dry . . . She shook her head to clear the disturbing image.

What bothered her was the part where she lost her voice. Stood there like a mooncalf, unable to speak. The opportunity she had been waiting for, even tried to arrange, and when her very wish arose in front of her, she'd acted like a little girl gawping at her first lollipop.

The duke had not mentioned his plans or departure date. Besides, time was not on her side. How could she demonstrate her womanly wiles in the presence of her family? Her father would not approve of her actions. He would be mortified at the idea of his daughter chasing after an important guest. Her brothers would not aid in her brazen scheme. They might love creating mischief, and she knew they partook in some improprieties she shouldn't know about. But when it came to her, their sister, each one had limitations on her range of freedom. Even though her brothers indulged her every whim, she could just imagine their reaction if she asked for advice on seduction.

A slight shiver rippled through her spine.

She paced the floor in her bedroom. What if she picked just one?

Kit was definitely out. He was the oldest and the most level-headed. Sam was the youngest and the wildest. He might be a good choice if she intended to pursue every man alive. But she was only interested in one. She chewed on the end of her finger. That left Ben.

If she could get past the embarrassment of asking. She would never survive the humiliation when he locked her up and told the others why. She stomped her foot with impatience.

Scanning her wardrobe, she debated on which gown to wear today. Earlier she had donned her breeches and took Blackie for a morning ride. Alex released a sigh. She needed to find a new name.

She fingered the gowns hanging in her wardrobe. What good would a dress do if she could not get the duke alone? She paced from her bed to the open window. Pulling the curtain to the side, she glanced at the blue sky. A beautiful day.

Today would be the day. If opportunity did not present itself

. . .

Her eyes widened as two riders appeared in her side vision. Papa and the duke, once again headed for the stables.

Giles might think her a mere girl—but his assessment was about to change.

She forgot all about changing and dashed from her room, hurried down the stairs and darted outside. By the time she entered the building, no one was in sight. She looked in each stall, to see if perhaps her father or Giles had stepped inside with one of the horses. Sadie snorted and nudged Alex with her nose. Voices drifted within her hearing as she walked closer to the back.

Her brothers.

When Sam mentioned Ben being with a girl last night, Alex's attention went on full alert.

Slipping behind the tack room door, she hid and peeked through its hinged opening. She knew better than to spy on someone, but how else was she to learn anything?

"I don't kiss and tell."

"Come on, Kit. How am I supposed to know if I'm doing it right?"

That was Sam's voice. He was with them.

"There is only one way to do it." That was Ben.

"Show's how much you know." Kit sounded sure of himself.

"You mean there's another way?"

Gee Sam, I'd like to know the answer too.

She recognized Kit's laugh, and Ben joined him.

"What are you boys up to?"

Uh oh. Papa.

"Just jawin', Pap."

"You got back earlier than we expected," Kit said.

"I have a meeting this afternoon."

Alex angled her head to see better. Giles stood next to Papa.

"I'll take care of your horses." Ben caught the lead of Papa's horse, then accepted a leather strap from Giles.

Oh, no. He was coming inside. She hunkered down on her knees. Scooting back, she crawled through the tackle doorway, and crept inside just in time.

"Nathaniel Hardcastle owns a plantation a few miles south. He's having a race come Saturday." Thank goodness, Papa and Giles were still in back.

Finding a shaft of light between the boards near the floor, Alex lowered to her elbows, and peered through the hole. From this angle she saw five pairs of boots.

"No better way to examine stock than with an impromptu racing event. Several gentlemen will be there. Some to show off their steeds, some to bet on the outcome." Papa settled his hand on Sam's shoulder. "Sam will be racing."

"Brusor. A gelding. Three years old. The fastest horse around these parts." She could imagine Sam puffing up his chest.

Huh. My new black could win.

Something furry brushed crossed Alex's back and she jerked, hitting a bridle, which knocked into the others, causing a jangling noise. She grabbed the straps to hold them still, then glanced down at the cause of the commotion.

Tom. How did you get in here?

The cat purred and stretched his back. She quickly shooed him away and retook her position of spying. When she spotted Giles, her breath caught. He stared straight at the tiny opening as if he could see her. He must have heard.

Her father kept talking, so perhaps her guilt triggered her imagination.

". . . and most times he won."

"Pardon me, Mr. Carmichael. You have a visitor. Mr. Daggett."

Papa's manservant. How many more people would show up before she could leave her hiding place?

"Yes, I was expecting him this afternoon." James pulled at his gloves as he swung to Giles. "Sorry to cut our afternoon short. If you will excuse me."

Finally, Giles pulled his gaze from her peephole. "Of course."

Good grief. Did he suspect she was spying on them?

"Kit. Come with me."

Ben stepped into view just as Papa and Kit left. "Sam and I are heading to the river. One of the steamers is bringing a few crates from New Orleans for us. Want to come along?"

"Thank you, Ben. But I believe I will take a look about your fine plantation at my leisure."

"Suit yourself. Come on, Sam."

～ell～

Giles quietly opened the door of the tackle room, and halted abruptly. He found himself confronting a very fetching derriere in lad's breeches. Propping one arm against the doorframe, he smiled to observe the little minx hiding, face down.

"Lose something?"

Alex flopped like a fish on dry land. When she settled down, her hands were fisted at her sides and her face flamed. "Uh, yes. Uh . . ."

"Or maybe you were snooping."

She braced one hand on the wall and stood, brushing straw from her clothes. A mass of tumbling blonde hair surrounded her shoulders, with springs sticking up, here and there. Her skin, already tanned by the sun, had a good amount of freckles on her finely boned cheeks. She looked as fetching as a maiden in jeweled finery. Actually, he preferred the tussled look. Full pouting lips boasted a hesitant smile of seduction no young girl should have. And her body? Displayed to distraction in her boy's clothes, molding and shaping every curve to perfection.

No man would mistake those curves for a lad.

Her dark brown eyes flashed. "I was getting a bridle."

He stepped forward and lifted a leather strap from a hook. "This bridle, perhaps?"

She bent and scooped a grey cat into her arms. "Tom distracted me."

Giles hung the bridle back on the hook and braced his hands on his hips. "Do you make a habit of spying on your brothers?"

"I was not spying."

"Of course, you weren't. Judging from the conversation I interrupted, no young girl would know the subject they were discussing anyway."

Her face flushed scarlet. He arched a brow. Surely, she had no idea the boys were speaking of tupping a girl's skirts. Just how long had she been listening?

"You are very handsome," the chit stated baldly, expanding a breath as if she'd kept her mouth closed too long.

He didn't know whether to be flattered, or feel concern at some unspoken purpose behind her words.

"What do you know of handsome men?"

"I've grown out of pigtails. I am a woman now."

Swallowing his amazement, he nearly choked. "Donning a dress does not make you a woman." His gaze dipped in a slow, silent perusal. The damn girl's breeches emphasized her curves, leaving nothing to a man's imagination. And he should not even notice, of course, but . . . Damnation. She did not look the least like a child.

"My brothers, are handsome, I suppose. But they are my brothers. I don't care enough about other men to consider them handsome."

Care?

"Why then, are you here?" He gave her his best glare.

"As I said, I was looking for ... never mind."

"I see you have resorted to breeches again. After your brothers' reproaching insults, I would think you learned your lesson."

"Learned my—" She thrust out her chest. "I am not unwise. Papa says I have spirit."

"Do you think it wise to hide in a tackle bin?"

"I was not hiding."

Damn the girl was tenacious. And that made her all the more appealing. He took a step closer, lowering his voice. "Do you think it wise to be alone here with me?"

"You're a duke. A gentleman."

He gave a harsh laugh. "Being a duke does not make me a gentleman."

"But Aunt Cornelia said English aristocrats live by their honor. You are a nobleman. You have integrity, and morals."

"Morals? Honor? A man lives by his own decree." He took another step. "What if I were to take liberties?"

"I can handle you." Her eyes lit up and she seemed much too sure of herself.

The gall of the chit.

With one quick movement, his hands shot out and jerked her against his chest. A gasp rushed from her throat, but she boldly held his gaze. With deliberate daring, his arms imprisoned her. He watched the emotions flitting over her face. He meant to punish, to teach, to frighten. His gaze lowered to her mouth.

He would send her fleeing for good.

He captured her lips in a forceful kiss. But was completely unprepared for her sweet taste.

Her fingers twisted his shirt.

Good God, she was kissing him back. With such enthusiasm, he was flabbergasted.

Unconscionable, that one so young should kiss with such skill. Had the damned girl been coached? She should slap him, call him a knave. Push him away, scream at him. Instead, she twined her arms about his neck while her warm, seeking tongue pirouetted in a mating dance with his.

He lost himself. He pulled her tighter, thoroughly enjoying the dancing of her tongue, simply taking delight in the movement itself.

Sweet.

Delicious.

Sensual.

He heard himself moan and was about to press her lower body against his aching bulge when reality slapped him in the face.

He grabbed her shoulders and shoved her away.

"Where the hell did you learn to kiss like that?"

Languorous eyes flew wide in surprise. And delight.

"So, you liked it?"

Anger and bewilderment had Giles seething. His intention to scare the chit had missed the mark. Did the girl have no humility? Did she have a bloody clue how close she had come to losing her virtue?

Her head tilted, and then she took a coy step forward. Her pouting lips swollen with their lovemaking. "I know you did." Her voice was as sultry as a siren's.

Was there no end to her audaciousness? This was not the result he had anticipated.

Before he knew what she was about, she smoothed her hands up his chest and pressed closer. "Are you afraid of a mere kiss?"

"You are too damned young to kiss a man like that."

"Language, sir Giles. Besides, *you* kissed *me*."

"This is madness." He pulled her arms from creeping further around his neck and shoved them to her sides.

"What? That you desire me?"

"How could a mere child know of desire?" He frowned. How *would* she know? She sure as hell didn't kiss like one. Twirling her tongue with his, pressing her body against him . . . His head was nearly ready to explode at the possibility the girl *did* know.

"I am not a child."

"You are not a woman," he nearly shouted.

"Then why did you kiss me like that? You kissed me the way a man kisses a woman."

He could not deny it. But his intentions had been honorable, meant to scare her away. Not create a yearning he felt all the way down to his toes.

"You can't get rid of me so easily. I think your silly attempt to scare me backfired."

Hoist by his own petard. By God, the woman was astute.

Woman? His jaw cracked as he ground his back teeth.

"I don't know what your game is, but it will not work with me."

"There is no game," she said quietly. "I saw you years ago. I decided then I would marry you."

Shock did not begin to describe his bewilderment.

Marry?!

Obviously, the brat had lost her mind.

Chapter 9

S he'd done it now. Alex clapped a palm over her mouth too late. Her nerves bristled with dread. She had not meant to say that. Trying to be a woman without really knowing how was taking its toll. Presenting a bravery she did not feel, she fisted her hands on her hips.

"When?" Giles growled.

Puzzled, she repeated his question. "When?"

"You said years ago. When?"

She blinked and tried to swallow, but her mouth had gone dry. "I was twelve years old." She looked down at the ground beneath her feet, wishing she could disappear. "Go ahead. Laugh."

"I am not laughing." His deep voice rumbled.

When she peeked at him, he stood there glowering. His dark eyes gave no impression of his thoughts. In that instant she knew she had to make him see her as a woman. There might never be another chance. She took a deep breath.

"Two men laughing and deep in conversation would not be expected to see anything outside their realm of events." She turned toward the nearest harness and lifted her hand to the leather. "When a small dog was nearly run over by a wagon, one of those men ran out to save the dog, while the other chastised the driver for not controlling his team of horses. Then, those same men calmed two hysterical young girls and delivered the mutt into their loving arms."

She peered over her shoulder into perceptive dark eyes.

"I see you remember the incident. Do you know which one was me?"

Giles cleared his throat. "The dog was not yours."

"No. He belonged to Winnifred. My childhood friend. I'd been allowed to visit and her mother took us to town. We were to wait outside the milliner's shop with her driver while she went inside to purchase a hat. Winnifred had begged to bring along her new puppy. He was so cute. And as puppies are, his energy overtook his body. When I tried to hand him back, he jumped out of my arms."

"You are the child who dashed after him. I grabbed you. Morgan took after the mutt."

When she turned and fully met his eyes, she knew the longing in hers must be apparent. "You saved me."

"You scared the life out of me." Giles shoved a hand through his raven-black hair, curling against the collar of his white shirt.

"Your friend brought the dog back and gently placed him in Winnifred's arms. She fell in love with him."

And I you.

"A child's hero worship," he replied dismissively.

"You may think my infatuation a child's whimsy, but you were more than my hero. You saved a dog. And me. I'd never seen a man so caring." She took a step closer. "Notice I did not say daring. My brothers are daring. To the point their actions are on the brink of folly. They would have let Winnie's puppy get trampled, and blistered me for chasing him."

"Surely not."

"Who knows?" She shrugged. "But you and your friend rushed to save two girls. Save their hearts. Save them from grief. And you did save my life, for I would have been trampled by that wagon."

"You make me out to be some hero. Let me assure you, I am not."

"No, you still don't see." She raised a hand to his cheek. "You noticed me that day. You looked at me . . . maybe with sympathy. But I saw in you a kind, soulful man. A man with heart. A man with secrets."

When he didn't pull away, she caressed the prickly skin beneath her fingers, absorbing his warmth.

"You created a flutter in my core. Something new and deep. Something I never felt before. I decided then and there you had my heart."

Confusion crossed his features. She could tell his thoughts disturbed him. Yet, he did not pull her hand away. "You were twelve years old."

"When I saw you again, only days ago, the same throb slashed my chest."

With a grunt he stepped back. "You know not what you speak."

"I may be young in years, but my father and mother taught me responsibility. Some see me as foolish, but I am independent. I possess good judgement. You have seen for yourself that I am determined. Aunt Cornelia has schooled me on the customs of the English. I'm not a complete illiterate."

"I would never think such a thing." The slight smirk on his mouth suggested otherwise.

"I know you've heard stories of me in boys' clothing, prancing after my brothers. But as I said, Aunt Cornelia taught me how to be a lady."

"Well, you sure as hell don't kiss like one."

Her heart lifted. "Such language for a duke." She pretended coyness as her lips curved in a mischievous smile. "You liked it. Do not deny it."

"*You* never answered *me*. A girl does not kiss a man the way you did without being . . . promiscuous."

"You wound me, Sir Duke." Her temper boiled suddenly, right under the surface. "I will admit I had practice. I knew you would never look at me seriously unless I could show you, prove to you that I knew how to act like a woman."

"Those are not the actions of a . . ." He glared at her. "What kind of practice?"

"At least I have your attention."

"You snared my attention when you had your tongue down my throat."

"I did not have my tongue down your throat." Her face heated. "However, I did have trouble swallowing since you took my breath." She placed her hand over her middle. "I even had a flurrying in my belly."

"Dear God, do not speak of your belly." He grasped two handfuls of his lovely hair.

He seemed more reachable with his floundering. "Why not? It's true."

"No matter if it is true or not. Now answer my question. How much practice?"

Clearly, he was losing patience. And if she were to guess, the duke was wound up good and tight. "Lots. I had a bursting curiosity. And the same hunger to learn as your inquisitiveness in asking me all these questions."

With a throaty growl he took a step closer. Broad shoulders towered over her.

"Don't look so ferocious," she admonished.

"What the bloody hell did you do other than kissing?" His thunderous expression made his eyes appear black.

"Nothing. I am not a woman of loose morals. When Henry tried putting his hand on my . . . well, I smacked him."

"You should have smacked *me*."

"Oh, no." She shook her head and took an impatient step, bringing her chest flush with his. "You see, I want you. I want to kiss you. I want you to touch me. Only you."

Her duke looked like he was strangling. His cheeks puffed out and his eyes grew darker.

"Good God. You cannot say things like that."

"But it's true."

"Again, that is not the point. You are a child. And I have no time for foolishness."

Anger filled her. His arrogance was wearing on her nerves. She wanted to stomp her foot in frustration but quickly realized he would see it as the action of a child.

Instead, Alex aimed for what she thought would be a purr, and laid her fingers on his chest. "Kiss me again, and I will show you I am not a child."

Flinging her hand away, he snorted and jerked back. His expression had become so outraged, she struggled not to giggle.

"You play with fire," he growled. "Next time I shall not be so tolerant. If you want to act like a grown up, you will suffer the consequences." He left the storage room, his strides long and brisk as he strode through the stables, headed for the outdoors.

"One day you will see me as I am," she called after him.

"God help the man you set your sights on when you grow up." His voice echoed harshly as he disappeared around the corner.

I am grown up.

And I have set my sights on you.

"Harrumph!"

She'd been caught spying—again. By her aunt, no less. Alex turned from the library door and found Aunt Cornelia with her chin elevated and her hands overlapped in a chastising fashion.

"And just what are you about?" Aunt whispered coldly, the sound of disapproval in her voice.

"Uh . . . I, um, nothing."

"Since you are about *nothing*, why don't you join me in the parlor?"

She followed her aunt down the hallway. Once inside, Cornelia gracefully sat and perched her elbows on the arms of a wingback chair, giving Alex the impression she was about to receive a lecture.

She pursed her lips and blurted, "Aunt Cornelia, I need your help."

Cornelia's stiff posture relaxed, and a look of concern flittered across her face. "My dear, is anything wrong?"

"No, no." Alex quickly answered to alleviate any concern. She marched over to the sofa and plopped on the cushion. "I know you think my behavior is inappropriate for a girl. So, I want your help to become a lady."

Cornelia sucked in a breath, clutching her abdomen. "You are an imposter. Where is Alexandria? What have you done with her?"

"Oh, for heaven's sake. I'm not that bad."

"I have been laying the groundwork for a while. I was beginning to think my coaching would never take root." Her aunt raised a painted brow. "Why this sudden change?"

Alex blew out a breath, sending a lock of hair flying. "Aunt Cornelia." She leaned forward and lowered her voice. "I must confide in you. There is no one else I can ask."

"Not even your mother?"

"Mother lives here, and it is because you live in England that I seek your advice."

"I see," Cornelia said slowly. Then nodded. "I will do what I can."

"Do I have your confidence?"

"My dear girl." Cornelia leaned forward, as well. "You have my heart, Alexandria. You may tell me anything." Then she shot Alex a hard glare. "As long as it is not something which will put you in dire straits or wish me to my grave."

"I want the duke." There. She'd said it in a rush.

Cornelia's expression became blank, her eyes narrowed. "Beg pardon?"

"Giles Litscomb. The Duke of Nethersall. I mean to marry him."

"Oh, Alexandria." She waved a lace-edged handkerchief about her face, before tucking it into her sleeve.

"Have you ever seen a man more handsome? He is kind and tall and . . ." She scooted to the edge of her seat. "Oh, Aunt Cornelia, please. If I am to have a chance at all, you must help me."

"The Duke of Nethersall." Her voice measured indulgent disbelief. "I see why you came to me and not your mother. Is he aware of your interest?"

Alex thought of her attempts at seduction. She cringed.

"What have you done?" Cornelia frowned fiercely.

"Followed him. But he catches me at my worst."

"That has to stop immediately. If you want his interest, you must not appear desperate. A lady should be coy. Mysterious. Enticing."

"Will you help me? I must be a lady to acquire the duke."

"Is a duke what you want?" Her aunt tilted her head and—as was her habit—looked down her lofty nose.

"I don't care if he is a duke or a farmer. His title or position is not important."

"Of course, his position is important. You could do no better than Nethersall. A title *and* a fortune. His reputation is beyond reproach. He is a man of honor, integrity, of moral character. He must pass the dukedom to a son." She clasped her hands. "Some members of nobility trade old English titles for American money. In this case, your duke could make an alliance with an American family who is still of noble birth. You would be the envy of the *ton*. And I will sponsor you. What a splendid idea."

"Sponsor me?" Aunt Cornelia's excitement nearly matched her own.

"Think of it, my dear. First, you would live with me, of course. You would have a coming out debut before a betrothal is announced. An entire wardrobe of new gowns. I must inform my *modiste.* You will be decked from head to toe in the latest fashion."

"Aren't you getting ahead of yourself? The duke has not agreed. He thinks I'm too young for him."

"Balderdash. You are of a marriageable age. The perfect age for Almacks."

"Almacks?"

"The Marriage Mart."

Marriage Mart? What had she gotten herself into?

"We have a lot of work to do if you are to be presentable at court. I will instruct you on all that is necessary to make you a diamond of the first water. Only a few months before the start of the London Season. You will be the belle of the balls. Men will take one look at you and profess undying devotion."

"But I don't want anyone else. I want Giles."

"My child, you cannot address a duke, thus."

Alex didn't miss her aunt's look of horror, but she concentrated on the word *child*.

"Aunt Cornelia, this is the very crux of my dilemma. The duke thinks of me as a child."

"He is not a young man, but he is not in his dotage. Men much older take young brides right out of the schoolroom," Cornelia explained. "Besides, we will change all that. We will turn you into a woman even His Grace cannot ignore."

Alex liked the sound of that. She threw her arms around her aunt's neck and pecked a kiss on her plump cheek.

"We must devise a well-laid plan. First, you must learn to walk." Cornelia disentangled herself and rose, gesturing toward the door. "Come with me to the library."

Walk?

"Why are we going to the library?"

"To get a book, of course."

"I need a book to learn how to walk?"

"You balance a book on the top of your head."

An image of her performing such a feat quickly appeared. It was all Alex could do to avoid laughing outright.

"You must pay attention, Alexandria. The clock is ticking."

Chapter 10

Scents of oranges and cherry blossoms dawdled on a gentle wind. Giles lounged in a meadow on a bed of grass with his hat pulled low over his eyes. His boots crossed at the ankles, he laced his fingers behind his head and chewed on a twig. He could not remember a day when he'd lolled without watchfulness or caution. There was something to be said for a life of leisure.

His eyes heavy, his body tired, he may as well take a nap. Throughout the night, visions of Alex had kept him awake. When sleep finally claimed him, he woke with the blasted girl on the edge of his dream. Deny as much as he liked, a vivid awareness assaulted him. He desired her company.

Alex was lovely. She appeared older than her years. Good God, he had peers older than himself who married maidens the first year of their coming out.

He liked women. Experienced women. But there was something that drew him to Alexandria. Could it be the shared memory of a little girl and a dog?

Mind boggling.

Yet here he was, an afternoon to himself, and who was he thinking of? Not a buxom woman. Not one of his past lovers. But a young woman with amber flecks in her dark eyes, bright with eagerness, desiring his approval. All she wants is him. When had he ever been truly desired for himself? A young woman with no motive other than she wants him.

You see, I want you. I want to kiss you. I want you to touch me. Only you.

He fisted his hands to keep them from trembling.

Surely, he had lost his mind. A child should not affect him so. *A child should not kiss like a bloody courtesan.*

He'd thought to shock her, but the minx had in turn stunned him. The girl was alarming.

Terrifying.

Tempting.

She had him at sixes and sevens. Since his first introduction to the opposite sex, he'd been chased and pursued by all manner of females, enjoying each and every one. Yet he had never settled on a particular woman. One day, he would choose. There were no delusions of happy-ever-after. Honor bound by his duty to marry and produce an heir, he would have permanence with a wife.

Why was he even thinking of such considerations now? Did it have anything to do with a certain obstinate urchin, with that small chin of hers hinting to willfulness? Or her chocolate eyes full of adoration and exhilaration?

The chit dogged his heels. Everywhere he went, somehow Alex showed up—in a gown showing her agile body, accenting her curves, leaving nothing to a man's imagination. Not that he should notice, of course. But . . . Damnation. She did not look the least like a child. Her eyes seemed always sparkling, a youthful ember in her gaze. He fancied the vibrant color of her hair, golden wheat shining like the sun's rays.

A rather incredible wrench jerked at his insides.

Never had a female had such an impact on his sensibilities. Thinking of her, his heart sped up an anxious beat. He imagined her rosy cheeks while his calloused fingertips traveled over buttery, youthful skin. If he had been standing, the powerful jolt in his loins would have knocked the legs right out from beneath him.

He shook his head to clear his imaginative musings, and tried to enjoy the quietness around him. But before long, he found himself thinking again of his fingers twined in blonde silk, cascading over velvety flesh.

God's teeth.

He'd always prided himself on his self-discipline. He controlled his actions. His desires did not control him. This weakness astounded him. Never before had erotic thoughts commanded him. The girl was half his age, and beyond his reach. Considering a courtship with her was impossible. Especially with three brothers ready to protect their sister's honor.

"There you are."

He came to his feet with the speed of a panther. The very object of his deliberations stood before him.

"Goodness, you're quick," Alex said. "You startled me."

"You are the one sneaking up on people." Damn. He hadn't heard the girl. Seemingly, he'd let down his guard. Who thought he would need it while basking in a moment of privacy-enjoying solitude?

"I am not sneaking. I thought you were asleep."

"So, you decided to wake me?"

"Maybe I just wanted to watch you."

Good God. The thought of Alex ogling his body while he slept sent a surge of blazing heat to his groin. On top of that thought pounced another. Would the chit restrain herself to mere looking?

"Somehow I doubt that."

"You spend most of your time with my father, either in the library or touring the plantation. I hardly ever see you alone."

It was too dangerous to be alone with her. So, he practiced avoidance. But he had seen her in the corridor, in the sitting room, at her mother's elbow. She and her decorous aunt seemed to have their heads together a lot of late. The abrupt halt of Alex's coquettish actions did not go unnoticed, either.

So why was he hanging around Louisiana when he clearly should be on his way back to England?

"Why would you want to see me alone? Don't you have your new stallion to keep you occupied?"

"I want to spend time with you. I think you've been avoiding me."

Where had he slipped, thinking Alex demure? Giles scraped a hand over his face, wishing he could just as easily wipe her from his existence. "We've already had this discussion."

"I want to kiss you again."

This girl is a bloody loose cannon.

"You should not be playing grown up games."

"Why must you see me as a child?" She angled her head and tilted her nose slightly in the air. Then ruined the effect by stomping her foot.

He raised a brow and dropped his gaze to her boot before returning to her face—clearly signifying her very action did not support her statement.

"You did not treat me like a child when you kissed me."

"Well laid plans gone awry," he mumbled.

"I'm not unschooled. Aunt Cornelia has taught me many things, and I am a quick learner."

He thought to appease her. Giles stretched to his full height. "Very well. What kind of things?"

"Your English customs."

"Why are you bothering with those? You live here in the Americas."

"Aunt lives in England. Maybe one day, I will visit, or . . . live there, too."

"Your aunt is quite a *dame of the haute ton*. One would do well to follow her example."

Her brow scrunched, as if making an important decision. "Will you sit and talk with me a while?" She bit her lip.

"I should . . ." *Get the hell away from her*. But his gaze returned to the flesh caught between her teeth.

"Please. I would very much like to hear about your home." She sank gracefully to the ground, arranging her skirts around her, much as a young debutante would.

"My home?"

"Yes." She glanced up at him with a stunning smile. "You are a duke. What does a duke do? Where do you live?"

"I live in a house. Most of my day is spent in Parliament." With his arms crossed, he stared at the bit of fluff on the grass.

"Are you vexed with me?" She looked at him with wounded eyes.

Now he felt guilt-ridden. Damned females, and their manipulative ways.

"No, I am not vexed with you."

Her mouth curved up in another blinding smile.

He dropped on his arse and draped an arm on his propped knee, unwilling to admit how much her smile affected him.

"I live in a house, too."

He glanced over and found a mocking expression on her face. He couldn't hold back a response. His lips lifted at the corners.

"If I were to tell you about my home, I would describe the rich land along the Mississippi. The two-story house with its white walls and curved stairs on each side adjoining the balcony." Her eyes met his. "See? It's not so hard."

"A man does not wax poetic about his home the way a woman does."

"Ah. Then you are ready to admit I am a woman?"

Did he think her keen? Admirably so.

"I admit you are a female." He frowned. "An exasperating one."

"It's a start." Her fingers smoothed a wrinkle in her gown. "Do you miss your homeland?"

"There is no place like a man's home." He studied the sun in the middle of a clear blue sky. Swirls of white gave hint of the clouds lingering on the horizon. On the other side of the ocean lay the land of his birth. He missed his old life more than he missed Nethersall Castle. His chest rumbled with a deep sigh.

"My house is made of stone and timber, built in the thirteenth century. Generations of dukes have lived there." He snatched a blade of grass and stuck the thing between his teeth. "With each generation, the new duke expanded the structure, adding more rooms, another tower—as if it wasn't big enough. Three stories, five towers, a maze of rooms such that you would need a charted map to navigate. Iron grillwork, stone stairs on the outside, polished oak on the inside. Trees, meadows, flowerbeds, high-climbing rose bushes. A vineyard. The Okeanos Tower, which means 'ocean,' borders the cliff's edge. Oft times I stand on the balustrade watching the waves smash against the rocky shore. Do my best thinking then."

"It sounds enchanting."

Her voice echoed too close to his ear. Her breath grazed his cheek. He jerked back. When the hell had she moved so close? He tossed the weed aside.

"Don't you like me?"

He tried thinking of an answer that would not wound her. "As much as I like any member of your family."

"I mean, you might like me a bit more. Like a—"

"The daughter of a friend," he finished for her.

She chewed her luscious lip again. "Well, yes. And . . ."

"And what?"

"Do you desire me?"

God spare me. When he kissed the girl, he should have spanked her instead. The thought created an image of her body spread across his lap, her rump covered in tan breeches, sticking up in the air waiting for the hand he'd rather use for caressing instead of delivering punishment.

He bounded to his feet. "I think this conversation is over."

"But we haven't settled anything yet." Large brown eyes pleaded.

"Heed me well." Hands fisted on his hips, he glared down at her. "You are a child." He was the one who needed to remember.

Skirts shuffling, she climbed to her feet in exasperation. "I think you are trying to convince yourself. I am a woman."

"And I am a man. You should not be alone with me."

A blonde brow rose in impishness. "Because you might kiss me again?"

The scamp.

She sashayed closer, her arms out toward him; a spitfire playing the seductress.

Preposterous.

Shouts drew his attention to the paddock. A gathering of men yelled in earnest. A horse snorted and bucked, trying to dislodge the rider on his back. Then, the man flew into the air. Another jumped the fence, distracting the steed while the rider tried to avoid getting stomped by the incensed beast.

Small fingers wrapped around his arm. "Giles."

He glanced back to Alex. Her eyes fluttered while she leaned in for a kiss.

"That does it." He bent down, grabbed the urchin by her thighs and tossed her over his shoulder. With angry strides, he marched the distance to the paddock, her fists pounding on his back.

As he drew closer, Alex's indignant yells drew the men's attention. Three in particular. He paused and dropped the wriggling bundle on the ground. Right in front of her brothers.

In the middle of a cloud of dust Alex fumed, and glared daggers.

Giles scowled at her and then turned to three stunned faces.

"Keep the brat away from me."

Chapter 11

Humiliating. Never had Alex been so embarrassed. Giles stormed off like a stallion bolting through an open gate. Kit studied her with both bushy brows raised.

Sam belted out laughter. And Ben looked mad. At her.

"What did you do . . . *Brat*?"

Him repeating the same term Giles had used only added to her mortification.

"I kinda like the Brit," Ben said.

How come no one went after Giles? Weren't her brothers supposed to protect her? She thought things were going swimmingly. A lovely conversation. True she flirted and pushed his boundaries. But Giles had come at her like a raging storm cloud. At first, she'd been excited—even though she gave a shriek while her arms spun like the wooden slats on a windmill. She had no idea her brothers were close by.

Alex crawled from the dirt and brushed the back of her dress. "What did *I* do? *He* dropped *me* on the ground."

"Gor, Alex. You're wearin' a dress." Sam acted like it was the first time.

"Yes, you clod-head. And now it's dirty."

"Let me get this right," Kit said. "You didn't do anything." She stuck her nose in the air.

"Our little sister? Of course, she didn't." Ben's smirk only made her madder.

"You're worried about your dress," Kit continued. "Am I supposed to go after a man because he got your dress dirty?"

"Uh . . . no." She couldn't have Kit fighting with Giles. No, she didn't want that. She waved a hand. "Never mind."

"Wait a minute, sister dear." Ben blocked her way. "What were you doing with the Brit?"

"The Brit has a name. And it's none of your business."

"Well, I'll be darned." Sam shook his head, drawing Ben's attention.

"What's that, Sam?"

"Haven't you noticed?"

"Noticed what?" Kit asked, turning his scowl on her.

Her cheeks heated as her irritation grew.

"Can you not see, Brother? Our little sister has set her sights on the Englishman."

"She *what*?" Ben shouted.

A lump clogged her throat.

"That true, Alex?" Kit's voice might have sounded calm, but his eyes challenged her to deny Sam's accusation.

"I like him, that's all." She drew a circle in the dirt with the toe of her boot.

Kit crossed his arms over his wide chest. "It's not going to happen."

She glared at Sam. "Traitor."

"What does she mean, 'traitor?'" Ben asked Sam.

Angry fire brightened Kit's irises. "You knew about this?"

Ben grabbed Sam by the collar of his shirt. Sam fought to get free. "Been holdin' out on us?" Ben tightened his hold.

"No." Sam struggled. "I just figured it out."

"You three go ahead and beat on each other," Alex shouted. "You are not telling me how to live my life."

"So, you admit it?" Ben dropped Sam. "You fancy the Brit?"

"Why do you think she's been wearing dresses?" Sam rubbed his throat.

"Figured Aunt Cornelia's influence had Alex finally acting like a girl."

"She was in trousers only last week. Before the duke's arrival. And very much after Cornelia's."

Why couldn't Sam keep his mouth shut? She could not allow Kit to find out her intentions. Alex stomped her foot. "I am eighteen. Old enough to make up my own mind."

"Not about this, you're not." Being the oldest, Kit had always thought his siblings should obey him.

"I am old enough to marry!" she shouted back at him.

All three of them looked at her as if she'd just sprouted horns. When would she learn to curb her tongue?

Alex spun on her heel. "I will not abide your bullying."

Kit grabbed her arm and practically dragged her to a wooden stool.

"What do you think you're doing?" she sputtered, trying to jerk her arm away.

He pointed. "Sit."

She opened her mouth to argue.

"Now!"

Glaring, she plopped on the wood and immediately regretted it when her bum stung.

"Explain what you just said."

"What?" She wanted to rub her aching bottom.

Ben and Sam watched as Kit pummeled thunder on her.

"Don't play dumb. You said 'marry.'"

Uh-oh. "You misunderstood."

Kit held up his hand in a silencing gesture. "I know you, little sister. You decry too strongly."

She huffed and straightened her back in peevish chagrin.

"You've been behaving differently. Do you fancy the Brit?"

When she remained silent, he snapped, "Answer the question. Do you have your eyes set on the duke?"

"Papa always said her impulsiveness would get her in trouble," Ben grumbled.

Papa. Good Lord. If they tell him . . .

"I might remind you of the man's station," Kit continued. "He is a duke. Let me count the reasons why any flight of fancy in your mind is absurd."

"You tell her, Kit." Sam wasn't that much older than she. And he'd had his share of mischief.

"I am old enough to marry." She clenched her teeth around each word.

"Over my dead body," Kit growled.

"You—you're not even a woman," Sam stuttered.

She stood, fisting her hands on her hips. "Just what am I then?"

"You're our little sister." Ben answered in a tender voice.

"I am a female. I am a woman." She stared at each one individually.

"You are *not*."

Her gaze flew to Sam. His throat convulsed as if he'd swallowed a bug.

"He meant you're not grown up enough to be a woman," Kit stated.

Fuming, she swung around and stomped off, to anywhere away from her three irritating siblings.

"Now just a darn minute," Ben shouted.

Sam yelled, "Wait!"

Why she stopped, she didn't know. Maybe because, for the first time, her brothers sounded uncertain.

Sam stepped forward. "All right. You are eighteen. Almost a woman." Her face tightened with temper. He quickly held up his hands. "We're just concerned. As brothers should be."

"That's right." Ben stepped closer. His voice lowered. "We care, Alex."

She glanced to Kit. Frown lines deepened his scowl. "Women don't always know what they want."

Seeing his concern, her shoulders relaxed. Her brothers did care for her, and she loved them, too.

"I want to know what the Brit did to entice our little sister." Ben's words were filled with anger, and carried a threat.

"He *is* a nobleman." Kit's tone sounded suggestive.

"The scoundrel," Sam burst out.

Her hackles rose. "What is wrong with you three? He's done nothing."

"He just dropped you on your bum."

"Didn't look to me like there was a lot of *charming* going on," Kit added.

"If anything, seemed to me like *she* was pestering *him*." Sam hooked his thumbs in his belt loops.

Her mind couldn't keep up with their thought process. Were they mad, or just plain witless? "Not that I care what you think, brother of mine. Just don't stick your nose where you do not belong." *Brave words standing before these three.* Her tongue too oft spouted before she gave herself time to think.

"You're my sister. And if I think the duke needs a lesson, I'll be glad to give him one."

"You big oaf." She stood toe to toe with Ben, angling her chin so she could glower into his face. "You leave him alone."

"You have no say in the matter." His voice hardened.

"Alex. Has the duke done something to lead you on?" Kit asked.

If he only knew. She'd thrown herself at Giles and in return, he dumped her in front of her brothers. At her silence, or maybe her flush, Ben chose his own answer.

"There are boundaries a man does not cross." He swung around with harsh intent.

"No!" She lurched forward and grabbed his arm. "He . . . he thinks I'm a child."

"You *are* a child!"

She hated her brother right now.

"Don't split your spleen, Ben. 'Tis obvious this infatuation is one sided." Kit chuckled. "After all, he did deposit our sister almost in our laps."

"Keep the brat away from him," Sam laughed. "That's what he said."

This time when Alex turned to walk away, no one stopped her.

Chapter 12

Apparently, races often took place in this county, and Nathaniel Hardcastle had felt the need for adding a race-course on a large section of his property. Giles scanned the crowd at the Hardcastle plantation. Eager participants and energetic steeds waited for the race to begin. Meanwhile, several gentlemen bickered and haggled, bets were made, and many crowed for their preferred horse.

Sam was racing his favorite. Being the smallest of the brothers, he'd been the favored choice to ride—not to mention he claimed to have the fastest horse. The others decreed him the best at racing. Several declared he seemed to have a camaraderie with every horse he greeted.

James quibbled with men he knew, and Giles made a few wagers of his own. He almost expected Alex to enter her black stallion in the race, but there was no sign of her. Either she did not know about the race, or her father denied her permission to join the men.

Sam pushed his way around a group of gentlemen. He looked flustered and rushed to his father's side.

"Something is wrong with Brusor."

"What do you mean, something's wrong?" James asked.

"He's not behaving normally. At first, I thought it was his hoof. He paws the ground. I don't have time to figure it out before we start, and I don't want to race him if I don't know what's wrong."

"Did you check his leg?"

"I did. It appears fine. He seems fit." Sam took off his hat and combed his fingers though his hair. "I just have a feelin', Pap."

James put his hand on Sam's shoulder. "You know best, son."

"Does this mean you will not be in the race?" Giles asked.

"Like I said, Brusor seems fine. But, no. I'm not willing to take a chance."

"Sam's instincts are spot on with horses," James said to Giles. "He talks to them. He understands them."

"Speaks their language," Nathaniel affirmed. "Never seen anything like it."

"He's trying to tell me something. I won't be able to race flat out if I have this on my mind."

"That's too bad, Sam," Giles added. "I was looking forward to collecting some winnings. I heard you were the one to keep an eye on."

"Well, now." Nathaniel rubbed his hands together in enthusiasm. "Dancer has an even better chance of winning."

Sam stepped closer to Giles. "I have an idea, if you agree to it."

"What's that?" The youngling seemed anxious.

"Gent. After what you told me about him catching Alex's stallion, I think he could win this race."

"You do?" Giles pondered the idea and decided he'd rather not race on unknown terrain with a newly acquired horse. "No matter how tempting, I'm not sure that is a good idea."

"Just hear me out." Sam held up a hand. "I looked him over. Had a chat, so to speak. If the idea is agreeable to you, I'd like to ride Gent. I want to give it a shot. But I need an answer fast. So, I can get him used to me being on his back before the race."

Being a good judge of character as well as making tough decisions in short order, Giles delivered a quick response. "Looks like Gent will be entered in a race."

Sam's face lit up, making Giles glad he could help out. Together, he and Sam hurried to Gent. Giles felt the steed should know Sam had his owner's approval. Sam pressed his face to Gent's ear. After a discussion between horse and rider, Sam pulled on his gloves, grabbed the reins and nodded in thanks. Then, he led Gent over where the horses were kept before the race.

"Make me proud," Giles called after them.

He joined James in the spectator area. Viewers watched as each horse and rider made their way to the starter line. Sam leaned forward and stroked Gent's mane.

"Is that your horse," James asked.

"Sam seems to think Gent belongs in this race. 'Twould seem they had a *conversation*."

"Even as a youngster, the boy talked to horses," James said.

Giles studied the pair. If the boy had any ideas of keeping Gent for himself, he best get the notion out of his head. Giles had taken a liking to the beast and planned to take him home to England.

The blast of a gunshot signaled the race was on. One gelding spooked, jumping into Gent. The horse showed his mettle. Seemingly unaffected, Sam quickly got Gent under control. With one hand on the steed's golden mane, Sam lowered his body, and Gent leapt forward in a burst of speed. With their coattails flying, men bellowed, compelling their horses to a faster pace. Sam's white shirt stood out amongst the other riders.

Steeds bolted down the road, around the pond, and pushed through the tree line. In a mere matter of moments, a rider broke through the trees with news of who was in the lead. A man waited at every checkpoint to assure the rules were met by each contender.

The excitement of the crowd was contagious. Giles cheered along with men he didn't know. Wagers were placed, pledges were made, and stakes heightened as each chap brought news from his checkpoint. Ale flowed freely, men chewed cigars in anxious expectation—a good time to be had by all.

Pride filled his chest when news came that his horse had caught the others. Gent proved to be a favorable investment. And with Sam in the saddle, the two had a remarkable chance of winning. Someone slapped him on the back, and he nearly spewed a mouth full of ale.

"Lookie. Here they come."

Three horses abreast of each other, tearing down the road, with several stragglers behind. Sam crouched low and Gent's legs stretched out a full half-length beyond what Giles could comprehend. Magnificent creature. Beautiful lines. With graceful strides, Gent surged forward, overtaking the other two.

Riding hell for leather, the middle rider slashed his whip on his horse's flank, prepared to overtake the third man. All the while, Sam inched farther ahead. Shouts and curses filled the sky.

Sam claimed the finish line.

The crowd roared. Cheers so loud, Giles might never recover his hearing. Backslapping and foot stomping commenced.

"Lost by a nose, Nathanial." James pounded his neighbor on the back.

Nathanial jerked his hat off his head and threw it on the ground. "Dad blame it. I got eyes. Half a length is more'n a nose."

"Come now, Nathanial. No need to get all riled up."

"Ain't riled, James. Your boy knocked the spots off Dancer. Thought I had you this time. Especially with a newcomer, since Sam didn't ride his own horse. Who owns that steed?"

James nodded toward Giles.

"That would be me."

"Let me shake your hand." Nathaniel grabbed his hand with a firm grip. "Fine animal."

"Thank you. I bought him at Hudson's auction."

"Never saw him up on the block."

"He wasn't. I met a man who needed a bit more blunt for the animal he wanted to bid on. The gold gelding caught my eye and we struck up a deal."

"Well, you got the better end, I'd say."

Giles grinned. "After today, I think so, too."

Nathaniel turned back to James. "Here's your ten dollars, James. Don't go spending it. I'll get it back next race."

"I'll keep that in mind, Nathaniel." James gave a hearty laugh. "Well now, Giles. Looks like your horse won the purse."

"I believe Sam had something to do with that. As for the purse, it belongs to Sam."

"Mighty generous of you. Proud of my boy." James glanced to the finish line. "Would you look at that? A smile big enough to show all of his white teeth."

Sam slid off Gent's back among a bellowing group of congratulating enthusiasts. His smile damned near split his face.

"Not generous at all. He earned it. I must say I am impressed with his skill. Not racing, but knowing his animals. Sam has a gift."

For the second time, Giles wondered if Sam would be interested in going to England.

Chapter 13

As the midday sun climbed to the middle of a blue streaked sky, Giles stood on the veranda staring beyond the courtyard. With a leisurely stride, he made his way down the curved staircase and took the path leading away from the stables. Chrysaor, the white stallion, danced along the fence line of the enclosed meadow. Breathtaking. There was no other word for it. Pranced as though he were on exhibition. A prideful animal. Well deserving. Morgan would love to get his hands on this stallion. But he had Pegasus. And Carmichael had been adamant about not selling Chrysaor.

How relevant, the animals had been named after a winged horse in Greek mythology. With his mane and tail in the wind, the magnificent stallion appeared as though he were flying.

Restless, Giles headed for the stables. Yesterday he'd spent the day with Carmichael, touring more of the man's plantation. James had a grand and lordly life. Such ethnicity caused Giles to long for his homeland. As soon as his business concluded, he would make haste to his ship.

So why had he not already departed?

A movement from the corner of his eye snagged his attention.

He ignored the leap in his pulse.

"Good afternoon."

"Spying again, Alex?"

"Nope. Just thought maybe, since Papa is busy, you would like to go for a ride with me. But, please don't expect me to ride sidesaddle. Those things are atrocious. And I am wearing a proper riding outfit."

"So you are." He studied her. She presented the appearance of any debutante. Although riding with a young woman sporting blind adoration in her eyes might not be a good idea. He shrugged, he had nothing else to do.

"I thought we could head over to the west end. Papa hasn't taken you there yet. We could visit the stud farm."

If the little minx wanted to visit studs, he'd just have to oblige her—for now. When the animals did their mating, he'd embarrass the stockings off . . . well the hellcat probably didn't wear any stockings. Even though she had donned the appropriate clothing. At least for today.

He tugged the front of his hat. "Very well. Lead the way."

"Are you game for a race?" She broke out in a smile that could equal the luster of the shining sun. Excitement added to her allure.

His heart's rhythm lurched with unbidden enthusiasm. He needed to watch his step.

Alex gathered the reins around her gloved hand and spurred the black with a light kick of her riding boots. The horse shot off at a furious pace. Good God, the girl would break her neck, yet. But her experience as a horsewoman showed in the way she handled the stallion. The two raced as one with astonishing swiftness over the field of grass and clover. What a sight they made.

Gent tossed his head in an anxious bounce, determined to be away. With a firm hand, Giles urged the horse faster as he sprinted to catch Alex.

In a matter of moments, Giles gained ground. When they reached a grassy knoll, Alex pulled back and eased into a walk alongside him. Fresh spring air blew the silvery tendrils hanging in front of her tiny ears. Exhilaration seemed to encompass her in waves as the shiny black stallion pranced and snorted with pride.

"I have been proven wrong. You can ride."

"I love to ride." Alex turned her arresting smile on him.

His insides warmed. "I noticed."

"He's as preen as any peacock strutting his feathers."

"It's difficult to say who is more proud of his performance. You, or him."

When she flashed her self-assured smile, again, Giles felt more pleasure than he dared admit. He admired her spirit, nothing more. An excellent rider, he granted. As though she were made to be on the steed's back. She seemed so carefree.

"I love the freedom and I feel his energy." She beamed as she patted the horse's mane.

Alex truly is stunning.

Giles heart softened.

When they topped the hill, she pulled at the reins. "This is a good place to give the horses a rest."

Giles agreed and dismounted. When she remained atop the black, he arched a brow.

"Well?" She waited.

A sound much like a groan escaped him as he mumbled under his breath, "Impertinent scamp." Reaching up he gently grasped her beneath her arms, the pads of his hands touching the sides of her breasts. Sensations as sharp as hot coals burned his palms.

She smiled—the teasing minx. He could wipe the grin right off her face in an instant. A slight turn of hand, a quick squeeze of her breasts—shock the little baggage. He swallowed. As tempting a thought, he feared the action might be too enticing for him to ignore.

She leaned over and placed her hands on his shoulders. He lifted her with ease and as she slid to the ground, her breasts brushed against his chest. *Bloody hell.* Caught by his own stratagem.

Naughty and full of guile, she flirted as well as the most practiced lightskirt in England. Where had she learned to be so bold? He set her on her feet with a jar. That ought to rattle her teeth a mite. He quickly dropped his hands and stepped back, damning his body for responding to the unexpected contact.

Instead of shrinking away, she looked him in the eye and grinned. If she were any other woman . . . God's blood, she was his host's daughter. He could hardly throw her to the grass and have his way with her. Even if she were curved in all the right places. Even if she did smell sweet and feel lissome in his arms.

He swallowed a groan.

She tossed that mane of glorious hair over her shoulder, took a step forward, and stumbled in a hole. Shock slashed her face, but she quickly recovered. She thrust out her chest, put a hand on her hip, and gave him what she must have thought was a come-hither look.

Giles couldn't help it. He opened his mouth and laughter burst out.

Her heated gaze quickly changed from allure to anger. God, the woman was beautiful with her stubbornness. A heightened sense of awareness strummed along his nerve endings. When had he started thinking of the blasted girl as a woman?

Her eyes went all warm and glazed over. The lush petals of her mouth opened slightly and the tip of her tongue teased their fullness. The termagant wanted him to kiss her. And blast it all, he wanted to do just that.

Hell and damnation.

The chit thought she knew what she was doing. She had no idea she played with fire. And even if he burned, he refused to take a virgin barely out of the schoolroom. Grabbing Gent's reins, he took a few paces forward.

"We could sit for a while," she offered.

"I prefer walking. Besides, you don't want Blackie to run off again."

"Blackie," she spat. "I really hate his name."

"Why haven't you changed it?"

"Well, I want to." She quickened her pace to keep up with him.

He seized the subject as one to keep the chit's mind off an inept seduction. "Have you thought of any names?"

"None I'm satisfied with. Horace thinks I should call him Black Devil."

Giles stopped, then glanced over his shoulder at the black. "Is there a reason behind his suggestion?"

"Blackie wasn't very friendly when he first arrived at his new home." Alex patted the horse's mane. "But he took right off to me. He has adjusted well. He's the most splendid horse I've ever seen. He deserves a better name, just as beautiful and as proud as he."

"What do you like?" Giles turned and started walking again.

"Well, I think he is magical," Alex said as she kept in step with him. "He's special. I just can't decide."

"All right. Let's see. To get in the spirit of things, Demon runs along the line of Devil." He made a motion with his hand. "I consider Angel to be too mild for this spirited creature."

"I agree."

"Hmmm. Magical . . . Witch and Warlock sounds more like Demon. When I think of magic, I think of fairy dust."

Alex came to a halt. Her eyes blazed with determination. "I am not calling him Fairy."

Giles burst out in laughter. "I should think not."

"I thought along the line of something dark, like the night." She fell back into step. "I could call him Dark Night. Naw, it's still not right. Too . . . ordinary."

"There are stars in the night sky. Maybe Night Star."

"Too familiar. Someone else could pick the same name. You mentioned fairy dust."

He stopped in shock. "You are not going to call such a manly beast Fairy Dust."

"Heavens, no!" She laughed. "But something intrigues me along that vein."

"How about Stardust? You've got the stars in the night sky along with a little fairy dust." He smiled, pleased with his idea.

"That's it! Stardust! I love it." She jumped with joy, making the stallion rear in surprise. She soothed the black, calling him by his new name. "Stardust. Stardust you shall be." She stroked his mane, smiling in delight. "Stardust. I think he likes it."

His gaze followed Alex's hands, as they stroked down the stallion's neck. Soft gentle hands, yet strong enough to handle the black with expertise. His breathing grew labored as he stared at her fondling caress.

Fondling?

Abruptly he realized where his thoughts had gone.

He was envious of the damned horse.

The dinner hour came and went without Giles in attendance. After his eye-opener this afternoon, the best course for him lay in any direction other than Alex Carmichael. He leaned a hip on the stone wall of the veranda sweeping from one end of the massive wing across the full length of Carmichael's house. Giles lifted a cheroot and bit the end. With a flick of his wrist, he scraped the match stick against the stone. Flame flashed on the end. Torching the tobacco, he drew deeply, watching the cigar fire a luminous red glow.

A thousand stars sparkled like diamonds in a blanket of black velvet. The night was cool even without a breeze. He took a deep breath, hoping the quiet night would calm some of the restless energy bouncing about on the inside. Floral fragrance wafted to him from the baskets of flowers hanging over the balustrade. A night for seduction, if one had such a notion.

Alex's image popped into his mind. He recalled how she'd stroked Stardust, and he imagined those hands stroking him in the same fashion. Her long, delicate fingers slipping down the side of his neck, curling in his chest hair, gliding over his ribs and farther down between his legs.

He'd never had trouble controlling his lust. Why he was having these lascivious thoughts about a girl half his age, he couldn't fathom. It was maddening. Besides, she had three vigilant brothers who would stop this line of thinking for him. He didn't want, nor need, the inconvenience.

Being a self-possessed man, he remained calm in critical situations. With patience and a clear head, he had made life-threatening decisions without a moment's hesitation. Anger, frustration—he'd learned to control every emotion. Patience and disguising his feelings had not only led him to succeed in achieving his goals, but had saved the lives of many.

Which was why this unexplained loss of control had him bewildered. He had no constraint over his thoughts, and very little over his manhood when he was in close proximity to a certain beleaguering young woman. He could not get Alex's kiss out of his mind. From the moment his mouth feasted on hers, he'd wanted to kiss her again. She had been as eager as he. A mating dance full of fire and passion. She said she had been taught. His eyes narrowed.

Who did the teaching?

A tug pulled at his gut. He dare not acknowledge the inquiry, for it smacked too closely toward jealously. Why did he lose all sense of restraint when he was near her? Yet somehow, simply looking at her robbed him of caution.

Lifting the cheroot, he inhaled, watching the fiery red glow on the end, allowing the smoke to burn his lungs. What a pity he couldn't whisk her away and teach her how to use her skillful tongue on other areas. His groin tightened.

God's blood. The chit remained in his mind like a cancer.

He closed his eyes to shove away his licentious thoughts. Darkness only brought her image clearer.

A slight breeze stirred along his cheek. His instincts told him he was not alone. He opened his heavy lids.

Time suspended in the moonlight. The image of his dream emerged before him, like an angel. He stood there, drinking in her beauty. In a cloud of gauzy lace, the moon's glow revealed a surprising amount of curves for one so young.

A golden halo of hair fell in loose waves about her shoulders. One wild strand curved around a plump breast. Was it his imagination or could he see the darkened tip? His tongue felt too big for his throat. His hands prickled at the thought of tangling in her thick tresses, tugging her to him, holding her captive while he plundered her mouth.

Inch by inch, he lowered his gaze, absorbing every detail, down to a tiny waist his large hands would easily span with his fingers overlapping. Nicely rounded hips . . .

Air hissed between his teeth. Unable to tear his gaze away, he stared at the center of her enticing curves. Her nest of curls lay barely hidden from his view.

His mouth went dry. His palms itched, daring to touch.

His gaze snapped back to find her striking eyes drinking him in as well, and an alluring smile on her full, pink lips that made his head spin.

So soft, so sweet, so tempting . . . her very scent stirred him. While his subconscious fired barbs of warning, his body whispered an irresistible 'yes.'

A demon housed his soul, testing his strength. All he could think of was how she would taste. When the tip of her tongue darted out to moisten her bottom lip, a jolt of lust hit his groin. He uttered a low groan.

A man would have to be made of stone not to react to her beauty. While his conscience and his honor battled, the angelic vision drifted closer. He tossed the cheroot over the rail. Surely madness drew him forward.

She leaned into him. His hands automatically rose to her shoulders, clasping the flimsy material covering her upper arms. Her eyes yearned, pure and real. And trusting. His blood pooled low in his belly. His gaze latched onto her mouth . . .

Her lips puckered as his fingers grazed her cheek, traced the column of her neck.

She stood on her tiptoes with a smile luring him to his doom, while her hands slid around his neck. Twining her fingers in his hair, she tugged him closer. Without hesitation, she opened her mouth.

His tongue eased out and slid over his bottom lip. She felt soft and fragile in his arms. Giles tightened his hold. He had lost his mind. At this moment, he would gladly drown in insanity.

"Alex," he moaned.

Moonlight streamed across broad shoulders. Naked broad shoulders. Alex caught her breath. For some time, she had watched Giles' silhouetted profile, wondering how to approach him. She'd unwrapped the gown from her trousseau in hopes he would not reject her again. By the look in his eyes, she'd done the right thing.

A dark dusting of curls scattered over his chest and down to a lean, narrow waist. Muscles covered his torso and arms. The sight of him standing almost nude, bathed in the moon's glow, would be forever singed in her mind. This delectable man that she had scrutinized so carefully, far exceeded her illusions.

She'd dreamed of his kiss. She wanted him to kiss her again. And then because she simply could not help herself, she leaned into him. She studied his face—a long way up despite her own height. He edged closer and she could do nothing but stare at his lips. His smile was slow and filled with sensuous promise.

Sliding her arms around his neck, her fingers twined in the hair at his nape.

He secured one arm around her back, causing her to catch her breath. Finally. She hoped he would not change his mind.

He did not.

His lips came down with the silken touch of a butterfly's wings. So soft. So perfect. Bending her backward, he fastened his mouth over hers.

At long last, she had her duke. He kissed her willingly. She needed to remind herself this was really happening. When his tongue teased her lips, she opened to him. His arms tightened as he deepened the kiss, then boldly thrust his tongue inside. Sensations like nothing she'd ever known swamped her.

She floated.

She burned.

Time and space disappeared. The only thing that existed was him. Her. And the delicious awareness swamping her body.

Their tongues meshed while her heart pumped furiously. Unable to take a breath, her head spun in a whirlwind of emotions. When he broke the kiss, she clutched him tighter for fear of falling. The hand at her waist held her firm. The warmth of his breath fanning over her cheek enthralled her.

"You occupy my thoughts. You taunt my every waking moment," he whispered as is lips brushed her temple. "At night I cannot sleep for you haunt my dreams."

Her heart filled with joy.

"Your tempting mouth." He eased away, enough to see her face. "Your daring eyes." He nuzzled her cheek with his nose. "Your sweet smelling flesh."

His voice was rich and more seductive than the moonlight. If heaven existed on earth, it was right here in Giles' embrace.

Arms of steel with gentle hands and mesmerizing fingers. She melted into his touch. His mouth sprinkled riveting kisses on her eyes, her cheeks, down the side of her neck. She gripped his shoulders and angled her head, relishing the delightful tingles. When he licked the flesh across her collarbone, her breasts grew heavy and her knees weakened. She swayed. His mouth captured one tight peak through her night-rail, hot and wet. Her body jolted at the raw stimulation. Quivers shot to her core. His arm, encircling her waist, held her up for her legs no longer had substance.

She moaned her pleasure. Never had anything felt so blissfully sinful? Knowing Giles was the one who caressed her and created this agonizing need made her heart soar to tormenting heights. She was in his arms. She loved him. He had complete power over her body. She'd never imagined love could be so wonderful.

Or so delicious.

He took her lips once more, his tongue plundering within. His kiss swept her away with passionate abandon. All she wanted was him. Desperately she clung to him till she could no longer breathe. With a groan he tore his mouth from hers. His chest heaving, he pressed her against his pounding heart. Hers too, thumped a dashing rhythm. He cradled her, his hand pressing her head under his chin, while pliable fingers massaged her scalp.

Moments stretched into timelessness. Precious seconds of paradise, that before she could only sense in her dreams.

"What have you done to me?" he whispered.

Oh, such sweet music to hear. With a husky laugh, she stretched, cuddling closer, knowing he expected no answer. They held each other in silence, his hand stroking her back. Her pulse calmed, but she wanted him to kiss her again. Her breasts still tingled, and heaven help her, she wanted his glorious mouth there again.

All too soon he stopped.

"You must go back inside." He grasped her fingers and brushed his lips over her knuckles. He then placed her hand on his arm, and gently urged her forward. It was so nice, holding on to his arm, walking across the balcony. If only this moment could last forever.

When they reached her bedroom door, he gave her a light kiss on her temple. Silence hung between them as he held her gaze, watching her step inside. Those dark, beautiful eyes sending her so much emotion, they needed no words.

He seemed reluctant to let her go. The sudden urge begged her to fling herself into his arms, but she feared breaking the magical spell surrounding them. He squeezed her hand gently just before he allowed her fingers to slide through his, and softly closed the door.

She wrapped her arms about her waist and smiled.

The duke was hers.

Chapter 14

What the bloody hell was he thinking? At some point—soon—he needed to get his mind out of his trousers and back into the head upon his shoulders.

Did Alex look different today? Or had his perception changed after their clandestine meeting on the veranda? He'd agreed to this outing readily enough. Hell, his reaction to the chit alarmed him.

"Just drop the reins, they won't leave us."

"I'm not so sure about this one," Giles muttered. Although Gent obeyed every command—so far—Giles didn't want his horse to wander away. He had followed Alex to a clearing just beyond where he had first seen her—when he thought she needed rescuing. Dismounting, he dropped the reins as Alex suggested, then stepped to her mount. Reaching up, he gently grasped her beneath her arms.

She gave him a teasing smile.

A groan escaped him. He was succumbing to her coquettishness, the same as last night.

She bent, placing her hands on his shoulders, and he lifted her with ease. As she slid to the ground, her breasts brushed him, causing an expedient reaction. One only had to glance down to distinguish what lodged in his mind.

Instead of moving back, she looked him in the eye and grinned, naughty and full of indelicate mischief. Evidently their interlude on the balcony had only encouraged her.

What did you expect?

Torture, pure torture. This prolonging the inevitable was playing havoc with his wits. Her beauty beckoned him, that pert nose, her bow-shaped lips. Golden lashes, nearly invisible, swept her tanned cheeks. A dainty piece of femininity with a woman's curiosity.

Giles remembered her response last evening. When he pressed a kiss to the side of her throat, she'd arched her neck and welcomed him. His mind still rang with the sound of her purrs. His gaze dropped to the creamy expanse of her delicate throat. Soft skin drew him like a bee would seek the nectar of a delicate flower. He hovered, licking his lips in anticipation.

He damned near leaned in to have a taste of her, before he caught himself.

Giles shoved a frustrated hand through his hair. When had his cool nature deserted him? Why in bloody hell did his discipline over his own body disappear in the urchin's presence?

Because she used the wiles of a woman.

God's teeth. He was not a youth in short pants. Was he low enough to blame a child for his lunacy?

"Where are you?" Her voice drew him from the insanity of his thoughts.

He scowled.

She propped her hands on her rounded hips. "Don't tell me I have to revisit ground that I have already covered."

"I beg your pardon?" His brow arched.

"I suppose I mistakenly had the wrong impression that after last night, I would not have to chase you anymore."

He ground his molars as his gaze locked on hers and he stilled, as stolid as the massive oaks around them. "You are not going to let this rest, are you?"

"Not likely." She smiled with the confidence of a woman who had most assuredly hooked her man.

Good God.

"You know you are spoiled, don't you? Just because your father has handed you everything you've ever wanted from the day you were born, do not think you can lead every man you meet by the crook of your little finger." He held up his smallest digit in mock demonstration.

"I'm only interested in one." She stepped closer, and laid a hand on his chest. The contact struck deep and sudden, firing his blood. He backed her one step at a time until he pinned her against a tall oak. One arm braced on the bark, he crowded her, sandwiching her between him and the tree. Though he knew his face wore a scowl, what started as irritation, quickly grew to magnetism. And awareness.

Her breathing grew ragged and her eyes glazed over. When her fingers tugged at the front of his shirt, he could no longer resist.

Her tenderly-curved bosom, soft and warm, molded to his chest. Her hand crept up and curved to the back of his neck. Her eyes held a mystical power that drew him in, without his will. He pressed his lips to hers in a gentle coaxing, then lightly sucked at her bottom lip. Her fingers curled, tightening her hold, and she brashly opened her mouth.

Sweet bliss engulfed him. His tongue, firm and daring, slipped in to tease. She reacted with gusto, the kiss now a maelstrom of parry and thrust. When breathing became a problem, he drew back for air, eliciting a whimper of loss from her throat.

"Hold on to me, imp. I won't hurt you," he whispered. "I only want to give you pleasure."

Once again, Giles found himself lost in the sweetness of her kiss. Blood surged like fire through his loins. Eager to be inside her, he pulled her tighter and ground his hips into hers.

Instead of being frightened, his wonderful, brave darling gripped his hair and tugged. Following his lead, her tongue tangled with his in a mating dance. A blazing inferno burned in his gut when he felt her mimicking his movements. Sucking, arching ... a quick learner, but with a natural, curious passion he was sure she had not experienced before.

It pleased him, rocked him, knowing this desirable maiden wanted him as much as he wanted her.

As if she could not get enough, her body writhed and squirmed, which in turn fed his raging hunger. The need to touch her consumed him, guiding his fingers. He tugged at her bodice until it opened, then pulled the ribbon free that held her chemise. His eyes lingered on her woman's breasts as they came into full view.

His heart pounded madly. Alex was a treasure beyond words.

Creamy flesh beckoned, and he surrendered to his desire. He took one pouting bud between his lips, his wet tongue laving her nipple. A mewing sound escaped her and instinctively she surged toward him, telling him with her body that she enjoyed what he did. He took advantage of her delicious offering and suckled, giving her what her instincts were telling her she craved. The more he tasted, the more he wanted. Wonderous need drove him. The more he caressed, the tighter she clutched him. Like throwing fuel to a burning flame, her response fed his appetite, triggering his desire to please her.

He inserted his thigh between her legs and rubbed against her feminine mound. Even wedged between him and the oak, she still managed to arch her back and ride his thigh. He wanted to heighten her senses, intensify her pleasure. Devouring her mouth in another heated kiss, he tightened his fingers on her hips, pulling her higher, showing her a rhythm while riding his thigh. Higher, nearer, to his aching rod. He angled and pressed, and absorbed her passionate cries.

God Almighty, it felt good. So good.

In the back of his mind, something told him to slow down. He didn't want to hurt her. But she was ferocious in her raging ardor. Alex moved as if a violent storm had been roused in her body. Their love-play dented what little control Giles had over his fevered mind. Her vigorous reaction to his caresses nearly undid him. With everything in him, he fought the urge to throw her to the ground and thrust his throbbing member into the wet warmth he knew awaited him.

This moment was for Alex.

Thank God she'd taken to dresses of late. Alex whimpered when he halted the thrusting motion. Pulling up her skirts, he quickly settled his hand where his thigh had been, applying pressure against her mound. A soft groan erupted from her throat, and she pushed herself against him.

His fingers probed and searched. Moving the material aside, he found the slit in her drawers. He traced the crease of her inner thigh, finding her slick, swollen cove. God, she was wet and ready. He sucked air through his teeth, restraining his own urge to let the wild stallion in his trousers free. She wriggled and arched. He was sure this was virgin territory, but her female instincts had her writhing with enthusiasm.

His finger moved over the sensitive peak of flesh and slipped inside. A small cry echoed in his ears. Fire shot to his center. Blood pounded in his temple.

Bringing his thumb forward, he caressed her bud while his finger dipped, withdrew, and thrust inside her again. Her hips rocked. Her gasps fired his craving. Logic gone, he hungered for completion. As his fingers worked their magic, she became a wild woman in his arms. He kissed her deeply, the stroke of his tongue in her mouth a mirror of the way his finger delved her slick folds.

Her hands dug into his back, groaning. The sound was music to his ears as he ravaged her thoroughly, intensifying her need.

She rode his hand, her body trapped between him and the tree.

Lost in the sensation of his own making, Giles' fingers plunged deeper, his breathing harsh, relishing her heightened desire. When he knew she was close, he broke the kiss so he could see her face.

Alex stiffened and ground her head back in the rough bark. He watched her explode as tremors shook her core. An awestruck expression swept across her face—from burning fever to conflicting bewilderment. Her body quivered, and her fingers clutched him like steel bands.

He gentled his movement until she calmed. Her hands gradually relaxed on his shoulders as her head fell forward against his chest. Utterly spent.

Utterly beautiful.

His heart thundered in his chest. Warmth spread through his center knowing he had pleasured her beyond her control. She was as beautiful as any woman could be. This magnificent creature trusted him. His heart swelled with emotion.

Minutes trickled by as their breathing slowed and their hearts returned to a normal rhythm. The sudden tilt of her head cautioned him. Shock covered her face as she quickly glanced down between them.

"Giles?"

"Hmm?" He kissed the fleshy curve of her breast.

"What . . . what just happened?"

"Ecstasy," he breathed roughly. "I gave you pleasure."

Her palms met her scarlet cheeks and her eyes widened with realization. "You simply lifted my . . ." Dropping her hands, Alex pushed at her skirts to restore them to some semblance of order.

Giles cupped her chin, raising her eyes to meet his. "Oh no, my dear. Don't turn all shy on me. You wanted this." His voice gentled. "You wanted to know passion between a man and a woman. Now you do."

Her teeth caught her bottom lip. "But you never removed or unbuttoned any of your clothes. And, you did not . . ."

He could not miss the whirl of activity going on in her calculating mind. His vixen was not as shy as she was curious. His lips formed a satisfying smile. "This was for you, sweetheart. I received my pleasure in watching you."

She sucked in air and released a heavy sigh. Then her eyes grew wide. "I had no idea. Uh . . ." She glanced down again, staring at his groin. Her hand strayed toward his thigh. He was hard as a stone, and yet her glance—and the vicinity of her reaching hand—had him ready to erupt. He caught her wrist just in time.

Bringing her fingers to his mouth, he brushed his lips over her fingertips. "No, sweetheart. You tread into dangerous territory."

"I think we have already soared into danger." A mischievous glint filled her dark, molasses eyes.

He held her hand over his heart. "As I said. This was for you."

"Please, Giles," she purred like a contented kitten. "I want to touch you. I want to give you pleasure, too."

She wriggled her hips against the bulge of his maleness. A harsh gasp escaped him. God, what a bloody coil.

He wanted.

She was willing.

His control ready to snap.

"Giles," she whispered. "Show me."

Chapter 15

Alex knew she should not linger. She should hurry to the house. But she wanted to enjoy those precious moments over and over before greeting any of her family. With her arms wrapped around herself, she embraced the aftermath of when the duke held her in his arms. *Oh, my.* Her heart raced at the thought of what they had done.

Mating, she understood. After all, her father owned studs. But she never knew—never dreamed—such delight existed between a man and a woman.

The duke had touched her, *there.*

She was still floating. Although her curiosity had been roused to recklessness, he had not allowed her to caress his hardness. *He simply smiled, bundled her up, and carried her to her horse.*

She danced a little jig and screeched aloud, unable to contain her joy.

"What are you up to, Alex?"

Guiltily, she swung around. Her eyes widened at being caught by Ben. She only hoped he couldn't read her mind. Heat rushed to her cheeks.

"Uh . . . nothing." She tried to calm her racing heart.

"You're up to something." His eyes narrowed and penetrated. "What is it?"

"I told you, nothing." Ben might be the most hardheaded of the three, but growing up she'd been closer to him than the others. She positively could not share this bit of information. She chewed on her bottom lip.

"Now I know you did something. You only do that when you've done something you shouldn't have."

Her hands flew to her cheeks, knowing they were red. Her heart took off at a gallop. How could he possibly know?

"Out with it."

"Out with what?" Sam stepped around the corner of the stables.

Oh Lord. "Nothing."

"Didn't sound like nothing the way you two were going at each other."

"Our little sister is guilty as sin." Ben shoved up the tip of his hat with his thumb.

"What did she do?" Sam asked, pinning her with his stare.

"That's what I'm trying to find out. And it ain't *nothing*. You gonna tell me, little sister?"

"Stay out of it Ben," she said.

"Gor, Brother. I believe you're right." Sam studied her more closely. "And it must be something we won't approve of," he declared.

"You too," Alex snapped at Sam. "I don't need either of you sticking your noses in my business. I am a grown woman."

"And when did this happen?" Sam bent over, clutching his belly as he burst out a laugh. "Don't half the lads 'round here call you a tomboy? They say you're considered to be in the domain of boys."

Of everything Sam could have said, that had to be the cruelest. She had no idea others were talking about her to that extent behind her back. No wonder no one had ever tried to tempt her. No boy had ever claimed to be sweet on her.

Well, it didn't matter. She shoved a curl behind one ear as she pushed away the hurt. With a deep breath Alex released it along with the insult. She had set her sights on one man long ago. He was the only one who mattered.

"I've set my cap for the duke."

Ben and Sam stared, agog.

"Kit made it clear," Ben said in a low voice. "And in case you didn't hear him, I'll tell you again. You can't have him."

"I *will* have him."

"Just wait till Kit hears about this," Sam warned.

A fist seemed to grasp at her lungs. "You can't mean to tell him."

"Of course, we're going to tell him. Right, Brother?"

"Right, Sam." Taking her firmly by the arm, Ben propelled her toward the corral.

"How can you do this to me?" She dragged her heels.

"Then tell us what's going on."

"I'm not a child."

"How many times we gonna have this discussion?" Sam braced his fists on his hips.

"The man is too old for you." Ben took off his hat and brushed his fingers through his hair. "The duke lives in England. What's wrong with the boys around here?"

"You just said they think of me as a boy."

"What do you think the blasted duke is going to do? Write you a sonnet to pledge his eternal love?" Sam held up his hands, at a loss for words. He looked as frustrated as she felt. He ground the heel of his boot in the dirt.

Ben tipped his hat back on his head and dropped his arms by his side. "I asked you before and I'll ask you again, did something happen?"

Sam's head jerked up.

Oh, no. She never could hide her exploits. With her face flaming, they were bound to jump to the wrong . . . well, not so wrong conclusion.

"Did the Brit do something?"

"Answer Ben. What the hell happened?" Sam never swore in front of her. She felt like a lit fuse attached to a powder keg with the flame way too close to the explosive.

"That whoreson," Ben shouted.

Sam spun on his heel and before he could take two steps, Alex screamed, "Wait! Where are you going?"

"To find me a Brit."

"Stop," she shouted. Ben grabbed her arm to keep her from following.

"Is it true? Did the Brit do something, Alex?"

"You can't let Sam take off like that. You've got to stop him. He is mistaken."

Sam halted. "Mistaken?

She chewed on her lip again.

"Alex," Ben growled.

"I told you. Nothing." She jerked her arm free.

"I don't believe you. Something happened. If you won't tell me, you'll just have to face Kit."

"What's been going on around here?"

Speak of the devil.

"Now we'll see what's what." Ben crossed his arms over his chest.

"Well?" Kit asked. "I just heard Sam shouting. Then I find the two of you yelling at each other. One of you going to talk?" He stared at her face and his eyes widened. "Alex?"

"Nothing." With a toss of her head, her long hair flew across her shoulder. She swung around in the opposite direction, intent on escape.

"Hold!"

By Kit's tone, she dared not take another step. She turned with reluctance. And immediately regretted not running. She took a tentative step backward, which earned her a scowl. Unable to stand his scrutiny, she dipped her head.

"What mischief are you up to now?"

"Sneaking around. Our dear sister is up to no good, and I'm going to kill me a Brit." Ben's low growl befitted a wild bear.

"Someone better start talking." Kit stepped closer, his voice taking on a cutting edge.

"The duke." Ben glanced to Kit. They stared at each other for only a moment, communicating some unspoken message.

Kit's eyes were hard when he glanced back to her. "Alex, you seem far too comfortable with the man for my satisfaction. Do I need to wring the bastard's neck?"

Exactly the reaction she expected from her brother.

"Kit, no." God, they were such hotheads.

"Did he take advantage of you?"

"No. He did not." She had been a willing participant. But she couldn't tell her brother that. How did she get into this mess, anyway?

"You have no idea of a man's—"

Ben interrupted Kit. "Damn it, Alex. You know nothing—"

"Will you two just stop! Nothing is wrong. Nothing happened." She would go to hell for lying. "I am tired of you telling me what to do. I know what I want!"

"And just what is it you want?" Kit asked.

"You're too young to know what you want," Ben shouted.

Ben was yelling, Kit accusing, and Sam swearing—how had her world crashed in a matter of moments? Damn her brothers. "You're ruining everything. You've got it all wrong." Tears ran down her cheeks in exasperation. Anger raged from her bones.

Her fists shook, her body trembled. She flashed her most ruth-less glare. "I'm getting tired of being told I'm a child."

She spun around, ran to her horse, and swung into the saddle, kicking Stardust in his ribs. He took off quicker than a flash of lightning.

Chapter 16

In all Giles' born days, he'd never met a woman as bold as the elfin brat. He fully ignored the nagging voice of his conscience reminding him he had aided her impertinence. Sharing zealous kisses was not the actions of a man who did not welcome a woman's diligence. Therefore, his conduct needed to be more principled.

Yet his pulse increased at the mere thought of this outing. He glanced at the sun overhead. Midday. A few clouds speckled in a canvas of blue. A bird or two soaring with a gentle breeze. His eyes crinkled as he took in the form swaying on the black in front of him. Excitement? An unusual feeling, this. Different from anything he'd known in all his years. How a slip of a girl snaked under his barriers, attacked his sensibilities, procured an emotion totally foreign to his being . . . His lips tugged at the corners. He liked it.

"This is a special place. No one else knows of it. At least, I've never seen anyone near here." Alex spoke over her shoulder as she led Stardust through a thick copse of trees.

"Your father's land is immense. I'm sure there are a number of areas you could get lost in."

She eased Stardust to a halt. "It's just through here." She dismounted, holding onto the lead strap. Finding her excitement infectious, Giles swung down from his own mount. Lifting some of the hanging brush, he followed her.

And stepped into one of God's creations.

A high wall of dark-gray rock sheltered a waterfall more glorious than any he'd ever seen. Waves spilled over the ledge to splash in a resounding rush, creating a whirling circle in a pool of crystal blue. Sun-glinting ripples flowed in a waltz to the edge of the embankment, while golden rays formed a mystic cocoon of enchantment. Lush green foliage hung in abundance, decorating the private lagoon which intimated at a lover's paradise.

His blood heated several degrees.

"Do you like it?"

He gazed at the fetching angel before him. "It's beautiful."

Like you.

"At night you can see a thousand fireflies." She glanced about the picturesque landscape. "Green diamonds glowing through their gossamer wings."

"You come here at night?"

"In the summer sometimes, when it's too hot to sleep. A nice dip relaxes me as well as cools the skin."

He did not even want to think of the image that thought created.

"When I was younger, I would dance and chase the lightning beetles. The most wonderful feeling centered in my chest when I captured them. Their tiny feet tickled my palms. Their light glowed through my fingers like a magical mist. Then I would open my hands and watch them fly away. My heart lifted with them."

A warmth spread through his chest. Such conflicting emotions, he could not begin to sort them out.

"The sky is so blue today," she said on a breathy sigh. "Enhances the impression of a perfect haven hideaway."

Giles couldn't find fault with that. The isolation alone proposed a clandestine rendezvous.

Food.

When one needed a distraction, food was a good diversion. At this moment the only thought in his lusty head—the one below his waist—involved the removal of Alex's clothes.

"A perfect spot for a picnic." He spun, hissing out a breath, thankful for the few paces of retreat to his horse.

He laid out a blanket, placed the hamper on one corner, and then admired the graceful way Alex arranged her skirts. Cornelia clearly had her niece practicing genteel ways. The girl's comportment had changed considerably. He had to admit, he no longer saw her as a child. She was a soft, inquisitive, responsive woman.

A smile as innocent as a babe crept over Alex's lips. Big brown eyes glinted, and for just a moment he remembered how they had burned bright in passion. A jolt of hunger shot through him, having little to do with food. Suddenly he wanted to discover whatever adventure this day might hold.

"Let's see what delicacies we have in this basket." Jerking his attention away from his licentious thoughts, he opened the hamper lid. "Ah." He lifted a slice from a cheese wheel wrapped in cloth. "This looks divine. We have bread, chicken, and strawberries."

"I see you've thought of everything."

He glanced over and gave her a sassy wink. "I added something special."

When he brought out a bottle of wine, her face lit up.

"I had to sneak two wine glasses from the cupboard."

"If Phebe had caught you, and knew I was sharing your find, you would have received a good tongue lashing." She let out a gleeful chuckle.

"My dear girl. Don't you think I could have smoothed Cook's ruffled feathers?"

"I have no doubt." She gave him an adoring smile that wrenched at him. Damn, she was desirable.

Lifting one glass, he poured from a bottle of French wine, then handed the delicate crystal to her. After filling another goblet with the burgundy liquid, he drank slowly and watched Alex as she sipped hers. His gaze moved to her dainty throat as she swallowed.

"This is some picnic. And I'm hungry."

"I like a woman with an appetite." He'd not been exposed to the full force of her personality. He smiled and looked forward to what the minx would deliver next.

"I like food. And I like to eat." When she grabbed a piece of chicken and tore a chunk out with her teeth, his eyes flew wide. Suppressing the ache in his loins, he belted out in laughter. She was no English damsel playing the part of a coy maiden. This girl was hungry and ate her fill.

Alex blinked, and her face flushed. Then she shrugged her shoulders and her lips turned up in a playful smile. "I like chicken."

"You are pure delight. I cannot say that I have ever seen a young woman attack a piece of chicken with such enthusiasm. Or pleasure."

Curse him, everything she did led to lustful imaginings within his thoughts.

As they ate, he repeatedly glanced at Alex. The longer he remained in her presence, the more enticing she grew. She really was quite lovely.

"I like the way you look at me."

"You do?" He raised a brow. "How do I look at you?"

"Like you want to eat me."

He choked on his wine.

"You should not be surprised. You have heard me speak my mind. I've wanted you—"

"Yes, I should be accustomed, and normally I am not shocked." He swiped at the spilled drink. "But you do have a way of taking me by surprise."

"I'm glad you have finally stopped running from me."

"Running?" His hand froze, holding a napkin in midair.

"Yes, running. I know you were afraid of me."

"I was not afraid."

"I love you. I have for a long time. All I desired was your attention."

Good God. The girl had him muddle headed. Just when he relaxed in her company, she threw another punch to his gut. And then another. He inhaled a deep breath and blew air out slowly. "I think perhaps you mistake infatuation with love. You could not possibly love me."

"Can't I? And after yesterday . . ." She dropped her head, but he saw her cheeks flush with embarrassment.

He should not be discussing his lapse of good judgement. He should not be thinking of her soft moans while he gave her pleasure. Or how she arched and pleaded, or the way she clutched him in her moment of bliss. He should not see her face swathed in ecstasy and remember how he'd lain awake all night thinking of nothing else. And he sure as hell should not be considering doing it again.

But, recalling her expression the moment she crested . . . his groin tightened and he ached from the fire poker between his legs.

"You are confusing a body's desire with love. A healthy amount of lust was involved."

"You let down your guard. You touched me . . . like . . ." Alex tilted her head. "Why? Why did you change your mind? Do you really like me?"

He stared into her beseeching eyes, noting the golden flecks in their dark hickory color. Another punch. Soon he would be battered and bruised from her aspirations. Aiming for a natural tone, he struggled to keep any emotion from his voice. With a shrug of his shoulders, he glanced to the swirling pool.

"You have captured my fancy."

"Is that all?" By her tone and the naughty sparkle in her devilish eyes, he knew she was thinking of the pleasure he'd given her.

"Every moment I spend with you, I find myself more intrigued." He seized a strawberry and held it to her lips, teasing the corner of her lips. She opened her mouth and sprang for it. He jerked his arm back, enjoying their game.

She took a deep breath, drawing his gaze to her bosom. The linen clung like a second skin, revealing tantalizing curves of what lay underneath. Her gown afforded little protection. Raw desire shot through his veins.

Exactly the kind of thinking he should avoid. His body had a will of its own. God Almighty! He had to stop thinking with his cock.

Wiggling her fingers in the air, she made a grand showing of plucking a strawberry. With a naughty glint in her eye, she held the plush fruit to her lips, and ran her tongue around the red surface before popping the thing into her mouth.

Lust threatened to choke him. For a man who seldom let anything unravel him, Giles was spellbound. Before he knew what she was about, she lunged at him, knocking him onto his back. With a siren's grin, she filched the strawberry, the one he'd forgotten dangled in his hand. She held the blasted fruit between her teeth.

He quickened. There was no hope for it. The chit enticed him with a magnitude unbelievable. He swallowed convulsively. For the life of him he couldn't resist stroking the backs of his fingers over her cheek. Bloody hell. This was not like him. Under any other circumstances, he'd grab her and make short work of getting the deed done. But she was an innocent, her father his host.

She closed her puckered lips, and the fruit disappeared. The tip of her tongue darted out to wipe the strawberry juice from her lush lips. His throat went dry.

He deserved a taste.

What was happening to him? Good God, his common sense had been stolen by the devil. He risked becoming a half-wit to an eighteen-year-old girl.

"Alex. We should not." He dropped his hands on her shoulders, intending to push her away. But once his palms covered the warmth of her skin beneath her clothing, the last thing he wanted was to let go.

"Should not what? Kiss you?"

He forced his gaze from her lips. "But a kiss can lead to more. I showed you that."

For a long moment they stared at one another. Her eyes glazed over so soft and warm, and her body angled into him. She made him feel something beyond what he knew, beyond what he could ever hope to have. A woman who gave her love freely. Unconditionally. Expecting nothing more than love in return.

How the hell could he think of her as anything other than a woman when she looked at him with desire? When she pressed her perfect curves into his hard maleness?

"The knowledge you desire me wrenches my vitals in a painful knot," he rasped, his voice ragged with longing. "Your curiosity stirs my body. I ache with the passion you arouse in me."

"Kiss me, Giles."

He shoved a strand of hair behind her ear. "You tempt me beyond my ability to resist."

"Then don't resist. Kiss me the way a man kisses a woman he wants to make love to." Her eyes blazed with innocent need, her passion lurking beneath the surface. He wanted her. And he had no desire to stop the heat surging between them. Ignoring the danger signals going off in the back of his brain, he surrendered.

"Oh, Alex, you have much to learn." He slid his fingers through her hair and gripped the back of her head. "Not make love *to*." At her confused expression, he pulled her head down as he whispered, "Make love *with*."

He took her mouth as a man dying of thirst in the desert. His blood heated. His loins hardened, burning to make her his.

Giles' lips moved over hers with the surety of a man who'd kissed a hundred women. Oh, how she thrilled at his surrender. He coaxed her mouth open, interlacing his tongue with hers. His arms, like bands of steel, crushed her to a chest solid as rock. When she thought she could no longer breathe, he broke the kiss and trailed his lips to her cheek, her neck.

"I'm tired of fighting you. Tired of denying myself what I desire most."

Alex could barely think. "What . . . do you desire most?" Her heart leapt with hope. More so because she wanted him to mean the words he spoke.

"You," he rasped. He tilted her head and eagerly covered her mouth with his again.

Finally. This was what she wanted. What she had been waiting for. What she had practiced with the butcher's son. But a boy's kisses had not prepared her for the onslaught of the duke. A man's touch. And oh, what a man. The powerful emotions swamping her body made her yearn beyond the bounds of reason, powerless to deny the mounting heat spreading from her chest to swirl low in her belly.

Was it possible to drown in a kiss? The impatience in his kiss quickly grew more insistent, more passionate. Opening her mouth wider, she welcomed his tongue sliding, coaxing, then delving deeper, ravaging her sensibilities.

Her lungs demanded she gulp for air. He held her immobile with his blistering gaze. Eyes dark and hot, melting her into a pool of desire. Gentle hands lingered, strong fingers spanned her waist, caressing, creating warmth. Surely a wicked spirit housed her soul, for she craved the feel of his hands touching her naked flesh.

Her mind whirled as he ran his hand down the curve of her waist and hip. Heat flared in her body, knowing what might happen again. She pressed closer, her hands clutching his neck, pulling him in for another wild kiss.

Shifting, he settled her between his legs. She barely had time to register their position for the delicious sensation swamping her while his hands slid over her back. She relaxed as he massaged her shoulders, and lower, liquifying her body. Her head fell forward. She melted against him.

He gently blew a breath across her ear, then nibbled on her neck. A tiny moan escaped her lips. Her body's response had her cupping the back of his head. Clutching his silky hair. Instinct compelled her actions. Giles was creating a frenzy within. She swiveled her hips.

In a smooth motion, he slipped her beneath him. A raven lock fell over his eye. Love for this man filled her chest. A woman's love. Tenderly, she raised her hand to his chest, feeling his heartbeat beneath her palm. Such leashed power should terrify her. Right now, his strength stirred curiosity rather than trepidation.

"I've hungered for you, Alex." His harsh breath rushed through his lips, almost in desperation.

Her heart lifted with hope and joy, to think she had driven him to *lust* for her.

"It hasn't been easy keeping my hands off you." One hand skimmed from her shoulder to her breast.

"You don't need to anymore. I'm here. I am yours." His eyes darkened and blazed with fire. She clung to him, thrilled that she could do this to him.

"Don't think, Giles. Just love me."

Chapter 17

G iles stared down at her, his stomach twisting in knots. "One day I fully intend to unravel you."

"Why not today?"

A jolt of need thrummed his belly. Coming here was a mistake. His head dropped to rest against her forehead. Desire warred with reason and conscience. A torrent of sensation soared through his blood. Pounded in his temples. His heart battered against his ribs.

He wanted Alex. God, how he wanted her. He longed to touch, tease; find sweet oblivion in her delectable body.

Raising slightly, he watched the emotions play across her face. Yearning. Hunger.

His control tumbled to dust. His gaze dropped to her mouth, where her tongue darted out to caress her bottom lip. Lust slammed at his endurance. He traced the outline of her mouth with a light touch of his index finger.

"Alex. Are you sure?" He could not deny her any more than he'd been able to resist their first kiss. His endurance weakened with each breath. Hoping to find some sense of fortitude to calm him, some stranglehold on his building need, he dallied.

But the look in her eyes, giving him her complete trust, snapped his last shred of resistance. Knowing he had no intention of following his own good advice, she suddenly became the one thing he must have.

He devoured her mouth, sliding his tongue in, then out, and back in again. Tasting, delving, so delectable he could not get enough. Breathing heavily, he kissed a path to her ear and nuzzled her neck. He swept his knuckles down her ribcage. Meaning to entice, and in turn he created torment for himself. His hands inched from her torso to the top of her bodice.

He glanced up and saw her provocative smile coaxing him further. He gladly obliged. He unraveled the laces of her gown, drawing the bodice apart to expose her creamy breasts. She gasped and shivered, with what he was sure was excitement. Through half lidded eyes, he gazed down at her, drowning in her perfection.

"Beautiful," he whispered.

Good god, he needed to taste her. And he wanted to savor every moment. With agonizing slowness, he adored her skin with his lips as he smoothed the gown over the curve of her shoulder. His fingers trailed down her side, to the indentation of her waist, and over her shapely hip to her thigh. At her knee, he drew a circle, then traveling the same path, his fingers drifted upward, relishing every delicious inch of bare flesh. Higher, over a taut belly and sensitive ribs.

A hiss escaped her lips.

He cupped a breast. Her body quivered and she moaned her pleasure. He relished the sound as he continued to fondle. With every caress, he wondered how he ever thought he could remain detached. His fingers kneaded, teasing the swollen buds into hardened peaks.

"Touching you this way knocks the very breath from me."

"I don't know what to do," she whispered.

"I will teach you." Languorously he removed the rest of her clothing while giving a kiss here, a nip there. Soon, every enticing inch was exposed for him alone. With the tip of his finger, he traced the vein at her throat. Her pulse beat a battering rhythm. He kissed her tenderly, then more forcefully as her response drove his hunger.

He shifted, tugging his shirt from his trousers. With a flick of his hand, the linen landed in the grass. When his gaze returned to her face, large brown eyes glowed with curiosity and awe.

"You're beautiful," she said.

He chuckled. "Men are not beautiful."

"You are. I have seen my brothers without their shirts." Her gaze lowered to his chest. "But to see you . . . to actually touch . . ."

Her fingers skimmed through the hair covering his chest. While she toyed and played with the curly strands, his reaction astounded him. Her touch sensitized his skin with a counteracting force. He had no idea his body could burn so hot. He sank against her velvety breasts, melding their skin together.

"You feel so good." The words she moaned rained havoc over his self-control. He dipped his head, kissing a pouting breast. Taking her nipple into his mouth, his tongue drew circles around the bud, then flicked it gently. She gripped his hair, holding him prisoner.

He loved her with tender kisses, soft touches, and warm caresses over every part of her body, memorizing each detail and curve, every valley . . . saving the temptation between her legs for last. His fingers drew close to his goal, then he'd change course; teasing, taunting, lulling her into submission.

While his fingers skimmed over her smooth skin, he kissed the other puckered nipple, and then drew the tender tip into his mouth. His tongue laved and he opened his mouth, taking more of her flesh, gently sucking.

She squirmed. Her little whimpers encouraged his already feverish lust.

He ran a finger over her knee to the inside of her thigh. Growing bolder, he moved higher, and higher to the juncture of her center. He swallowed her gasp with his mouth. When his fingers lightly skimmed her curls, she gripped him with urgency. Whether reflex or instinct, her enthusiastic fervor would be the death of him.

Giles told himself to linger. But one touch led to another, and another, until he reached his prize. He cupped her mound. Brushing her entrance, his fingers found her wet. Relief and hunger ripped at him as he probed her with a sure, swift stroke.

She shivered and jerked her hips while digging her fingers into his back.

He made no sound, only stroked her tenderly, massaged her swollen nub, then thrust one finger inside her slick passage.

Her breath hitched, brokenly.

Joy swamped his chest. How could the simple act of giving her pleasure affect him so?

Fierce hunger slammed his gut. He kissed and nipped behind her ear. "Alexandria. You are driving me wild. I want you." He stroked her harder, adding more pressure. She squirmed and shuddered; her moans grew louder. He swelled with elation, watching Alex in the throes of her passion, basking in her breathless gasps of pleasure.

He grinned, knowing he was the one to send her on her flight to ecstasy.

Her hips rocked in rhythm to his caress. Faster and more urgently, until she stiffened and cried out.

His chest ached with the need for air before he realized he was holding his breath, waiting for her to reach her climax. His chest ached. He marveled at the delicate creature in his arms. Bliss covered her features. Her moans made his rigid shaft ache. Desire boiled in his blood.

Summoning the power over every raw nerve he'd been taught to control, Giles wrestled with the desire to possess her. And lost. There was no denying himself now. He quickly worked the buttons on the falls of his pants, and tore his trousers off, kicking them aside. Slowly, he moved between her knees, bracing his arms to keep his weight from crushing her.

"Alexandria, will you let me . . ."

"Yes!" she cried with no hesitation.

His breathing ragged, he thought to soothe her fears. But his golden nymph seemed as eager as he. "I don't want to hurt you, but I'm afraid it is inevitable. You may feel some discomfort."

"I am not completely uninformed. And I have been riding a horse since I was four."

Her flesh cushioned his shaft. He angled himself, searching for the small entrance.

Holy Christ.

Raging want threatened to sweep him away. God help him, he wanted to thrust. Wildly and hard. Deep. He groaned at the restraint.

Narrow, the way inside her, and so very tight. And so very spectacular. He nudged, retreated, and nudged a little deeper. Sweat broke out on his neck. Slowly, by tantalizing inches, he sank into her, stretching and filling her with his rigid length.

God's blood.

He felt her stiffen, and wished he could save her the pain that pierced her body. Her breathing quickened, yet he was the one who trembled.

"Relax. I've got you." He gazed into her smoldering eyes. There was no turning back now.

Sinking into her virgin flesh, he kept his eyes locked on her face, taking in her beauty, her passion enflamed expression. And with one last push, he thrust his full length through her maid-enhead.

Blood roared in his temples. Pleasure spread from his cock through every nerve in his body. Rapture beyond his reckoning, his head threatened to explode.

He gasped for air in hopes to slow the impulsive urge to thrust and end his madness.

But her body clenched and stole his breath.

An explosion of fire singed his core.

Her dark eyes flew wide and a harsh groan escaped her lips. Her grip on him tightened. Then she smiled, giving him the assurance he craved.

Need forced him to move. Unable to remain still any longer, he drew out slowly, then carefully pushed back in, embedding himself deeper.

"Are you all right?" His voice barely more than a growl, he prayed she would not halt him now. For he had little control, and if she denied him, he would surely die.

"I am astonished. What are you doing to me?"

"I'm making love to you, little one. Am I hurting you?"

"No," she replied breathlessly. "You could never hurt me." She suddenly sucked in a breath. "Oh, Giles. Do that again."

"Sweet girl. I will do that . . ." He pulled out, then pressed in, driving deeper. "Again . . ." He took a breath, slid out and thrust in. "And again . . ."

She caught his rhythm and joined him, matching his thrusts.

"Now, you will make love *with* me." He tangled his fingers with hers. "Together."

He surrendered to the enchantment spell she wove around him, hungry for every ounce of her sweetness, her passion, all that he could have. Famished for so long, he became driven, enmeshed in his need with wild and free abandon.

God, her body gripped him so snugly. She clung to him, her fingers holding on to his. Her hips gyrated beneath him.

The world disappeared. Heat and friction pushed him over the edge, the flame of his desire burning his reason to ashes. He kissed her again and again. He worshiped her with lips, hands, and the powerful embrace of passion. Her body arched, then her walls contracted as spasms of pleasure made her tighten around him. His vision faded and his belly clenched as he choked out a groan.

With one hard thrust, he embedded himself deep inside her.

Wave after wave crashed with mind-numbing pleasure as her name wrung from his lips.

❧

Tingling started in Alex's stomach and radiated out toward her fingers and toes. Ripples of sensation coursed through her body—it was more than her mind could take in all at once. Whatever hesitation she might have had completely vanished under Giles' careful guidance. She trusted him. Lost in his ministrations, she'd been eager to experience every emotion, every sensation.

Becoming a woman was not as terrible as she had envisioned. With Giles, the transformation was most pleasurable. She had wanted him so badly. She loved him. And he loved her. Even if he did not say the words.

With soothing strokes, the pressure eased. He kissed her cheek, her ear, her neck. Which made it all the more difficult to gather her wits. She had no energy left. Her mind and body in complete lethargy. Yet she tried to digest what had just occurred—that gentle, passionate joining.

He lowered his face to the curve of her neck. "Alex, I did not mean for that to happen."

She sucked in her breath. "Do you regret what happened?"

He caught her wandering hand and linked their fingers together. Raising her hand to his lips, he kissed the back of her knuckles. "Not in the slightest."

The anxiety in her chest eased.

"However, I should have behaved more in a gentlemanly fashion," he added.

"Do you think me too wicked to admit that I'm glad you didn't?"

The outlandishly sexy smile he gave her set her belly fluttering.

She had been unsure of what to expect, but determined to have him. She'd yearned to make him hers. Dreamed of his making her a woman. He could not call her a child anymore. Excitement shoved away any insecurity, any notion of anxiety, and she basked in the unbelievable rapture he made her feel.

She was not too young to realize that Giles offered her nothing more than this moment in time. But she was determined to imprint her mark on him.

She curved her hand around his neck, and pulled him in for a burning kiss. One she put her whole heart into. Her pulse pounded in a wild rhythm. She had wished for this for so long. His mouth over hers, his arms holding her, his flesh against hers. If only they could freeze this moment.

He gave her a squeeze, then his body eased away as he rolled to his side and gathered her within his embrace. His hands, strong yet gentle, caressed her shoulders and back. Her head rested on his silky furred chest, and she smiled, ecstatic. This had to be the most wonderful feeling in the world.

Giles had made love to her.

Correction. *With* her.

Alex emitted a heavy sigh and curled into his warmth. Her body still tingled. Lying together, his arm around her, she now knew what it was to be one with a man. One heart. One body. One soul.

They didn't speak of their thoughts, or the sentiments in their hearts. But he had to feel the same as she.

Sinfully good.

Wavy tendrils of her hair streamed over her arms, onto his chest. He reached for a curl, worrying the strand between his fingers. "Your hair is the color of champagne shimmering in the sun." His voice thick with contentment, his lips vibrated her scalp as he mumbled into her hair.

Alex savored his words. She raised her head. "I am deliriously happy," she giggled.

"Judging by the smile on those well-kissed lips, I would agree. But we mustn't tarry. Someone could come upon us." He stretched, reaching for his trousers. "I would not want to meet any of your brothers."

"Please." She stayed him. "They don't know of my secret lagoon."

He dropped a kiss on the end of her nose. A deep sigh escaped his chest as he wrapped her in his warmth. She curled her fingers in the scattering of hair angling down his nicely firmed ribs, a few tuffs trailing to the . . . "Oh, my," Alex sighed.

The roguish grin on his lips was sinful indeed. She must be in heaven. To lie with him like this, her head on his shoulder, skin against skin, silk against her fingertips. He held her for long moments. Raising her head for another kiss, she ran her fingers through his raven mane, and tugged.

When he took her mouth, white-hot heat filled her again. She crawled on top of him, but he lifted her away.

"We must talk, Alex. We need to get dressed."

The tone of his voice caused her to scrunch up her nose. Its timbre sounded too much like her brother when he threatened to chastise her. She eyed Giles warily.

"Don't look so worried," he said as he tugged a golden strand lying over her breast. "You tempt me beyond good sense."

Fearing he regretted their interlude, she gulped.

Troubled eyes stared down at her.

"I don't regret what we did," Alex blurted out.

One corner of his mouth lifted in a smile while his fingers traced her cheek. "Neither do I."

She heard the words, saw the sincerity in his expression when he spoke. Still, a pending doom threatened her peace of mind. Suddenly, she didn't want to hear what he seemed determined to say. Her breath came out in a rush as she threw her arms around his middle, merging their naked flesh together. Could she keep him here forever if she held him tightly enough?

"You do realize this changes things." His voice rumbled under her ear while his sturdy arms cradled her. Warmth. Security. Safe. Loved. She felt every emotion exuding from his body to hers.

She leaned back. Afraid to ask, yet needing to hear. "What do you mean?"

"I must speak with your father."

"You don't mean to tell him?" she shrieked. "You . . . You can't!"

"Alex. I won't tell him I took your virginity. But I will speak with him and ask for your hand."

Pure bliss flooded her and made her head spin with happiness.

"You want to marry me?"

"Yes. Are you so surprised?" His grin melted her heart and curled her toes.

"A bit, yes."

"You chased me until you caught me. Now you do not know what to do with me?"

She wanted to kiss the smile on his face. "Oh, I know *now* what to do. And you will not get a chance to change your mind." Suddenly, a thought popped into her head, and her mouth pursed with worry.

He placed one finger under her chin, lifting her gaze to his. "What is it?"

"Is it because I threw myself at you? Is it because you took my virginity? Do you care anything for me?"

"I care more for you than I ought. I care more for you than I have ever felt for any woman. You charmed your way into my heart, little one. What we just shared, nothing compares to the ecstasy I received in your arms."

"I love you, Giles. I knew you would be mine."

His dark hair fell over his brow. Her rugged, strong duke, with his devilish grin. Hers. All hers.

"It's a shame we wasted so much time." His thumb caressed her chin.

"*We?*" She punched his shoulder. "You mean *you*. If I had known then what I now know, I would have attacked you."

"You did," he teased and pulled her back into his arms.

"Sooner. When you were more vulnerable." She cuddled closer, rubbing her hand over his chest. "Which is not even in the realm of possibilities, for there is not a vulnerable bone in your body."

"Wrong, my dear." He smoothed a curl over her shoulder. "You were too damned tempting. I finally had to succumb."

"What about now?"

"Hmmm?"

"Can we, um . . . do that again? You um . . . look like . . . Giles? Can I touch you?"

If eyes alone could start a fire, his heated gaze would burn her to cinders. Her hand trembled with want. She could not seem to pull away. Her gaze lowered to him . . . *there*.

"Please, Giles."

"Yes. You can touch me, Alexandria. I would like that very much." She loved the way he said her name, drawing it out like a caress. Looking into the depth of his penetrating stare, she could fall in love with him all over again.

He said yes.

Nerves and anticipation churned within her.

She lifted one finger and gently poked. His hardness jerked. A soft sound of surprise escaped her throat. Excitement spurred her on. She covered him with her palm. Hot. Hard. Silky soft.

She stroked him from the satin head down to the base. To her further amazement, it grew. Bigger.

"Careful, my love."

She glanced up into glazed midnight eyes. He gritted his teeth.

"Am I hurting you?" She tried to withdraw, but he covered her hand with his own.

"No, love."

Love. He called her 'love.' Not once, but twice. In her elation, her fingers tightened around him.

He groaned. Such an intense reaction from such a fleeting touch. A fuse fizzled along her nerve endings, flaring to life. She quivered in anticipation of doing it again.

"I want to please you." She caressed with her hand while her foot slid along the tense muscles in his legs.

"Anxious, my love?"

"Show me," she whispered. Rising up, she ran her tongue over his lips, hoping to create a like sensation in him as when he'd created a fire in her blood hot enough to burn through her veins.

"Right there. Stroke me." While one hand gave direction, his other shoved through her thick hair. He covered her mouth with his, devouring her lips, and with such passion. Sleeping areas of her body flared anew.

She learned what he liked, and soon her strokes grew more determined, more forceful. Eyes closed, his head thrown back, his rigid body shuddered.

"Good God, Alex. Tell me you did not practice this."

"Only with you." She gripped his shaft tightly and stroked him harder. She needed, wanted more. The tips of her breasts, the pit of her stomach, and . . . oh, between her legs ached.

As if he knew her need, he covered her mound, slipping his finger deep. Her mouth opened in an arousing sigh. His hand teased, gliding in a wicked rhythm that had her writhing and twisting. Yearning.

"Alexandria," he gasped.

The sound of her name from his throat thrilled her. Heat shot through her body. She pressed closer to his relentless fingers, her hand groping him while a moan slid from her lips. Giles taught her cravings of her own body she never knew existed. The depth of this euphoria took her breath.

She clung to him, and kissed him with mindless abandon.

A groan escaped as his tongue twirled with hers. His fingers plunged deep. Pressure burst and shattered in a million tiny pieces.

Giles stood and swept her into his arms.

"Hold on to me."

Limp and sated, she tightened her arms around his neck. Snug in his embrace, he carried her to the spring. With each step he took, every beat of her heart sang with love. As the cool water covered them, he placed her legs around his hips, then took her mouth again, his hands cradling the underside of her thighs. His lips left hers and kissed a path over her cheek and along her jaw. He placed a hot, open-mouth kiss in the curve of her neck, and squeezed. In one swift move, he thrust. Sheathed to the hilt, he filled her completely.

And branded her his forever.

Chapter 18

G iles glanced down the curved mahogany staircase with deliberate intent. No time like the present. Alex wasn't the sort of wife he had originally intended to acquire. But suddenly, she was the only one he wanted. Once he made up his mind he wanted something, he saw no reason to delay. He'd never been one to avoid confrontation. Not that he expected one, but he doubted Carmichael would be thrilled, or give up his daughter eagerly. Giles was about to meet a lion in his own den and ask for his cub.

He had thought of nothing else since yesterday afternoon when he'd made love with Alex in the secluded lagoon. A buzz of sensation quivered down his spine. He could still smell her essence. Still feel her smooth skin against his fingertips, her soft cries of ecstasy echoing in his ears. God, her body had wrapped around him like a tight-fitting, velvet glove.

While he held her cradled in his arms, deep in his soul he knew she was the one. The woman he belonged with. The only one he wanted to spend the rest of his life with.

His mind spun with possibilities.

He had a conscience. He'd taken her virginity. A precious gift, though seized in a heated moment, was not to be trampled upon. His honor declared he do the proper thing. Admittedly, his honor had very little to do with wanting Alex. Accepting the difference in their ages, he finally conceded he cared for the girl.

Cared? He had bloody well been captivated.

He might feel guilty for his rashness, but some part of him had been remarkably pleased, for now she was bound to him. The idea created an unsteady rhythm in his heart. He had spoken the truth when he told Alex his proposal was not because he had taken her virginity. Deep down, he wanted her. Amazing, how much delight he received at the thought.

Asking her father for her hand in marriage was no hardship at all. Actually, he looked forward to shackling himself to the spirited vixen. Life would not be dull.

With a spring in his step, he trekked down the stairs and went in search of his host.

"James. I wonder if I might have a moment." Giles felt at odds greeting him with such a casual address, but the man insisted he be called by his given name. He respected Carmichael and due to the topic Giles wished to discuss, even more reason he should formally address the man properly.

"You have the look of a serious discussion," James said.

"This is a matter of great import."

"Very well. Let's go into my study."

Giles followed James down the hall into the large room and closed the door behind him. The click of the latch resounded in the silence. Two leather chairs faced a huge oak desk.

"Have a seat." James gestured with one hand as he strode to the sideboard. Lifting a crystal decanter, he spoke over his shoulder. "I find it better to discuss matters over a glass of brandy. Would you agree?"

"Yes. Thank you." Giles lowered his tall frame into a cushioned seat of fine padded leather.

James opened a glass door and retrieved a pair of beakers. After pouring a generous portion into both, he handed one to

Giles. Then he stepped around behind the desk. His features held no expression—curiosity or otherwise.

"All right, Giles. What do you have on your mind?" Direct and to the point.

"First, James, let me thank you for your generosity. You have made me feel most welcome in your home." As soon as he could, he wanted to dispense with decorum and get to the heart of the matter. Carmichael presented himself as a no-nonsense sort of man.

"Glad to hear it. Hope Alex is not giving you any trouble."

Being a self-possessed man, nothing much surprised Giles. He had learned from experience to keep his mouth shut. However, this took him aback, for James hit dead center on the subject uppermost in his mind.

"Actually, she is the reason I've asked for a private audience."

"Pestering you, is she? I thought as much." James leaned back in his chair. "She's my daughter. I know her."

Giles studied the amber liquid in his glass as he contemplated James words. "I will admit she followed me around, but we have become friends."

"Friends? I think the girl fancies you. Being a man of nobility among other things."

This time, Giles nearly did cough in astonishment. How astute.

"Cornelia has filled the girl's head with England's aristocracy, parties and balls. She spins yarns and praises the English customs, making them appear grand and romantic. Alex soaks up Cornelia's stories like a sponge dropped into a pan of water."

"Yes, I overlooked, for a moment, Cornelia lives in England." A point in his favor. After all, being Alex's aunt, she could be an ally.

"Loves it there. I've asked her to live with me here, but she will not leave England. My dear sister refuses to reside in a country which she considers barbaric." James gave a bark of laughter. "England has her share of cut-throats and aristocratic ne'er-do-wells. Glad to leave all that behind me."

"Yes, you have made quite a life for yourself here. A grand plantation. A lovely wife, a fine family. I envy you."

"A strange statement, coming from a duke." He raised a brow and placed one hand on his desk. "I know while you're in America you prefer not to use your title. But you are a highly titled lord of the realm. Why would you envy me?"

"Your family." Giles took a hefty drink. "I am at a point in my life where I am ready to settle down. As you pointed out, my title demands a certain way of life. To carry on my lineage, I require a wife and must produce an heir."

James' gaze bore right through him.

"I am more than fond of Alex. I would ask your permission to court your daughter. As you mentioned, I believe she has taken a fancy to me, and I have developed a *tendre* for her as well. I have several estates, and the ancestral castle. Investments in a profitable shipping line, dabbling in thoroughbreds. I do not make a habit of boasting my wealth—actually not at all—but to give you an idea, I am a wealthy man without my dukedom holdings. So you see, I am able to provide for her, give her everything she could possibly want."

Giles studied the man's closed face. James gave no outward sign of his thoughts. At least he was not shouting.

Silence stretched for long moments, before James rose and sauntered over to the window. Giles felt like a lad waiting to receive his comeuppance.

"You have given me a great deal to think about."

"My intentions are most honorable. With your permission, after a proper amount of time, I plan to ask Alex to be my wife." May as well get it out there. Let her father know he had more than courtship in mind.

Another moment stretched in time. James nodded his head as if he had made a decision. Whether he approved the idea, or had just plotted Giles' demise, he uttered not a word, but returned to his chair.

"I find honesty is the best approach to any matter."

Every muscle in Giles' body tensed. "I would expect no less."

"Very well. Please, hear me out."

Those words did not bode well for his cause. The man seemed to hold Giles in high regard, but at the moment he looked like the bearer of bad news. Definitely not in Giles' favor.

James reached to a carved box on the corner of his desk. Opening the lid, he held the small chest out toward Giles. "A smoke for a serious discussion."

With years of masking his feelings, Giles had perfected the art. He called on those days of perseverance to aid him now. Lifting a cheroot from the chest, he lit the end. He watched the tobacco fire red as he inhaled, then leaned back, propping an ankle over his opposite knee.

"I appreciate your intentions," James began. "However, I must ask some questions and express my opinion on a few things."

"Of course."

"Alex is my only daughter. I love her very much." James lit his cigar and tossed the flaming stick into a glass bowl.

And you would more than likely kill me if you knew I had already touched her.

Giles was not a rogue. Even when he'd come close to throwing away his heritage, he had always been a man of honor. Morals.

Principles. As his father would say, 'One makes their own bed and must lie in it.' The damage done, he was more than willing to lie in the bed of his own making—with Alex.

"An attribute, sir. Your love for your family."

"Alex is young. I know by English standards she is of marriageable age. But she is only eighteen. Very impressionable."

"I understand. I treated her like a child, at first. But I learned she is a responsible woman for her age."

"We are talking about my daughter, are we not?" James gave a grin. "Responsible?"

James need not remind him of her impetuousness. Visualizing those breeches caressing her curvaceous bottom, his loins stirred. He shifted in the chair, uncomfortable for the first time since closing the study door.

"I've seen the change in her. She's been wearing dresses and the like. I thought Cornelia's influence had taken root. Now I see you may have been the one to bring about the transformation."

Is this the honesty part?

James Carmichael did not dawdle or drag his feet. He spoke his mind and said what he thought straight out. However, he sure seemed to be taking a long time getting to the matter that most likely lurked just behind his teeth.

"Even Sam and Ben remarked on her appearance. They might tease her and give her a hard time, but they spoil her."

"I've noticed. The bond between each member of your family is in full view for all to see." A little ache of resentment trickled in his soul. He'd never had a loving family. No siblings. With a dominating father and a mother's love taken from him at an early age, only bitterness cloaked him in his youth.

"We are close. You would take Alex away from her family?"

The crux of the matter.

"Only if she wants to go. I promise to take care of her. And she would have a family member there. Your sister would help Alexandria get settled into the scheme of things."

"Hmmm." His heavy sigh did not sound encouraging.

"I have a ship. She could visit, and you could come to England to visit her. I would never keep her from her family, or force her to do anything she would not willingly want to do."

And he wouldn't. He suddenly realized he would move heaven and earth to give her anything she desired.

"What if you take her to England and she doesn't like it there?" James leaned forward, bracing his arms on his large oak desk, his dark eyes piercing. "What if she cannot be without her family?"

God forbid that should happen.

When had he become so infatuated with the girl?

"Alex seems like a very spirited girl. She has a craving for adventure. Her aunt would be close by. I would assure they visit frequently. I hope Alex would make her home with me in England. But," a pang stung his beating heart, "should she choose to leave, I would bring her back to you."

"Then I must save you the trouble. Alex may think she is grown up, but she has lived a sheltered life. Cornelia has filled her head with exciting stories, but when it comes right down to the bone, she will not leave her family. Forgive me, Giles, but I really believe she will not survive without us."

His beating heart stopped. His arm hovered, the brandy inches from his lips.

"At first, of course she would be excited—at first." James paused, holding Giles gaze for several heartbeats before he continued. "Marrying a duke would be grand. Traveling to England would be grand. Alex has mentioned going back with Cornelia. But I'm afraid it's the novelty, the exploration. Embarking on a new adventure. As time passes, when the newness wears off, she will miss her family—her life here."

"I know I am asking a lot." Giles stared into intense brown eyes, recognizing the man's concern. But he did care for Alex, and he would protect her with his life. Now to give her father the assurance he needed.

"I accept your feelings, and I understand you will miss your daughter. I give you my word as a gentleman, I will keep Alex safe. I will provide her with furnishings she is accustomed to. I am financially able to give her anything she desires. I assure you, I will protect her with my very life."

"I have no doubt about your intentions, nor your honor. I trust you would do exactly as you promise. But, what will her life be like? She will be a duchess. I know I'm repeating myself when I say this sounds exciting. But what will Alex do? How will the *ton* treat her?"

"They will bloody well treat her with the respect she deserves," Giles said with abrasive force. At his outburst, he realized his calm facade was disappearing fast. An urchin with chocolate eyes—glowing in passion, radiant with desire, gleaming with love—had stolen his composure. He'd been unable to keep a disciplined thought in his bloody brain since meeting the chit.

"The *ton* can be cruel. Alex does not do well following rules. A spirited girl, her impulsive actions are not thought out. Only weeks ago she wore breeches, and those of her age taunted her. She has a temper. I love Alex, but I know my daughter. She is rebellious, stubborn, tenacious, at times unmanageable. She would be under scrutiny. Her position would require her to behave a certain way. The first matron who spouted nonsense or insults would receive a tongue lashing. Alex would disgrace you."

"Alex would and always will come first," Giles said with resolve. "She will be my wife. She will be above reproach."

"I would not have her spirit crushed."

Giles' voice dropped to a whisper. "Neither would I." Little snippets of doubt began to invade. Alex loved her family and they doted on her. Could he take her away from them? Would the move crush her spirit? With the brandy in one hand and his cigar in the other, he wondered if either vice would improve his disposition. He expressed a solution for every argument—but one. Her spirit. The one thing he loved about her the most.

"For now, I am not in favor of this match. I like you. I think you would be a good husband to my daughter—in a few years."

His chest constricted. Until this moment, he had not realized how much he wanted James to agree to the match. He cared more for Alexandria than he realized.

Good God. What if there were a babe?

"Come now." James shot him a quizzical look. "It can't be as bad as all that. By the look on your face, one would think you have lost your best friend."

Chapter 19

How did one break one's heart? Giles' blood froze at the cruel thought.

He stood by the window staring at a blue sky. Instead of enjoying a beautiful, sunny day, he agonized in a hell of his own making. Clamping down on his wayward thoughts, he sighed heavily and hoped he did the right thing. His belly clenched thinking of the event about to transpire in the next few moments. The confrontation with Alex.

If he followed through, her heart would shatter like glass. He knew this as surely as he knew sinners burned for eternity, for did not his own heart break?

For a time, he dared to dream. God had given him a taste of heaven only to throw him back into the bowels of hell. How could he have expected Alex to share his world? A fool indeed to even think such matters. Her nickname alone was speculation for ridicule. His nobility predicted his life. Shaped his life. Demanded he live his life accordingly. Years of rebellion had proven nothing. Other than he had to return to the very existence from which he'd fled.

Duty. Responsibility. Obligation.

Aristocracy be dammed. Why had life been so cruel as to saddle him with a title? And why had he been reared to honor the task and all his title imposed?

When his ship sailed to America, he'd feared months of boredom. Look where that thinking landed him. A young sprite with chocolate eyes had melted his heart. If he'd known foolhardy events would have led to this day, this moment, the deception he was about to perform, he would have taken the first ship back to England.

No matter now.

It was done. Alex's father had made it perfectly clear he would not allow his daughter to suffer the hardships of being a duchess. Unable to survive in a world a thousand miles away without her family. He'd convinced Giles what she thought of as love would fade. She was just too young. Excitement of the unknown, the enthusiasm of a young mind, a mettle worthy of her brothers—all as a result of her family's love and affection.

According to James, his daughter's courage and bravery stemmed from being spoiled, but her brothers watched over her. No amount of explanation on Giles' part could persuade the man that he, Giles, would give her the life she deserved. He would protect her as well, beyond the measure of her blasted brothers. And yes, he had grown more than fond of her.

In the end, he relented.

Alex could not live in his world. And he could not remain in hers.

The door to the drawing room opened, and swiftly closed. The back of his neck tingled. Without turning he knew Alex stood behind him.

Comrades praised him for his serenity, his composure. Years of secret missions had taught him patience. Given him nerves of steel. Ballocks of iron. His serene, relaxed manner had earned him great respect. Well known for his tranquility in a crisis, he'd been given a leadership role.

The task before him once again demanded a tight rein on his strength of will.

Masking his emotions yet again, he turned. His treacherous heart jolted.

Sensible words failed him. The beautiful woman standing there took his breath.

Lovely.

His gut tightened as the image of her face submersed in ecstasy flashed into his mind. God save him.

As Alex darted toward him, his arms opened of their own will. She landed against his chest. God, she felt too good in his arms. His jaw tensed.

Damnation.

"Oh, Giles. I don't know how you managed, but I'm so thankful."

"Thankful?"

"For this time alone." She pulled back to meet his gaze. "How in the world did you manage this private meeting? When Father told me—"

"Alex." Giles loosened her hold and captured her fingers. "I must speak with you."

He studied her features. Wheat colored hair elucidating the sun's reflection. Big, brown eyes sparkling with amber, flecks of gold that would haunt him till his dying day. Plush lips, enticing and promising heaven here on earth. Every feature, so endearing to him that his heart wrenched as he branded her features to his memory. Whatever he wanted to savor, today would be their last day together.

"Oh dear. Something must be terribly wrong to put such a hard look on your face."

"Forgive me, but I know of no other way than to be forward. I am not a man to mince words."

"My love, what is it?" Imploring eyes with a hint of apprehension stared at him.

My love.

Good God. There it is. Surely, there must have been a time in his life he'd felt this uneasy, yet he could not imagine when.

"I have much to say to you. Please sit down." He guided her to the sofa.

"Giles, you're making me very nervous. I'm not sure I want to sit."

"Please." He gestured.

"All right. You're not going to pace, are you? Will you sit with me?"

Her nervous chatter had again reminded him of her age.

"I need to speak with you regarding several matters." He cleared his throat.

"Please don't tell me you have regrets." Distress filled her pleading gaze.

Would he ever get used to her outspokenness? He had no choice. Sitting beside her, he lifted her hand and stroked his thumb over her fingers. "I have no regret of my feelings for you."

Her shoulders drooped with her sigh of relief.

"I have no regrets you expressed your—"*Dare I use the word love?*—"feelings for me." He lifted her hands and kissed the back of her knuckles. "I will treasure those moments forever."

Although one corner of her mouth wilted, her smile speared his heart. Her eyes still held a bit of distress.

"Alex, I have been here for an extended amount of time. I have duties and a home in England which I've neglected for far too long."

"Oh. You are leaving?" she gasped.

"I must." He tightened the hold on her hands.

"For how long? When will you return?"

His gaze plunged to her trembling lower lip. Lifting one delicate hand, he brushed a kiss into her palm. "I won't."

She stared—as if she had not heard him, nor the import of his words. Silence stretched for several moments.

"I don't understand," she said in a feverish whisper. Her obvious attempt at bravery lanced his soul.

This damned torture was of his own making. He'd given in. Surrendered to his lust. Guilt weighted on his shoulders like a block of iron. But he must plod forward.

"We live in two different cultures. Our worlds could never coexist."

"But . . . wait. Even though we've been acquainted only a short time, we developed a bond. I'm sure I could fit into your world, with Aunt Cornelia's help."

"Alex. You're young. You've never been away from your home. You're a lovely young girl whom I admire very much."

"Is it my years?" She recovered from her flinch, but he'd seen her balk when he'd used the word *girl*.

"My time with you has been important to me." He held her fingers so tightly, he had to remind himself not to crush her bones. "You are very dear to me. I cannot stay in America, Alex. My home is in England. I can neglect my duties no longer. I must leave."

"Are you asking me to go with you?"

Bloody hell. He dug the pit deeper. He would give anything to spare her his answer. Maybe he should just take her. Carry her away on his ship like a pirate and damn the consequences. But her father's words halted the action before he could put any deed to motion.

Would Alex hate him later, when she grew bored, or when she missed her family? Or God forbid, if she no longer wanted him. Would a quick break now spare her agony in a few years? If

he only knew . . . if he could trust what she felt now would last .
. . But he'd never been a man to dwell on 'ifs.' He was a man of
hard facts.

"I'm afraid not."

She jerked her hand free, covering the gasp on her lips. After
a heartrending pause, she murmured, "I see."

"It has never been my intention to hurt you. You gave me a
gift I will treasure to my dying day." He was doomed for unconscionable damnation. Even though, unbeknownst to her or
any member of her family, he'd secretly made preparations in the
event of a babe. Any word of such would end this unwarranted
charade. The burning pits of hell would not keep him from
claiming the child and his mother, should the status arise.

Pain burned in her eyes. Her palms covered her chest—as
though they could provide some small protection against her
breaking heart—and she sprang from the sofa.

Maybe the best thing would be to place some distance between them. He ran a frustrated hand through his mop of hair.
Ballocks. He hated this. Damn his soul to hell. And damn her
father for forcing him to do this.

Force?

Giles closed his eyes and swallowed his agony. This was best
for Alex. He did it for her. He could not bear to see the light
leave her eyes, or suffer her resentment when she wanted to
return home to her family.

Leaving me.

Yearning for her to turn around, see the lie for what it was, he
stood. Hoping she would not turn, praying she did not cry, for
then he would surely confess all. His love, his need.

*Foolish, foolish man. You learned long ago, dreams were for
others?*

"You are special, Alex." Her name rolling from his tongue was enough for him to struggle with the words clogging his throat. "You are wonderful. But my time here has come to an end."

"You no longer want me." Anguish laced her words.

And ripped his heart.

"There is no future for us. The English insist on the eldest son—in my case, the only son—doing his duty, to marry and produce an heir." Giles fought to keep his voice even. "A dukedom. I must follow my path. The course plotted for me. I have no choice in this matter." With every word, he knew he carved another chunk from her ruptured heart.

She whirled with a vengeance. "Your duty? What of your *duty* when you held me naked in your arms?"

Images punctured his mind of an innocent face, a sultry gleam in beguiling eyes before she kissed him so shamelessly. Her fire and spirit while sharing their bodies in passion.

He hated being the villain in her eyes. Drawing on years of self-discipline governing his emotions, he dredged up every ounce of strength of will to form his next words.

"You are too young." At her gasp, he held up a hand. "I know what happened between us was not your fault. I am older, and supposed to be wiser." God, he hoped there were no consequences of his foolishness.

"Wiser?" Her hands shook with anger. "You . . . you're leaving? And telling me you plan to marry another?"

Giles nearly choked on his despair.

"What of love? Did you not profess your love for me? What of *our* future? Did you not make assurances to me?"

"In the heat of the moment, I declared my fondness of your body. My liking of your attributes," he said, trying to be reasonable. Good God, he bungled this. Why not rip her heart out and get it over with?

"I gave you my virginity. You held out a promise of affection and hope. Now with words of honor and duty, you cruelly snatch your pledge away?" She could hardly speak through her tears.

Rage threatened. He wanted to pound something. Break something. She had branded him with her scent, her taste, her zest for life. *God's blood.* His entire being felt twisted in knots. Knowing he would never see her face again, he committed to memory every detail, every fleck in her enticing brown eyes . . .Now filled with hurt and anger, her anguish sharp enough to shred him. Pain rawer than salt on a gaping wound pierced his chest.

Enough.

He had to end this torment.

"I am a duke. This is my heritage. I do not expect you to understand my way of life. Aristocracy allows no breach in etiquette. What's inside me demands I comply with the mandates of my ancestors. You may accept it, or not."

He shoved his hat on his head and spun on his heel. The devil collected his due this day. As Giles marched across the tiled floor, the doorman practically ran ahead of him. Grabbing the brass handle, he jerked the door open just as Giles stomped through, headed for his ship.

Destination . . .

Hell.

Chapter 20

E verything seemed to fade around her. The room dwindled and blurred before her eyes. Alex was aware only of the blinding agony that wrenched her soul. Like a body with no will of her own, she drifted, crossing the corridor, climbing the round staircase, padding down the hall to her room. Her feet moved, she saw the portraits on the wall, yet her mind floated in a dark cloud. Somehow, she closed the door and stumbled to her bed. She threw herself across the coverlet and clutched a pillow to her shattered heart. Grief nearly swallowed her whole.

Her eyes burned. Tears threatened. She could never let them start for she feared once begun, they would not stop. With her heart breaking, she needed a firm rein on her emotions. If she cried, she would sob uncontrollably.

The first tear ran down her cheek.

Then another ...

A knock on her door startled her awake. Eyes puffy, nose clogged, she shoved the hair out of her face. She must have cried herself to sleep. Another rap on her door.

"Yes?"

"It's Papa."

Oh. Maybe she could blame the puffiness on sleep. "Just a minute." She scurried from the bed and adjusted her clothes. No need to brush her hair. Father has seen her at her worst. She opened the door. When he extended his arms, she choked on a sob and the tears flowed again.

He held her for several seconds, allowing her to sob in misery.

"Papa. I love Giles." She swiped at the scalding tears on her cheeks.

"I know you think you do, Pet."

"I do." She shoved away. "You have no idea of what I feel for him. You think I'm too young."

"You're only eighteen."

"Aunt Cornelia was only sixteen when she married Uncle Toby. And they have a passel of children."

With a raised brow, he stared at her the same way he always did when he was about to give a lecture. "Things were done differently then. Your aunt lived in England and met her husband at a coming out ball."

"Still, she was but sixteen," Alex huffed.

"You are my only daughter. We do not live in London."

She threw her head back and glared in defiance. "But Giles does."

"My point exactly! He is an Englishman, born to wealth and position. A duke."

Seeing her father was trying to control his temper, Alex calmed her own temper. She knew better than to anger her father beyond his tolerance. She'd never been on the receiving end of his displeasure , but she had seen him explode on one of her brothers. She tried a gentler approach. "I understand. He is an important man."

He took a breath, as if needing to do so. "You are unfamiliar with English customs."

"Aunt Cornelia has been educating me." Alex absorbed every tidbit about England's traditions and all the proper behavior her aunt was willing to share.

"Cornelia," he spouted as if he had eaten turtle soup. And he didn't like turtle soup. "She's filled your head with fantasies. Life in London can be kind *and* cruel. It is an entirely different world. One I would hope to keep you from."

"But, Papa. It was your homeland."

"I was born there. I moved here and made a life with your mother. America gives a man opportunities, a whole new way of life. England is very confining. You are at the mercy of your peers. If you are nobility, you are under the *ton's* scrutiny. The gossip mongers can be harsh and ruthless."

"But Aunt Cornelia lives there. She likes living in England."

"All it takes is one mistake. Or one comment to ruin one's reputation. Aristocracy may accept you and welcome you into their midst, or cut you where no one would dare speak to you or call you friend." His shoulders lifted in a heavy sigh. "I would rather spare you a life of scorn and ridicule."

A sudden thought struck. "Papa. Did you send Giles away?"

"What? No. Why would you ask me such a thing?"

"You just said—"

"I know what I just said, girl. You do not need to remind me of my own words." He glanced to the floor as his hands closed into fists.

Alex stared at her father. She'd never seen him nervous, if that was what his fidgety behavior could be called.

"Papa?"

"I did not send him away." Papa's temper was back. "A member of the aristocracy does not ignore his responsibilities. Giles made the decision to return to his home."

Alex stepped to her vanity and plucked a kerchief from the top drawer. Dabbing her nose, she crinkled the linen in her fist.

"I love him, Papa. I thought he . . . cared for me, too."

"I'm sure he did, in his own way. But not as a candidate for a wife."

A pain stabbed her chest as if Giles had plunged the knife himself. She had made love with him. Did their joining not present her as a prospect for consideration of marriage?

"Your skin and lips are so pale. I'm worried about you." His voice so close, her eyes snapped up, seeing that he stood right behind her. She met his gaze in the mirror. Lines creased the corners of his eyes. Frown lines marred his forehead. "Time will heal. You must accept this. Giles is gone."

Her suspicions lingered. "Papa, I am old enough to marry."

"You are half his age. You're still a child."

Her last thread of patience snapped. She whirled around at his accusation. "I. Am. Not. A. Child."

"You are my child!" he shouted. His brows drew together and his jaw muscle flexed. A sure sign he would not budge on the issue at hand. "I am your father. You will give up this foolishness. Your life is here. The Duke of Nethersall will enact a duke's role and produce more generations of dukes."

While Alex hid in her room, days had gone by and the pain had not lessened. Mama had heard Papa bellowing. She must have questioned him. She brought Alex her meals, and made excuses for his anger. Still, his words smarted. But knowing her parents loved her, she felt even more miserable for causing their worry. She had no appetite for food, and even less for enduring another day of heartache.

Why did it hurt so much?

She leaned on the window seat, her knuckles propped under her chin. Dark clouds in a dreary sky threatened rain. Even the thought of Stardust had not given her any motivation.

Another pain pierced her at the black's name. Would everything remind her of Giles? She really should not waste tears over a man who did not want her. Who tore her heart out?

She should never have embarked on such a mad scheme in the first place. What a fantasy, thinking she could fill the role of a duchess. Yet it was not the excitement of being courted by a handsome nobleman. It was Giles himself. Handsome, adoring, kind . . .

Oh, her romantic heart.

Alex covered her eyes with a groan. Her cheeks felt puffy and her head hurt. A night of weeping would do that. She supposed she should leave her room. How would she face the day? Did she really want to encounter her brothers? If she stepped one foot outside her bedchamber, there would be no doubt. She could not bear their scorn, or their sympathy. *And Kit had told her not to set her cap for the duke.* Her humiliation grew by leaps and bounds.

A rap sounded on her door. She wished whoever was there would go away Although, her selfishness would only cause her mother more concern.

"Come on, Imp. You can't sleep the day away."

Kit. She ignored the cajoling voice.

"Alex, if you don't open this door, I'm coming in," Kit thundered.

She wondered if her thoughts had conjured him up. "Just a minute."

With a frantic glance, she realized she still wore the same clothes she had on yesterday. Tilting up her chin, she shrugged.

No sense in delaying the inevitable. She only hoped when he confronted her, she did not fall apart again.

"All right. You can come in."

The door knob turned, and Kit's shoulders filled the doorway. Alex took a deep breath and held it until he stepped inside. He shoved the door closed behind him.

"Don't you look a fright."

"Good morning to you too, brother dear," she huffed.

"You slept through breakfast." He arched a brow the way he always did when about to give her a dressing down. "It's nearly noon."

"I was exhausted."

"Your face betrays you. Your cheeks are swollen, and it pains me to see the haunted look in your eyes."

Haunted? I'm bruised. Crushed. I'm a desperate, pathetic creature wanting what is impossible.

She refused to cry. She drew air into her lungs, summoning the fortitude to put on a brave front.

"What a nice compliment." She moved back to the cushioned seat beneath her bedchamber window.

"May I join you?"

She continued to stare through the glass. "Would it matter if I said no?"

"Come on, Imp." Kit sat beside her, stretching his long legs out in front of him. "You've been cooped up for days."

She grunted in response—but secretly, she was glad for Kit's presence.

"Why don't you grab your breeches and we'll take the black for a ride."

"He has a name, you know." She stared out her bedchamber window, feigning a bored expression. Her heart hurt too much for any other emotion.

"Blackie? Thought you were going to change it."

"I did. Giles did. It's Stardust." She actually said his name without bursting into tears. If Kit noticed her stammer, thankfully he ignored it.

"Hmm. Nice name. So why don't we get Stardust and Brusor, and go for a ride?"

"Brusor?" She dropped her arm and stared suspiciously at her brother. "Ben gave you permission?"

"What makes you think I need his permission?" Kit angled a brow the way he always did when he wanted to lord his advantage of being the oldest over his siblings. His attempt to lift her spirits warmed her heart. He knew mentioning Brusor would get her attention.

"Sam won't let anyone near Brusor since the race at Mr. Hardcastle's." She turned back to the window in silence. Not that she didn't want to ride, she just preferred to sit here and bask in her brother's company.

"Funny thing, that. Seems the problem with Brusor was lu—uh, love."

If Kit's intention was to totally confuse her, he succeeded. "Huh?"

"Brusor was sniffing after a mare."

"A mare caused him not to race?" She crinkled her nose and studied her brother. "You are teasing me."

"Just checking to see if you were paying attention." Kit slapped his hands on his knees. "So, how about a ride?"

"Looks like rain." Again, she feigned tedium.

"Afraid you will melt?"

She glanced out the window to the trees beyond the meadow. Picturing Giles, racing Gent alongside her, to their hideaway lagoon. Envisioning his handsome smile, the dimple in his chin, watching his eyes darken just before his lips met hers ...

"If only he would have believed me when I told him I would leave my home," she sighed.

"What?" Kit glared at her like she'd grown another head.

Mama had tried to console her. Papa didn't comprehend. But all of her brothers were close to her. She needed a man's way of thinking to help her understand.

"Giles. I told him—"

"I heard what you said. I just don't think you grasp what you are saying."

She faced him fully. "Kit, I realize you think I am foolish to have once thought him worthy of my consideration." She spoke from her heart, her pleading eyes focused on his. "But I love him."

"You have other choices." His harsh gaze bore into hers. Clearly, he wanted to say more, yet held back the words he knew would make her angry.

"Do you honestly believe I do not know my own mind?" She tried to control her temper. She just wished her brother had more faith in her as an individual.

"Your actions speak louder."

"Because I dress in boys' breeches does not mean I am a child. You yourself have said my mind is quick. You also defended me when you told Emma Louise even though I dress like an urchin, I'm older and wiser than my years."

Kit took several moments to reflect on her words. Then, he lifted her hand and held it between his own. "Would you really leave your home?"

Alex hated to see him regard her with sympathy. "I love my family, but yes. I would have gone with Giles to England."

"Let us not worry about that at the moment. Help me to understand what happened."

A flicker of hope surfaced. She desperately needed to talk with him. Even though she might not like his resolution. At least he was willing to listen. He would help her sort out her thoughts. Nevertheless, baring her soul would place her firmly back in the very place she had been trying to avoid—the real world. The one without Giles.

"The first time I saw him I was twelve years old."

Kit jerked with surprise. "Where? I don't remember him."

Years drifted away as she went back in time. Remembering, as though the incident happened only yesterday. Once again, she stared out her window, smiling at the image of the little dog.

"Do you remember Winnie?"

"I remember the two of you getting into mischief. Actually, I think you were the leader and she just followed along."

Alex appreciated her brother's teasing. When his serious expression did not change, she realized he meant the slight. She shrugged with indifference.

"Do you remember the time her mother took us to town and I told you the story of the man rescuing her dog?"

"Yes, I seem to remember something like that."

"Giles was that man."

A faint whistle shot though Kit's teeth. "The staggering pieces of the puzzle are beginning to fit together."

"You see? I met him before."

"You fantasized over him. He rescued you, became your champion. Hero worship. Nothing more."

"No, Kit. I worshiped him, that is true. But you did not see him the way I did. He was a hero. He also was compassionate. Understanding of two young girls. After rescuing me, he blasted the man for his recklessness. Then, he checked on me a second time to make sure I was all right. Yes, Kit. We were two girls infatuated with heroes."

"You never said a word."

"Papa would have tanned my hide. But, the thing is, even at my young age, I saw real concern in his eyes. It stayed with me. I have never forgotten the way he looked at me."

"How did you know he was a duke?"

"After he and his friend left, Winnie's mother told us he was a duke. A very important man. When Aunt Cornelia came, I asked her. She told me all about a duke and his ranking position in England."

"Titles. I'm glad we don't need to worry about that in America."

She grasped Kit's hand. "Don't you see? According to Aunt Cornelia, a titled lord would not waist time with those beneath him. He would never save a dog, or talk to two urchins on the street."

"Urchins?"

"Riff raff."

"You are not riff raff. You are the daughter of the most prominent man in New Orleans."

"Giles did not know that. Yet, he did save us."

"What are you getting at, Alex?"

"Giles is a caring man, not at all like the way Aunt Cornelia explained a duke's position. What I saw in his eyes that day was real. My feelings for him were real. And I love him more now than ever." She squeezed Kit's arm. "Shouldn't I be with the man I love?"

If every woman born harbored certain wiles to get her way, she prayed those traits, whether charms, trickeries, ruses or guiles, would aid her now—for she would need every wily advantage to win Kit's support.

"You've always been a stubborn girl. You truly love this man?"

"With my whole heart."

She sensed him weakening.

"I believe Papa must have spoken with Giles. Everything was wonderful. And then . . . suddenly he was saying goodbye."

"Pap only wants what is best for you."

"I know. I also know Papa and you think Giles doesn't deserve me. You would probably think the same about any man who tried to take me away."

"You've got a point there," Kit relented. Then he stiffened. "But the duke hurt you."

"Because he left. I'm not sure he did so willingly."

"He's gone."

"He is the man I chose. I have pledged my love to only one man. Giles is the only one I will ever love."

Kit grunted what sounded very much like a snort. "Maybe if he had not broken your heart. I might consider your words if you were the same spunky girl as before his arrival."

"You think I would be the same after I *knew* I loved him."

Kit shoved to his feet. "No. Nothing ever remains the same. You have grown up. But, don't ask me to ignore his actions. I need to give this some thought."

"What do you have to think about? All I need is your understanding." She tilted her head, adjusting her gaze to his height. "And maybe a little help."

There went that patronizing brow again. His arms crossed over his chest and his gaze held suspicion. "What kind of help?"

She dearly loved her brother, but he sorely tried her patience. "Take me to him."

"Now I know you've lost your mind." He dropped his arms and spun toward the door. She lurched, grabbing him before he could retreat.

"Aunt Cornelia is leaving within a fortnight. I can go with her."

"No you will *not*," he thundered. "Listen and listen well. Do not mistake my understanding for surrender. I know you, Imp. Your tricks will not work on me. I came up here to cheer you up. Not to be hoodwinked. And you, my dear sister, need to face a few facts. The duke left of his own free will. What if you hie off to England and he rejects you again?"

Alex shoved back the emotions welling up inside. Doubt burgeoned at the possible truth of his words.

"I'm sorry, Alex." The look on his face told her he'd rather cut out his tongue than hurt her with the truth. "You must see reason in this."

She would not cry. Would not. Yet tears filled her eyes and brimmed over onto her cheeks.

"Come here." Kit pulled her into his arms. "You will not go to England." He took a deep breath and let it out in a heavy sigh. "But I can carry a message."

She jerked back. "You would do this for me?"

"Calm yourself." He wiped a tear with his thumb. "Pen a message. If in a year you still feel the same way, I will take you to him."

Kit slipped the missive into his coat pocket as he pulled the door closed behind him.

"Been in there long enough." Ben shoved away from the wall he'd been propped against. At the end of the hall, Sam stopped his pacing and spun around.

"Well? What's the verdict?"

He looked at Sam, answering them both "As I suspected."

"What did she say?" Ben asked.

"She fancies him. He told her no. He broke her heart." That about summed it up.

"The Brit will be missing his cods."

"Do we go after him now?" Sam rubbed his hands together.

Kit hesitated, thinking over what Alex asked of him.

"There's more, isn't there?" Ben frowned. "You were in there long enough to have Sam here, wearing the shine clean off the floor."

"He told her she was too young." Kit had perceived her anguish. He ground his teeth in anger. "Giles said he was a duke and his home was in England."

"All of that is true." Ben studied Kit's face as if searching for hidden truths. "But you seem a mite pensive."

"Don't tell me you're going to let the blasted Brit get away with this," Sam growled.

Ben had too much influence over their younger brother. The boy mimicked his speech as well as his actions.

"Of course not."

"Then what do you plan to do?" Ben asked straight out.

Kit gave a shrug. "I simply plan to kill him."

"I'm coming with ya," Sam said without any hesitation.

"I'm going, too," Ben declared. "At least let me get my pound of flesh before you shoot the bastard."

"All three of us can't go. Someone has to stay here and keep an eye on Alex."

"Yes," Sam agreed. "She just might take a notion to get on a ship and follow him."

"Over my dead body." Ben glanced to her bedroom door. Then he gave a meaningful glare to Sam. "Someone needs to stay here and make sure she stays put."

Sam's face screwed up the minute recognition dawned. "Why me?"

Ben pointed a finger at Sam's chest. "You're the youngest."

"I get the hind tit all the time." Sam grabbed his hat and smacked it across his thigh. "Dag blame it. I'm the last to do everything."

"Well, Brother?" Ben asked Kit.

"We sail with the morning tide."

Chapter 21

England

Lightning ripped violently across the night sky. The bellowing wind heaved, thunder roared, and rain slashed the windows. A fire burned low in the hearth. Leather and sandalwood drifted among the scent of scorched wood, suggesting warmth and comfort—the furthest thing from reality.

Dark clouds rolled in chaos, matching Giles' mood. He clutched the glass in his hand as amber liquid glided smoothly down his throat and warmed his belly. He took another swallow, welcoming the burn. With every sip, his determination grew. Blot out his pain. Drown his stupidity. Blur the image of the one he simply could not erase. The one he could not get out of his head.

He dropped the sheer curtain and crossed the carpet in his cherry-wood study, and picked up a packet from the heap of correspondence littering his desk. Perceiving nothing required his immediate attention, he tossed the report from his land agent to another growing stack, then strode to the sideboard and grabbed the brandy bottle by the neck, splashing more liquid into his glass. In an effort to ease the guilt gnawing viciously at him, he took a long swallow. A small coating of amber liquid remained. Another reminder of the one he tried to forget. A self-mocking smile twisted his lips.

He was not used to tucking his tail between his legs, nor licking his wounds. Venom coursed through his veins. Flames from the fire could not melt the cold rage chilling his blood, nor warm the hollow ache in his frozen heart.

He had done what he had to do. He cursed the duty and responsibility ingrained in him. Yes, he had granted James Carmichael's request. And somehow in the midst of it all, he metamorphized into his own father. The man he hated above all others. A man who had lived according to dictates with no consideration for another's feelings. Emotions were not allowed. Sympathy not tolerated. Transgressions not forgiven.

He glanced at the portrait hanging on the wall above the hearth.

"You have won!" he yelled to the man who sired him. Surely he heard, for his ghost haunted these walls. Had haunted *him* for years. Tomorrow morning the bloody painting would come down from that wall if he had to use an axe to do it. Giles tossed the brandy down his throat and slammed the glass on his desk. How foolish to think he had exorcised the demon from his soul.

As a lad, he'd had no recourse but to follow his father's wishes. A cane marked his back when he questioned, or moved too slow to answer, or administer the man's behest. For years he had suffered nausea, feelings of fear, and even manifested shadows at the corners of his vision. The happenstance of his birth had been drilled into him with words of steel, and an expectation clad in iron. Giles had accepted his duty. And there was no way out.

Until that fateful day. When he had grown to a decent size, and unable to take any more, he fought back. Where had the gumption come from? Young in years, but old enough to forge a different way of life, one that nearly got him killed. Anything to escape from the hell his sire put him through every day.

Yet hellish did not begin to describe the torment he inflicted on himself. Alex's pain-filled eyes would haunt him for the rest of his days. Like a moth drawn to a flickering flame, she lured him back to the one place he wanted to be—and could never go.

Nethersall Castle was where he belonged. The land on which he'd been born, birthed to aristocracy. A peer of the realm. He had no need for the money the estate would provide, as he owned an ungodly amount in his own right.

Taking the bottle with him, Giles leaned back in his favorite overstuffed leather chair, stretching his toes toward the fire in the stone hearth. His future loomed as dark as the blackness beyond the window. He tossed back another drink. The ghost of his father; the saintliness of his mother. He scrubbed a hand over his face and wondered what his life would have been like if she had lived.

The clock on the mantel struck ten bells. Sprawled in his leather chair, Giles stared into the blazing fire. After everything he had suffered, leaving this mausoleum . . .

"Why the bloody hell did I come back?"

"You know why."

Shock made him mute. Years of training to hear even the slightest sound of movement, and Morgan had entered his home without Giles having an inkling. He could blame the brandy, but even drink had not dulled his mind. Haunting specters had dominated his focus.

He spoke without turning around. "Taking up old habits of creeping about at night?"

"Has our friendship been restricted to the daylight hours?" Morgan stepped into view, brushing his wet hair from his face.

"Neither man, nor beast, should be out on a night like this. What brings you here?"

"Well, my good man. Quaint you should ask." Morgan removed his gloves, jerking on every finger as if each tug gave significance to his words. "When my good friend," tug, "returns from a voyage," tug, "an *extended* voyage," tug "one I sent him on . . ." He tossed the gloves onto a table and swung his topcoat from his shoulders.

"Where is Cuthbert? Did he not relieve you of your coat?"

"Blood and the devil. Forget the bloody coat." Morgan smacked it down on top of his gloves. "Why did you not send word of your return? You were gone a long time. Kat was beginning to worry. I will not have my bride worried."

Interesting Morgan still considered Kat his bride after nearly a year. "You think you do not worry your bride venturing out in this storm? I am surprised Kat allowed it. How is wedded bliss?"

"Wonderful. Now, what the hell happened?"

"Tuck away your boorish behavior and sit down." Giles waved a hand, indicating the twin chair in front of the fire. "I don't care to peer up at you at that height."

Morgan studied him, with a threatening scowl. Taking no notice, Giles turned back to the fire.

"Do my eyes deceive me? Is this the same man who, not so long ago, entered my house and gave me a trouncing for putting my head in a bottle?"

Giles smiled in remembrance. Yes, he had enjoyed seeing Morgan sputter about like a fish out of water. And he had been furious that his best friend had allowed self-pity to drive him to such lengths. What irony that he once saved Morgan when the bonehead sat in his study in the same sorry state. Galling as it was, Giles had to admit he cared not a whit if he drowned himself in drink. Even though it gave him little comfort.

"I plan to get drunk. But, unlike you, I am not sinking myself into a bottle to the point of oblivion."

"I beg to differ."

"You have no idea of my thoughts."

"Salient point." Morgan shrugged, uncaring of his intrusion. "If your thoughts pertain to the concept I have heard you express countless times, then you came home to face the samedevil."

Giles hoped his sire writhed in the pits of hell. He tossed back the contents of his glass. "A pity he took so long to die."

With his hands braced squarely on his hips, Morgan glared down at him. "I thought you had conquered those demons."

"Hard to conquer what you are forced to live with every day." Grabbing the empty bottle by the neck, he swung his arm toward Morgan. "Feel free to get one of your own." Amusing to think how in the past he had been the one to divert Morgan from submerging himself in spirits. One would imagine they'd had a reversal of roles.

"Care to enlighten me why you are sitting here in a very near replica of me, when I once endeavored to drown my sorrows?" Morgan pulled another bottle from under the cabinet and seized a glass. Leather creaked as he sat in the matching chair. "What eats at your soul?"

Giles' harsh laugh gushed forth. "What eats my soul?"

A spitfire of a girl with long, sun-kissed curls.

"The ghost of my father haunts my soul," he mused instead. "His blasted constitution. The title he gave me decrees the path I must follow. Responsibility, duty, honor—millstones I am required to do by moral obligation."

"This is an old issue." Morgan's brow furrowed. "I remember a man who once spat in the direction of duty. He carried his honor like a weapon."

Giles leaned his head back against the leather and closed his eyes. "How foolish we were then. My life was worth nothing, so I cared not."

"When I reflect back, I sometimes wonder if I wanted to meet my maker." Morgan gave a laugh which held more sorrow than humor. "I had no fear of death. I welcomed it."

"Two sorry lots. Undoubtedly, an angel of mercy watched over us." Giles stared at the amber liquid in his glass. "We each were hell bent on self-destruction."

"High-and-mighty overweening cocks." Morgan lifted his glass and took a healthy swallow.

"Rebellion was the only thing on my mind." Giles emitted a hard sigh. "Every mission meant more than a challenge. I looked at each as an adventure to slay my dragons. The ones I carried in my soul."

"Did we really think we were indestructible? Untouchable? It is a wonder I am still alive. Of course, if not for you . . ."

"Wasn't about to leave you in that hell hole." Giles extended the empty bottle toward the light, confirming what he already knew. Without a word, Morgan offered the one in his possession.

"You always were the calm one. The more levelheaded."

Giles shrugged. "Cunning and planning are my attributes."

"Others commented on your patience. Not envious. More watchful. Respectful of your calculating mind and your diligence. Yet each one keenly aware." Morgan quaffed another hefty swallow from his glass before continuing, "Think of a powder keg waiting for a lighted fuse to blow."

"Ahh, but what drove me." Giles measured the amber liquid flowing smoothly into his glass while the image of his father's harsh features stabbed his focus. "Bitterness of the man who sired me drove my passion. Like you, I cared not about death.

My only course was to strike at my father. Each mission was a blow against him. I fought for my freedom. And look where it landed me. Right back here in the bosom of my prison."

"The man is dead and gone." Morgan's words seemed far away.

"But his mastery over me remains."

Damn the man!

Even from the grave the wretch controlled him. Giles drained his glass, poured more, and reached an arm to Morgan, handing the bottle back to him.

"You allow it."

"Leave off, Morgan."

"You continue to allow your father dominance. To govern your life."

A sharp sting of acknowledgement targeted the truth of Morgan's words. Giles disregarded them. "I trusted very little in my life until I met you. We became friends. I grow weary of repeating myself."

Morgan's brow rose in skepticism. "As your friend—"

"As an earl," Giles interrupted, "you know the dictates of your station. I am a duke. A duke must cleave to the strictest rules of society."

"Rules instilled by your father. You can do any bloody thing you set your mind to."

"As it happens, I cannot escape my nobility, or what is expected of me. I will marry and produce the required heir."

Morgan shoved out of his chair and trudged to the hearth. With an arm braced on the mantel, he stared into the fire. Flames blazed, sparks popping from the burning wood. He swung to Giles with narrowed lids. Oft times his friend would do that. Study, dissect, speculate—an indication he had an inkling of someone hiding a secret. His mind was a well-oiled machine, and once Morgan had the idea between his teeth, he would gnaw away like a dog with a large bone.

"Give it up, old man," Giles said with a disheartened sigh. "This is my life. You have a wonderful marriage with a lovely woman."

His own future loomed dark and empty. He wished, resentfully, he could slide into blessed unconsciousness. Suddenly aware of how much he'd imbibed, he reached for the bottle next to Morgan's chair. The little amount remaining confirmed his suspicions. "Think we need another bottle." He rose and took a moment to steady his legs. "Bloody hell. I must have consumed a good amount before your timely arrival."

"No more for me. Kat will have my hide if I go home foxed."

"You can handle your whiskey, my good man. I have seen you drink me under the table."

"Do you suppose, perhaps you should conquer your demons before you bring a woman into the mix of things?"

"I did not say immediately. Still, a duke must have a proper wife. I believe I will ask Katherine to help me with an assortment for my selection."

"You jest." Morgan grunted his astonishment.

"Why would I quip about something so serious as a wife?" Giles held a new bottle aloft. "See what I mean. You have a bride to keep you on the straight and narrow. Do I not deserve the same thing?"

"You deserve to be happy. Maybe take some time in choosing a woman to spend the rest of your life with."

"Not all men marry for love, my friend."

"I once felt the same as you. But life with the right woman can be fulfilling indeed."

"For God's sake. You will find no pulpits in this dwelling. And if there are any, I will burn them along with my father's portrait in the morning."

"The devil you say."

"I do say." Giles swung his gaze to his sire's painting and held up his glass in a toast. "Enjoy your last night as oppressor. For tomorrow you go to a fiery grave."

Morgan shoved from the hearth and took the brandy from Giles' hand. "I think we've had enough of this." He placed the bottle on the table along with his glass. "I'm off."

"Are you seriously taking my drink away from me in my own home?"

"Go to bed, Giles. I will be back in the morning. I want a clear head for our discussion."

Giles angled a brow. "Am I to presume you are suggesting a reason other than a friendly visit?"

"There is more than just your father haunting you this night." Morgan gathered his coat and gloves, and strode through the door.

God's blood.

Galling as it was, Morgan would probe and press until Giles revealed all. Yes, they were more than friends. Together they had survived countless missions where each had depended on the other for their very life. Tomorrow morning, the man more important to him than an arm or a leg, would split his heart open and make him bleed.

When he lifted his glass to down the brandy, ruby and amber lights danced in the spectrum below the rim. A reflection from the firelight. He swiped a hand over his unshaven, whiskered face. He could drown in drink, tasting nothing but remorse, and Alex's image would still remain fresh in his mind. Oh yes, he had fought against his attraction, but in the end he succumbed.

Then, horror of horrors, he denied his love for her. The biggest betrayal of all.

He must not think of her mischievous smile, or those kissable lips. Or how her eyes fired in temper, and God help him, how her amber and gold flecks glowed in passion. How her pale blonde hair shimmered like sunshine radiating off a mellifluous cloud. He rubbed his forefinger and thumb together. Her soft skin as smooth as the finest China silk. Or how she clutched him when he was buried deep inside her.

Now he had something else to drown out. He marched over to the glass Morgan had placed on the table and tossed back the brandy in one gulp.

He would never accept his visit to America as simply a pleasant pastime. After all, he had asked to marry the girl. An undertaking he did not take lightly. He groaned, thinking of his conversation with Carmichael. Like it or not, nothing could come of their association. Her father made it very clear his daughter would not be leaving her home. Yet Giles heart splintered at the thought of never seeing Alex again. He shuddered with the knowledge that a mere slip of a girl had brought him to his knees. A girl who showed more caring and passion than any woman with whom he had been.

Fate dealt him a cruel blow. He would give anything to have Alex in his life. But her father was right. She belonged with her family. He could not rip her away. He had refused to be responsible for the separation. His heart would not survive if the day came when she would regret her decision, and want to leave him. That pain he cared not to subject himself to.

Fate.

He had left a slice of his soul behind. Although his love for Alex would never die, he must fulfill the duty his title proclaimed. He would marry. Not for love. Very few marriages were a result of love. Half the women in England would happily settle for a position as the new Duchess of Nethersall without him professing a hint of love. Noble women could be just as calculating as noble men. He would begin his search immediately. He did not need anyone's approval—sure as hell not Morgan's.

Giles strode to the hearth, leaning a forearm upon the mantle. He spoke in a tone as raw and searing as the red embers on the charred wood.

"Do your worst, my friend. Even if I bare my soul, destiny has decided my fate for me."

Chapter 22

G iles' impulse to visit his gentlemen's club in hopes of a distraction had been doomed from the idea. His hopes to forget Alex, of course, were impossible.

True to his vow, he had taken down his father's portrait. As for burning the damned thing, he'd reconsidered. Generations of dukes lined the ancestral hall of Castle Nethersall. Following sequence, Giles' own portrait was the next to take his father's place above the mantle. Another item on the long list of obligations.

Alex.

Now there would have been a true work of art. Alex's portrait hanging above the fireplace. He imagined gazing at her loveliness for hours on end. Could he bear the gut-wrenching pain? He wondered if a person could die from heartache. No doubt he had crushed Alex. What she did not know was that his own heart had shattered as well.

However, a duke must adhere to his duty. Certainly, he could not have the portrait of his lover hanging on a wall where his wife would see. His private chamber would have been a better place. But therein lay the problem. He had no portrait, no painting. No likeness of the woman he loved. Only her exquisite image, burned into his mind.

After months of hell bordering on despair, he decided to heed his own words. To beget a wife, one had to go through the motions. Almacks be damned. He made a bargain with Horace Pendorgrass, and now he would wed the earl's daughter.

Giles could not afford weakness. Not when years of anguish and rage had led him to this pivotal point.

Even with Morgan at his side, Giles' announcement of his intentions—taking the plunge into matrimony—caused the men around him to fall silent, while conversation droned in the background. In a circle of leather upholstered chairs, Giles gazed at each man. A cigar hung precariously from Witherspoon's mouth. Carstairs' eyes nearly bulged from his head. Hatheridge sputtered, his drink dripping from his chin.

"A wife? Are your wits addled? Do tell what you have done with the real Duke of Nethersall." Carstairs downed his glass and signaled for another.

"Bloody hell, Nethersall," Witherspoon croaked.

Roxborough's dark brows lifted above the edge of his newspaper. "Upon my word, Nethersall. What is this?"

"The clock is ticking." Legs extended, Giles studied the toe of his black hessians. "I need an heir to pass the dukedom."

"I would rather have a hot poker stuck in my eye," Hatheridge mumbled.

Roxborough gave a nod. "One day you may change your mind."

"May I never be that desperate."

"Desperate, you say. Marriage does not have to be a prison." Witherspoon shifted in his chair, flicking his cigar into a crystal bowl. "Look on the bright side."

"There's a bright side?" Hatheridge quipped.

"Of course, there is a bright side."

"Well, I for one fail to see it," Carstairs piped in.

"Nethersall can simply deposit his wife at his country estate, and then hie back to London to enjoy all the things that make life worth living."

Giles would have to disagree on that.

"Capital idea," Carstairs said, then nodded to Giles. "And I know for a fact, you have several."

"Several what?" Sedgewick threw back his tails, and gracefully lowered his tall frame onto the last seat remaining in their circle. He made a grand show of pulling on the cuff of his sleeves. "What have I missed?"

"You are late, Sedgewick. What kept you?" Witherspoon asked.

Carstairs gave a knowing smirk. "Lord Hardwicke's widow, no doubt."

Sedgewick smiled, neither admitting nor denying his whereabouts.

"Nethersall has just announced his plans to marry."

"Why in God's name would you want to do that?" Sedgewick's brows raised to his hairline.

"Another who agrees women are a plague upon men," Hatheridge crowed.

"The proverbial heir," Witherspoon muttered as he knocked ash from his cigar.

"Oh. An heir, of course. But it still flabbergasts the mind." Sedgewick shrugged and swung to Carstairs. "So, the several I heard you mention would be several candidates, hmm?"

"Several estates." Carstairs lifted his glass to a servant.

"Poor show, my good man, to make fun when I have missed most of the conversation. Would you care to enlighten me?"

Giles waited patiently while his cronies discussed his personal life as though he was not there.

"As Nethersall has several estates, he can deposit his new wife in any one of them."

"I see." Sedgewick relaxed back against his leather chair and crossed his boot over one knee. "Tuck the little woman out of sight and out of your hair?"

"Exactly," Witherspoon added. "The one farthest away from London would be my choice."

Giles thought about that. Mayhap he should live in a secluded estate. He preferred to be alone while he wallowed in self-pity. Of course, the duchess would want to be in London for the seasons.

Actually, Giles cared not where his wife lived. Perhaps, it would better for her if they lived apart. That way she would not have to witness his sullen moods when Alex entered his mind.

Which was most of the time.

Alex.

If she were his wife, he would never let her out of his sight. He smiled as he thought of a bride month with her. Like Morgan, he could imagine himself being gone for months. He would never tire of Alexandria.

"A man could conceivably change his mind. Am I not the example of wedded bliss?" Roxborough smiled with contentment, for he loved his wife as much as Morgan loved Kat.

"Nonsense," Carstairs huffed. "A man cannot let frivolous emotions control his destiny. Can you not see Nethersall has the proper idea of marriage one should? A man does not dwell on the attributes of a bride the way one chooses a mare for his stable."

The bloody fools had no idea of the nonsense they spouted.

"Are you saying I should pick my prize mare with more relish than I should a bride?" Declaring his plans, Giles had expected ridicule. Having his cronies discuss how he should choose a bride chafed on the raw.

"My mother has been crowing for me to pick a wife," Sedgewick announced. "She's dragging me to Almacks next week. Perhaps we can go together, old man."

Hatheridge choked on his brandy.

"What is the matter with you, pup?" Sedgewick slapped him on the back.

"I thought we were in agreement on the matter of marriage. You just said—"

"I said Mother was dragging me to Almacks. I never said I was going to pick a bride. Besides. You may earn favor with your grandmother." Sedgewick glanced to the ceiling in thought. "Hmm. A wife of good stock. Noble birth. 'Tis a bit like picking a horse, I suppose."

"Do you check her teeth?"

"Glad to see you got your wind back," Sedgewick told Hatheridge.

"Of course." Carstairs cleared his throat. "A man takes pride in the horseflesh he owns."

Giles raised a brow. "Should not a man take pride in his wife?"

"For appearances' sake, yes," Hatheridge agreed. "But a man loves his horses. A good steed, a good ride."

"Hatheridge. Cannot a wife give a good ride?" Witherspoon crowed.

Guffaws sounded around the room, verifying others listened in on their conversation.

"A wife is to be above reproach." Sedgewick reached inside his coat pocket for a cigar. "She is the adornment on a man's sleeve. If you want a good ride, get a mistress."

"A wife may object to such a notion," Morgan pointed out.

"She may object all she wants, Whetherford. It is none of a wife's affair if a husband has a dozen mistresses." At Morgan's glower, Carstairs quickly amended, "Of course, not every man is besotted with his wife the way you are."

"And not all wives are as comely as Lady Whetherford." Witherspoon received a glower of his own. "Come now, Whetherford. All work and no play makes for a very dull life."

The fool. He should know better than to dip his toe into Morgan's pond.

"I will wager his wife keeps him on his toes. Won't give him time for—"

"I will kindly thank you to keep your tongue behind your teeth and away from my wife, or I will gladly remove it."

Carstairs sputtered, "No insult, old chum."

Witherspoon placed his cigar in the glass bowl. "Let's drink to Nethersall finding the right woman."

"I'll drink to that." Sedgewick raised his glass.

"To debutantes and their matchmaking mamas," Carstairs said as he lifted his glass.

"May she be a sweet little miss who does not bore him to tears." Sedgewick saluted again.

"A weak-willed light-o-love," Carstairs added.

Witherspoon folded his paper and placed it on the table at his elbow. "A soft-spoken woman who will leave him in peace." Witherspoon lowered his voice and added, "If there is such a creature to be had."

"A paragon who does not have an old dragon for a mother." Sedgewick was getting into the spirt of toasts.

"Much rather have a feisty woman like my paramour." Hatheridge's words slurred, but his voice was loud enough to be heard.

"For a wife?" Carstairs choked.

"Good God, no. I'm remaining single until my dying day."

"He has a point." Witherspoon faced Carstairs. "Where is it written a wife cannot enjoy the marriage bed?"

"If that were the case, men would not have mistresses," Sedgewick declared.

Morgan chuckled.

"A mistress is fine until the veneer begins to crack." Roxborough did not have a mistress, but he joined in the toasts.

"You could show a bit more passion for your bride-to-be, Nethersall." Witherspoon gestured with his glass signaling for Giles to join in the spirit of things.

"If you have any doubts about this, then cease this course immediately." Morgan's caution interrupted Giles' musing.

Surrender—a word not in his vocabulary. At least, not until now. A duke must accept his fate, accommodate his new wife. *Yield to another.* How the thought tasted like bile.

"No doubts. I must have a wife. And Miss ...Pendorgrass is my choice."

"That empty-headed doll?"

Witherspoon kicked Sedgewick in the foot.

"Good God, Witherspoon, what—?"

"The girl is beautiful. Excellent choice." Witherspoon signaled for Sedgewick to shut his mouth.

Giles shrugged. "The girl's father is recognized for his proceedings in Parliament. A match with his daughter is acceptable to me."

"What about her dragon of a mother?" Sedgewick received another kick. He turned to Witherspoon with a harsh glare.

"Horace Pendorgrass is ambitious. He is a proud man. Not one bit of scandal has been connected with the Pendorgrass name. His daughter is an excellent choice." Roxborough gave a nod of approval.

"Then we shall toast Nethersall's betrothal." Witherspoon held up a glass of port.

"A beautiful dimwit . . . er . . . chit the *ton* will accept."

The ton will accept.

But what will Alex do? How will the ton treat her?

Carstairs and Sedgewick had pinned Harriett dead to rights. A meek, docile, mindless chit. Was this what he wanted? An adornment for his sleeve? If so, Harriett embodied an excellent choice. As a member of the aristocracy, she had been trained in every art, accepted among the *ton*, her character beyond reproach—yes, perfect.

With three daughters to marry off, Pendorgrass needed the quid to ensure his offspring's financial stability. With what he would receive from Giles, Harriett's sisters would shine in all their glory at the next coming-out ball.

True, this marriage would not be based on affection. A duke's title assured the best match for Pendorgrass' daughter, and Harriett had been groomed to be a lady in every aspect, including accepting a man of her father's choosing.

No, Giles would not wed for love. An heir for the dukedom must be provided, therefore he must tie the knot. Even if it felt like a noose around his neck.

Eyes the color of molasses, surrounded by a golden cloud of tresses flashed before his mind. If Alex were his wife, there would never be a mistress. He had no right to lust after a woman other than his wife. Yet, his future bride-to-be could not create a surge of passion the way Alex—

Damn and blast!

Giles quickly shook off his line of thinking before doldrums had a chance to take hold.

"I am in a hell of my own making."

The buzz around him stopped. He cursed himself for speaking aloud.

"It is not too late to change your mind." Witherspoon broke the silence.

"Of course not," Hatheridge nearly bellowed. "See the right of it, Giles. You can beg off."

Close friends though they were, Wesley addressing him by his first name in public lay claim the man was well into his cups. Suggesting Giles break the engagement had every man staring as though the cove had lost his mind.

"Gentlemen. I normally do not chime in, since I am a not a member of your close-knit group," Roxborough interjected. "Once an agreement has been made with the girl's father, the man would demand satisfaction if Nethersall were to cry off."

"That settles it. You must flee. We'll away on an adventure." Hatheridge was beginning to slur his words. And he was having difficulty accepting the news.

"Don't be a rodcock."

Hatheridge frowned at Morgan, clearly offended. Even so, he made a princely offer. "The Lady Mistress rides anchor in the harbor. Take a month, or three to clear your head."

The group sat in silence, waiting for Giles to reply. Even Morgan held his peace.

Finally, Viscount Roxborough spoke. "Do you need to clear your head, Nethersall? Do you want to stop this wedding?"

"Want?" Giles snarled. "Since when have my wants or needs mattered?"

He hated self-pity. He sounded like a bloody ass.

"It is not at all fashionable to wear one's heart on one's sleeve, Nethersall." Witherspoon studied him.

"What's this?" Carstairs straightened in his chair and sniffed like a hound on the trail of his quarry.

"I suspect there is more to this tale than just a wedding." Witherspoon's narrowed gaze plagued Giles.

The man sensed a skeleton in the cupboard. No one knew a thing. Except Morgan. And he bloody well would not tell a soul.

"Still, I think it's a deuced poor reason for a bachelor to resign himself to marriage." Obviously, Witherspoon's words had gone unheeded by Hatheridge.

Roxborough recognized something amiss and saved the day. "Well now, Hatheridge. When the day comes that you do change your mind, I hope I am there to witness it."

"I offer myself as your best man." Morgan joined in, steering the topic away from any more speculation on Witherspoon's comment.

"In fact, I will make a wager." Sedgewick was never one to be left out when a bit of sport was to be had. And when a wager was mentioned, a gentleman's hearing altered, taking notice quicker than a matron spreading gossip.

"A wager, you say?" Carstairs spoke louder than Morgan. Other men in the club drifted their way.

"Within the year, our man Hatheridge, here, will succumb to the wiles of a debutante."

"Not bloody likely."

"I'll take that bet," a bystander added.

"I will venture to go even further." Morgan joined in the game. "Hatheridge will be chasing the chit, not the other way 'round."

"God's blood. If I ever get that stupid, I hope someone foots, (hi-cup) shoots me."

"Let us be off to White's." Carstairs set down his glass with a crack.

"White's?" several echoed.

"Yes. To enter this wager in the betting book, of course."

"Now, see here . . ."

Witherspoon and Sedgewick grabbed Hatheridge by each arm, wrenching him from his chair. Carstairs slapped him on the back, nearly toppling him over.

"Come, my good man." Carstairs glanced to Giles. "We are off to White's."

Giles chuckled, threw back the rest of his brandy and stood with a burst of renewed energy. Word of the wager spread from one man to the next. In turn, several men hastily grabbed their coats and hats, and scurried for the door. Morgan helped navigate Hatheridge to the carriage.

"Wait a bloody minute. You cannot seriously be thinking of putting such a ridiculous wager in the betting book."

Sedgewick pried Hatheridge's fingers from the doorway of the coach and shoved him inside. "It is not unbelievable. I will even dare to say a few of our acquaintances will jump on our wagon."

"This is absurd. Putting that rubbish in White's book is laughable. Anyone who knows me will not aid your cause. I am a rogue, through and through."

"Sheath the blades on your tongue," Morgan muttered as he crawled into the coach behind Hatheridge. "This is just the distraction Giles needs."

Chapter 23

G iles stepped onto the veranda and inhaled the morning fresh air. The last time he had enjoyed such a morning, he could not remember. Going along with his bantering fellows last evening, in their playful tantalizing of Hatheridge, had been good for his self-esteem. He'd been wallowing in a well of defeatism since his return from America.

That needed to stop.

He had made his proverbial bed. Now he must lie in it.

Easy to tell his mind, but his heart disagreed by revealing its earth-shattering pain. An ache he would have to live with, since he'd made his choice and had no intention of changing his mind.

He turned to go back inside, closing the balcony doors behind him. As he strode to his study, he considered the correspondence that needed his attention. A stack of letters was waiting, and he would need to respond to at least three today.

When he entered his study, he smelled the aroma before he saw the steaming, silver pot. Ahhh, Cuthbert anticipated his need for coffee.

"What do you have there, Cuthbert?"

"Since you decided to skip breaking your fast, I brought sustenance to you. Coffee," Cuthbert said the word without distaste. It had taken the man a long while to understand that Giles preferred the dark brew to England's tea. "And some of

Cook's scones. Even though she had eggs benedict laid out in the dining hall, she prepared these for you knowing your habit of often skipping the morning meal."

"I shall make a point of complimenting her for them, so she will not take offense with the meal wasted in the dining hall. I have much to do this morning."

"Very good, my lord."

Giles sat down at his desk, as Cuthbert poured the wonderful smelling brew.

"Will there be anything else, my lord?"

"No, thank you." He sipped the hot coffee as Cuthbert took his leave. Mmm, just what he needed after the late night. Again, he thought of how refreshing the night had passed. Very different than his evenings of late.

Possibly an hour later, he was not sure since he was deeply engrossed in one item on paper that Parliament currently debated, when there was a sharp knock on his study door. Giles glanced up from the papers on his desk to find Cuthbert, stiff as the starch in his shirts.

"Lord Thornton is here, Your Grace."

Lord Thornton?

What the devil was he doing here?

"Send him in." Over the past few weeks Giles had collected an incredible amount of time to lament his errors. His mind leapt about, wondering why Thornton would want to see him. Being a prominent member of Parliament, the aristocrat debated pressing business in the House of Lords as well as overseeing secret matters. Amazing, how during Giles' spying days, he had not known Thornton had a hand in organizing his missions.

Giles stood, recalling the last time he had seen the man. Thornton had engaged Giles to find his nephew, Kat's brother. He could still taste the excitement at how his blood had spiked at the thrill of that dangerous escapade. His mission successful, he had not spoken to Thornton since. What could the man want with him?

"Your Grace." Thornton held out his hand for a hearty shake. The man commanded a room just by being in it.

"Thornton. Welcome to my home. It has been a while."

"Yes, yes. Glad to see you have taken your seat in Parliament."

"I'm filling my father's seat."

"Yours now."

"Please come in. May I offer you some refreshment?"

"No, thank you. My wife and I just finished brunch." Thornton glanced about as he took the high-back chair in front of Giles' desk. "I knew your father. He was harsh and exacting. When he addressed the floor, his eyes flashed fire with every word he spoke. Well-respected by his colleagues. As you know, money exchanges hands for illegal business endeavors. Your father never accepted inducements to line his pockets. He expected you to take your place in Parliament."

God save me.

His father had no love for his family, nor liking for his son. Giles did not give a whit for tales of how the man was respected for his integrity.

"Are you here to discuss parliamentary business?"

"Right to the meat of the matter. To answer your question, no." Thornton shifted in his chair. "Do you mind if I smoke?"

If he needed a smoke, this must be pressing business, indeed.

"Apologies," Giles said as he made to stand. "I should have offered . . ." Thornton waved a hand in casual dismissal.

"No need. I brought a special blend with me." He reached to his inside pocket and retrieved a gold case. Popping the latch, he offered a cigar to Giles.

"Ah, I remember those. I believe I will. Thank you." He ran the cigar under his nose, inhaling the spicy tobacco.

Thornton tucked away the case, and pulled a pipe from his pocket. At Giles' raised brow, he grinned.

"Like traveling with an old friend." He packed the tobacco, then put the pipe to his lips. The flame dipped several times before smoke swirled in the air like a dancing snake.

Obviously, Thornton was in no hurry to open the topic of his unexpected visit. Giles lit his cigar, leaned back and enjoyed its aroma. Whatever Thornton wanted, he would divulge in good time.

Thornton took a few puffs of his pipe, then tilted his head back, sending spirals of silver floating into the air. "Lives up to its reputation?"

"Yes." Giles knew Thornton meant the cigar. "As good as I remember." Giles relaxed his muscles in the comfortable leather, and enjoyed the flavor on his tongue.

"I have come to seek advice."

He controlled his surprise at the shocking idea of Thornton seeking advice from him.

"Of course you and Whetherford were the first two I thought of when the *situation* was brought to my attention."

"Morgan is retired. And so am I."

"But you would love to sink your teeth back in the game. Admit it."

"I will admit the idea has my blood thrumming. Days of monotony makes the thrill of excitement very tempting. What is this dubious circumstance?"

"As it turns out, there is no emergency. A case of kidnapping turned out to be a precocious daughter running away with her beau. Once the truth came to light, the father stampeded about like a wild boar. No amount of finesse would console the man. He wants to teach her a lesson. With discretion, of course."

"Of course." Giles gave a nod.

"He thinks the scoundrel hopes to gain access to her fortune. Poor girl. Has the harsh looks of her father, hairy brows and all. My thoughts on the matter, he should leave the chit alone." Thornton puffed on his pipe, then held it to the side while staring at the ceiling. "Hence the need for a trusted . . . shall we say go-between."

"I would think you would have an abundance of names."

Thornton met his gaze. "This is a unique nature for a significant friend. He does not suffer fools, and this young man who has trifled with his daughter will suffer dire consequences if I do not intervene."

Giles could easily read a man, but Thornton had him stumped. A private man, yet when he needed information, he gleaned particulars down to the last detail. No speculation. Only cold, hard facts. The king of discretion, mastering cloak-and-dagger operations, he held his secrets close to his chest.

"You plan to save this scoundrel?"

"My friend confided in me. I investigated. The scoundrel is no reprobate. He deserves a sporting chance."

"Before I can recommend someone, I will need more information."

"As you are aware, all of my informants are confidential. I guard my contacts' secrecy." Thornton leveled a compelling gaze. "I count you among my most trusted."

"I am honored."

"I'm in need of a man with exacting morals." Thornton's grin depicted a hint of mystery, and held the confidence of a man in control. "I need a man with your particular skills."

A rush went through Giles' limbs with the speed of a lightning bolt. Excitement only danger and memories could generate. He might have dropped out of the game, but he housed a wealth of knowledge, and certain skills could be taught.

An hour later, Giles shook hands with a satisfied Thornton. Closing the door, he took two steps before it opened again. Reflexes kicked in and Giles spun.

"What did Thornton want?"

"God's blood, Morgan. What are you doing lurking about?"

"Cuthbert told me Thornton was here, and allowed me to wait in the library."

"You were hiding in my library?" Giles taunted with a smirk.

"I do not care to be dragged back into my former life. Kat would have my head if even a hint of risk or danger reached her ears." Morgan studied Giles. "You are not considering his proposal, are you? Although, risking your life would be better than committing the suicide you plan for tomorrow."

Anger surfaced, then simmered. Silence stretched between them. Why should he be angry? Morgan was entitled to his opinion. "First you sneak about my home, then you hurl insults. Do you have so little respect for me?"

Morgan's jaw tightened in anger. "You know bloody well this has nothing to do with respect."

"You have come to collect, then? I have not forgotten you saved my life."

"Bloody hell, Giles. That is not what I said." He took several breaths, reminding Giles of a steam railway locomotive. "We have been friends for a long time."

Giles could kick his own arse for spouting such nonsense. He exhaled his frustration in a harsh breath, then went to his desk. "I am a fool"

"Would you not offer a gentleman a drink?" Morgan's voice echoed off the walls.

"Assuming, by your comment, I am about to be on the receiving end of your tongue, perhaps I should just throw you out."

"You may try," Morgan said with a mocking grin.

Giles strode to the sideboard and gathered another glass. He splashed a measure into the crystal, and thrust it toward Morgan before adding more brandy to his own.

Drink in hand, Morgan took his usual seat, a leather chair in front of the hearth. "I thought to make one last plea for sanity."

Giles settled in the matching chair. "You have come to my door to declare your sanity?"

"Mine is not in question." Morgan glowered. "However, yours is another matter entirely. How long will you continue this way?"

"By *this way*, if you mean wallowing in a mess of my own making, I have one more night of freedom."

"You must call off the wedding."

"Impossible." Giles brought the brandy to his lips.

"You just bemoaned this was a mess of your own making. Yet you offered yourself to the chopping block."

"I am a duke. You know I must marry." He closed his eyes and pinched the bridge of his nose, weary of this discussion.

"Marriage does not have to be a prison."

"No one said—"

"You just spoke of your last day of freedom. For God's sake, call off this farce of a wedding."

Farce?

A duke had to do what a duke had to do. "The wedding is no charade. Nor is it the travesty you make it sound."

"You are the one speaking of freedom on the eve before your nuptials. What of the American girl?"

Alex.

His grip tightened on his glass. "Best forgotten."

"Can you forget her?"

Forget Alex? Never.

Anguish quivered down his spine as an image emerged of a golden goddess with captivating eyes. She was a mere girl when he first met her. But she had grown into quite a woman. An extremely tempting woman. With a heart as big as the moon.

"She is unforgettable. She knocks me to my knees. Makes me weak."

One corner of Morgan's mouth lifted.

"Wipe that bloody smirk off your face."

"I know of what you speak. Kat affects me the same way. Every man who has been in love has felt the same."

Several moments passed in silence. Giles peered into the fire, but he felt Morgan's heated stare.

"You do not deny it."

Deny that he had been captured by irrationality? Him—the man of reason? Deny that he had fallen into lunacy by lusting after foolish dreams? A man who did not believe in fantasy? Yet his heart ached for a girl with wheat gold hair and molasses eyes.

"Far be it from me to argue with a man who yammers the truth," he mumbled.

"You admit you love this girl?" Morgan persisted.

"How else do you describe the feeling for one who constantly overpowers your thoughts? She would stare at me with a hunger no young girl should know." She'd surprised him. Then capti-vated him. She showered him with her warmth and determination, proving she would not give up. Every tender touch attested to giving her love. He had never experienced such devotion. No woman had given him intelligent conversation. Nor energized him to the point where he felt much younger than his years. She was feisty, resolute, adamant and unwavering in her purpose. Steadfast in her pursuit of him. Tenacious. Spirited. Stubborn.

And so loving, she boggled his mind.

He had no idea he could love a woman to distraction. His soul bled for the Yankee American. "How does one repair the hole she has carved into my heart?"

"I think this discussion calls for more sustenance." Morgan stood and strode to the sideboard. Reaching under the cabinet, he pulled a new bottle from the shelf. He opened it before returning to the set of chairs. "Our friendship began as mere lads, each fighting his own demons. We have come a long way since then, my friend."

Giles held out his glass. "Dwelling on the past makes a cold bedfellow."

"Do you not remember our rally cry." It was a statement more than a question. "Never give up. Never surrender."

"I need no reminder. You think I have lost the passion of those days?"

Wasn't that the reason he rebelled in the first place? Left his home when he was just a lad? Foolishly risking his life, daring the Angel of Death to take him. Oh, yes. He remembered too well.

Morgan leaned forward, bracing his arms on his knees. "When a man makes a mistake, he must live with the consequences of his actions. We made a lot of mistakes in the past, but nothing compared to the grave error you are about to make."

Giles stared into the fiery flames in the hearth. "What is one more over the course of many?"

"You cannot marry one woman when you are undeniably yearning for another."

"A wife is not a partner, not even a companion. A wife is not like a comrade or a friend who will see you through to your deepest aspirations."

"Kat is all those things to me, and more. A companion. A confident. An ally. She is my partner in everything."

Morgan's wife was a rare bird. The two of them fit together like a pair of gloves. Giles had seen it.

"I need not those things," Giles said sharply. But, oh, how he craved them. The ache in his chest would not go away. "Alex is lost to me forever. I need a woman who will not make me behave so foolishly. I simply need a vessel. One meant to deliver a healthy heir."

Morgan raised his brow. "Your father's words?"

Giles forced himself not to flinch. He hated the man. But somewhere along the way, he had become his sire. "An old man with generations of wisdom between his ears."

"And not one troy of compassion in his heart. Bloody hell, I don't believe this." Morgan shoved from the chair and stomped across the carpet, then he suddenly whirled around. "You ran away from your father."

"I am not sure 'ran away' is the right choice of words."

"You hated the man. You fled the home of your birth to get away from him. You swore you would never be like him."

Is that what Morgan thought? That Giles was behaving like his father? At this point in his life, he did not care. "He is dead." Giles shrugged. "Now I have obligations."

Morgan huffed in annoyance. Thank God Giles was not his enemy. "Good God, what happened to you?"

Giles ran a hand through his shaggy hair. "I am the same man. With the same thoughts and convictions. I have simply accepted the dukedom path before me. A marriage of alliance."

"Did you hear anything I said?"

"Hard not to." He took a swallow of brandy as Morgan grunted. Giles loathed his situation. But he was not one to express his discontent over what could not be changed. "What do you want me to do? Roar? Beat my chest? Throw a temper tantrum? I must follow the path fate has allocated."

"Are we not in control of our own destiny? *Fate*." Morgan heaved an exasperating sigh and plunged on, his voice rising. "We make our own fate. Would I have Kat if not for you? Would I have gained her if I had not fought for her?"

Had he not shouted the same sermon nearly two years ago when Morgan fell into his cups?

"You are angry and rightfully so," Morgan continued, "but you sit here like a man who is wasting away."

"Bloody hell, Morgan. I am not a sorry sod squandering into nonentity. My lot in life is too tasking to fritter away. Cannot a man enjoy his brandy on the eve of his nuptials?"

"You have never been one to bow out, nor give up," Morgan stated. "No need to commit lunacy and leg shackle yourself to the first conforming female. Nobility is not in the title. It is in the heart."

A searing ache tortured that very region. Giles lived with the pain every day. Yet the longing must be denied. Of all the women he could have had or ever wanted, the only one he desired with a hunger beyond his own imagining was forbidden to him.

Alex.

"If I were a fool to believe in dreams . . ." His throat clogged. He was a fool. A fool to linger in the land of imaginings. As if he could have her, hold her, protect her . . . Cherish her all the days of his life. He forced those thoughts away. "I do have some measure of control."

"We've known each other since we were ravaged and raw with grief." Morgan's voice vibrated in the stillness. "We took life by the ballocks, and lived to see another day."

"True, we took risks."

"Risks? We are lucky to be alive."

"Lucky?"

"Damned lucky! And I will never forget you saved my miserable hide." Morgan took a deep breath and let it out slowly. "Maybe I did not care if I lived or died then, but I am bloody well appreciative now. I have a wife I love to distraction." Morgan paused, and shoved a hand through his hair. "Never thought my life would take such a turn. Never thought I deserved such happiness. I find, not only do I like it, but I am worthy." He looked pointedly at Giles. "So are you."

"You misunderstand, my friend. I too, loved. But it is a complication I cannot afford."

"Not afford?"

"Her father convinced me." Giles tossed back the liquid in his glass and reached for the bottle.

All the air seemed to fizzle out of his friend. "What does her bloody father have to do with this?" Morgan asked, dropping into his chair.

"Quite a lot. Alexandria is an infant compared to me."

"An infant. You act like you are a doddering old man. She is of a marriageable age. She must be something of a woman if you love her."

Giles gave a harsh laugh. "I tried to convince myself she was a child. Instead, she convinced me she was a woman."

"Then get up off your arse and go get her. Do not marry Harriett Pendorgrass."

"You are asking me to commit social suicide. No doubt a grand scandal would come of it. The *ton's* delicate sensibilities would not recover."

"Scandal be damned! Fight for the woman you love." Morgan showed more energy being angry than Giles could amass.

"Come down off your pulpit, Morgan. I do not require a bloody sermon. Besides, the banns have been circulated." Giles tossed back the remainder of his brandy and poured more. He was bound to have a deuced headache on the morrow. Perhaps a fitting one to match the twinge in his chest.

Morgan shook his head. "Looking back, I appreciate your actions on the night you came to Whetherford and gave me a trouncing. Had no idea—being on the receiving end—how difficult your task of kicking me in my well-deserved arse."

"Thank you. But I do not see what reference your drunken squalor has to do with my situation."

"For God's sake, Giles. You expect me to believe you have not fallen into the same dark hole? Where is the man who kicked my arse that day? Where is your passion? Where is your spirit? You have been allotted only one life. Do you really want to live it according to others' wishes? Society's decree?" Morgan's voice lowered with a harsh edge. "Your father's behest?"

Giles' fingers tightened around the glass in his hand, so firmly, it should have shattered.

My father.

"A spawn of Satan himself." He breathed deep for control.

"Do not let yourself succumb to the temptation of giving in to his ghost." Morgan shot out of the chair again. For a big man, he paced the room like a deadly tiger.

Giles closed his eyes and leaned his head back against the cushioned leather. Did he do this for his father? His obligation as a duke? He would lose his mind if he continued this back-and-forth battle of indecision.

"Spare me your wisdom in how I should live my life," he growled. "You are my most trusted friend. As my friend, let it be."

Morgan stopped his pacing and pinned Giles with a hard glare. "If you refuse to listen to your heart, you will grow bitter. We cannot change the past. Even if it were possible, I would not do it. I found Kat. Our love is stronger for what we went through. If you give up your heart's desire, you will have another regret to add to your list of many."

"God's breath, I cannot bear anymore!" Giles threw his glass at the hearth, watching it shatter into a million pieces.

Morgan looked to the shattered glass, then turned with a stone-faced expression. He picked up his hat and calmly strode to the closed door. Giles thought his friend was leaving, but Morgan paused with his hand on the knob.

"You and I know exactly how short one's existence can be. There is nothing so cold as regret." Morgan crowned his hat, and left.

Chapter 24

G iles spent the night debating Morgan's words. Between the request Thornton had made and the insistence in Morgan's plea, Giles had not slept a wink.

As for Thornton's request, he wanted Giles to do a little investigating. Nothing as dangerous as his last entreaty.

Giles understood the need for discretion. Most of his life had been spent keeping secrets. On many missions, his very life had depended on concealing his identity and his true purpose for being where he should not have been. Behaving in such a way as to avoid attention or reveal private information was second nature to him. He had thrived on action and mystery. Yet he found propriety must be above reproach, whether he was acting as a duke, or working under cover. He lived and breathed decorum, so when in his natural habitat, he made no mistakes. While performing services in secrecy, he could not afford to make mistakes.

He supposed he should be tired. But then, it was not the first night he had gone without sleep. Looking back, he would have to say there were countless nights he'd spent watching, waiting, where sleep had not been an option. And when he had searched for Stephen, urgency demanded he do so by the moon's glow.

Before he rode down memory lane, he decided to clean himself up for the new day. After his morning toilet, he graced Mrs. Cook with his presence at the morning meal. The smile on the woman's face pleased him as much as his arrival apparently had her. He spent the rest of the morning and most of the day on his horse, touring the fields and visiting his tenants. Satisfied things were progressing as they should, he headed back home.

Thoughts of his impending nuptials soured his mood. *God's teeth.* If he were to get maudlin every time he thought of his betrothed, perhaps Morgan was right. Giles should reconsider this wedding.

What was he thinking? He had to marry. It was his duty to continue his line. Although, marriage did not bother him as much as the bride. If he must take one, any bride would do. For he could not have the only one he wanted.

The muddle in his mind still warred as he rode into the courtyard. His groom met him before he dismounted.

"Your Grace. Cuthbert said there was a gentleman waiting to see you and I was to direct you inside as soon as you got back."

"Thank you, Horace. Did he say who this gentleman might be?"

"No, Your Grace."

"Very well." Giles climbed down and brushed his horse's mane. "Pharaoh had a long day. See that he gets an extra ration of oats."

"I will, Your Grace."

Giles knew that the groom was required to call him by his title, but he liked it when his friends called him by his given name.

Cuthbert, met him in the long corridor.

"Your Grace."

"I understand there is a gentleman to see me. I shall hurry to make myself presentable."

"Forgive me, Your Grace. But your visitor is not a nobleman. As for your appearance, I shall take the liberty of saying your suit of clothes are appropriate."

"Who is my visitor, Cuthbert?"

"His name is Jack Gordy, Your Grace. If you will forgive my saying so, I believe he may be the sort ... that ... well ... he may share a talent you keep hidden."

Giles' mental instincts went on alert. Cuthbert never spoke out of turn. He knew of Giles' dark past. If he suspected the visitor had the same talent, as he put it, then it must be so. Giles wondered if Thornton may have had a hand in this. Giles glanced down the hallway to the drawing room door.

"Very well. I should not keep my guest waiting."

"I will announce you, Your Grace."

"No need, Cuthbert. If he is as you think, I do not want to intimidate him before I find out his reason for being here."

He strode to a set of closed doors wondering what he would see on the other side. If Thornton had anything to do with this, Giles would soon find out. He opened a door.

A man stood by the large stone hearth, staring into the fire. His head jerked up as Giles entered.

"Your Grace."

Of course, certain standards had to be respected. "I believe you have the advantage."

"Forgive me for barging into your home unannounced. My name is Jack Gordy. I have no title. My lineage is not one of noble birth. But I am an honest man. I shall try to prove my worth."

Giles gave a nod. He took the hand Jack offered and gave a shake. Strong grip. The man was no weakling. The man was tall, but not as tall as he. Dark eyes met his own in a direct stare. The man did not flinch, nor turn away. Giles prided his instincts. His gut told him this man was what he claimed to be. As for being honest, time would decide.

"Please, have a seat." Giles used his hand to point to a high back chair. He took the one facing it. "I hope you have not been waiting long."

"Only for a bit. I am grateful your man allowed me to wait. I am pleased to meet you, Your Grace."

Giles would dispense with pleasantries and find out why the man was here. "Tell me what I can do for you."

"First, let me say we share an acquaintance. Captain Radbourn. I met him in a tavern along the waterfront. He was looking for men to crew his ship. An unfavorable sort pulled a gun on him and I relieved the man of his gun."

"I am sure there is more to that story."

"Let's just say I helped Captain Radbourn."

Giles was one to get answers. He had a feeling Jack left out quite a lot, but Giles would worry about that later. Something else was underfoot."

"I will be straight forward, Your Grace. I have done some investigating."

The hair stood on Giles' neck.

"I hope you will hear me out before you cast judgement."

Giles studied the man under half closed lids. Since he was a man of great patience, and a curious sort, he would allow Jack to talk himself into, or out of, a cryptic situation. "Go on."

"I have been offered a voyage. During my careful inquiries, I learned about Captain Radbourn's rescue. I learned you were the one who brought him home." Jack paused. Seemingly, to gage Giles viewpoint on hearing such news.

Giles held his tongue.

"I was approached by a very mysterious man. An odd duck. More than a servant. He was contracting business for his employer. After our puzzling conversation, and much speculation, I wanted to find out what I was getting into. I hope I can trust you by saying this." Jack cleared his throat. "I believe the same proposition was made to Captain Radbourn."

Giles nearly lost his teeth.

What the bleedin' hell?"

He'd had plenty of experience receiving shocking news, and learned not to show emotions of any kind. He breathed in slow, then carefully asked, "Why would you think that, Mr. Gordy?"

"As I said, I did some investigating. I know you are a reserved man, Your Grace. I hope you will not consider this an intrusion on your privacy, but I assure you, I mean you no disrespect. I will not utter a word to anyone else that is spoken in this room. All I ask from you is honesty."

That was laying it out there.

Giles thought this over. Jack was putting his arse on the line.

"Might I offer you a drink, Mr. Gordy? I believe the coming discussion requires one."

"Please, Your Grace. My name is Jack."

"I see no need to stand of formality, Jack. Please call me Giles. I think we are about to become close, and very personal." He rose and went to the sideboard. He lifted the decanter sitting on a silver tray and poured a generous portion into two glasses. After handing one to Jack, he lowered his tall frame into the cushioned seat. "I too appreciate honesty, Jack. I do not suffer liars. A man in my position never gives information. Of any kind. And I do not believe in gossip. With that being said, please continue."

"My sources give me facts. My gut instincts tell me you can be trusted." He paused, as if waiting for Giles reaction.

Giles gave nothing away, simply sat there and listened.

"I signed on with Captain Radbourn. The Lady Mistress made it as far as the North Sea when the captain suddenly changed his mind and the ship returned to England. I now know a woman was involved. Women make men do strange things."

Yes, Giles could relate to that. He had thrown caution to the wind with Alex. He knew firsthand about how a woman could twist a man's gut into knots.

"The man approached me after Captain Radbourn's wedding. Since he is on his bride-month, I cannot speak with him. This mysterious man offered me a proposition, and has given a sense of urgency. That is why I came to you."

"And what is it you require of me?"

"I would not ask you to reveal secrets or confidences. However, anything you can share to help prepare me would be beneficial in accepting or denying this voyage." Jack went on to explain his situation.

After a brief conversation, Giles was certain Jack Gordy could be trusted. Who was the man who had approached Jack? Could this man be the reason Stephen had gone to India?

Intriguing.

"Tell me more about this mysterious man."

"He said his name is Jedidiah. Spoke about his employer. If I had to guess, I would say he worked for a very important man who wants to keep his identity secret."

Understandable. At least Giles now knew the man was not Thornton. Thornton would never go to a tavern to seek an emissary.

But he might send someone.

Jack took a swallow of brandy, then continued. "I have no idea what his connection is to India, but that is where he wants me to go."

A shiver attacked Giles' spine. Stephen had been tortured and his men killed. A man would be crazy to go there again.

"This man, Jedidiah. Exactly what does he want you to do?"

"That's the thing. He won't tell me until I agree to the voyage. And I can pretty much name my price. His employer must be quite wealthy. Jedidiah has an accent, and his complexion is dark. I would guess India to be his homeland."

"He wants you to accept his proposal without revealing his plans? That's absurd."

"I think he is shipping guns to the rebels there. I don't know much about India, and I have never sailed anywhere near there."

"You would be best to keep it that way," Giles nearly shouted. *Good God.* Torture and murder had been Stephen's plight. The same could happen to Jack.

Jack cleared his throat. "Will you tell me why?"

Giles took a hefty drink.

Bloody hell.

While he hesitated, Jack spoke. "I know you—a duke—risked your own life to go in search of Captain Radbourn. I know you brought him back to England. I also know he was in bad shape."

"It would seem you discovered quite a lot." Giles stretched his legs and stared down at his hessians. "In my younger years, I was reckless. I accepted excursions without a care. I am no longer at a point in my life where I live for danger. If I were, I would go with you." He glanced up to see Jack's reaction.

"At the time I signed on, I had no idea why Stephen, that is Captain Radbourn, was sailing to India. He did tell me it would be dangerous. After he changed course back to England, there were rumors. I know he was attacked, his ship sunk, and his crew murdered." Jack's eyes hardened. Other than that, he showed no outward emotion.

"Are you familiar with the skirmishes among the Indian princes? They do not like that the British military is taking away the rulers' independence."

"I have heard a little."

"There are warlike Rajputs who fight against being ruled by the British. Stephen ran into one. The Rajput prince was pure evil. Deliberately killed Stephen's men right in front of him. Apparently, Stephen had sailed into a secluded cove, and the Rajput chief did not believe it was an accident."

"He killed Stephen's entire crew?"

"Yes," Giles answered before turning his glass up and emptying the contents. He rose to get more, and brought the bottle back with him.

"There are citizens who fight for their livelihood. From what I understand, the Rajputs who go against England punish the poor devils. Their armies force the people to give up their independence." He poured brandy into Jack's glass. "There are those who believe in peace, try to maintain fair trade. Then there are the rebels who fight against tyranny. But if anyone should run into such a group that fights purely for evil, they are doomed."

Giles added brandy to his own glass, then settled back into his chair. "Perhaps this Jedidiah works for a man who is helping the citizens. Perhaps he is sending arms to the rebels." Giles studied Jack.

"What will be your answer?"

Chapter 25

Two men ambled along the London docks, undetected in the midst of other sailors. Even their size went unnoticed, for most crewmen sported muscles resulting from the hard labor necessary in keeping a ship topnotch. After months at sea tugging on ropes and swabbing decks, a man was bound to be in brawny form.

Sea Dancer had docked earlier this afternoon. The time of day made no difference to a sailor's thirst. Shouts and boisterous laughter came from the open door of a tavern. Kit and Ben stepped inside. A cloud of smoke hovered in the air. Barmaids scurried about serving drinks and flaunting their wares. Kit made his way through the crowd searching for an empty table. Spying one off to the side, he slumped onto the wooden stool.

"What say you, Brother? I'll flip a coin to see who pays." In the opposite chair, Ben pulled a coin from his pocket.

"Heads, I win. Tails, you lose."

The coin was in midair before Ben's face twisted into a scowl. "That doesn't seem quite fair."

"Well now, luv? Whatever's ailin' ya, a draught will take that frown right off yer handsome face." A buxom woman with fiery red hair balanced a tray in one hand while the other rested on a plump hip. A smile bright enough to illuminate the dark was aimed at Ben.

"And who might you be?" His grin showed a full set of teeth. Once Ben turned on the charm, a woman was bound to fall for his appeal.

"Gilda." The girl thrust out her bosom and twirled a lock of her dark hair.

"A lovely name for a lovely lady." Ben gave her a saucy wink. "Sounds like just the thing. Would you kindly bring my brother and me a pint of your best ale?" He flipped the coin again. "I would be most appreciative."

"Why, ya near blind me when yer lips turn up in such a winsome grin. What a handsome brute ya be." She winked right back. "Coming right up, luv."

Ben watched her backside as she sashayed away.

"Looks like you're paying for this round and a bit more."

Ben uttered a hearty laugh. "Well worth it." His gaze met Kit's. "Why so glum?"

"Not sullen. Just quiet." Kit shifted in his chair. "Best place to garner information."

"Information on what?"

"On anything. The latest scuttlebutt spreads the quickest in taverns."

"I thought we were here to see the duke."

"Never hurts to keep up with goings on in the town, and at the docks."

"Here ya are, luv."

Ben tucked a coin into the barmaid's plump bodice, taking an exorbitant amount of time removing his fingers. The girl laughed with enthusiasm and leaned forward while Ben whispered in her ear. She danced away with a promise in her twinkling eyes.

"A toast to the Duke of Nethersall."

Kit stiffened. Ben jerked his head in the direction of the voice.

"May he enjoy his wedding night." Loud guffaws followed clanking glass.

"Hear, hear," another man bellowed.

"To the bride. May she scream the walls down."

"Will she be screaming her pleasure or crying out in indignation?"

"She's a virgin bride. She'll not know how to pleasure a man."

Ben's eyes flashed with enquiry. Kit concentrated on the next man's voice.

"My money is on the duke. He'll be showing her the way of it."

"Come now, Buxley. All the man needs is to consummate the wedding night."

"Right-o, Saxon. A man's mistress does the pleasuring." More guffaws and shouts.

Ben made to rise.

"Where do you think you're going?" Kit said in a low voice. "Your last round of fisticuffs cost me a stint of months."

"You can't blame me for the squall that blew your ship south instead of north. Not to mention the damage to the vessel. Besides, there's the legacy of the Cape Verde islands. 'Americans are arriving. There are tears of joy, lighting up the women's eyes.'"

"You abandoned me," Kit growled.

"'Twasn't only me who jumped ship and dallied with the women of the island. Besides, you had to make repairs to your ship, and the whalers worked for much less money than American seamen."

"But I can blame you for the stretch behind bars." Kit leaned forward, bracing his forearms on the round table. "Or do I need to remind you of a certain woman and her brother who threw you into a shabby hold on his ship?"

"Whaler ships are revolting." Ben shivered, demonstrating his revulsion. "Mate thought better of the idea, once I pounded some sense into him."

"Still, we lost close to a year."

"Not to worry, Brother. We are in England now." Ben glared toward the celebrating men. "And I have not forgotten why we are here."

"I'm in no mood for fisticuffs in a tavern."

"Well, I am." Ben stood, taking his mug with him. "Pardon me, gentlemen. You seem to be celebrating. If you share your news, I'll be happy to join you in a toast."

Several pairs of eyes landed on Ben.

"Who might you be?" The man they'd called Buxley addressed him.

"Sailed in on the *Sea Dancer*. Docked this afternoon. Name's Ben."

The man seated to his right spoke up. "Was down at the warehouse when yer ship entered the harbor. She's a beauty."

"We're with Langston Shipping."

Ben glanced to the man who was standing.

He continued, "This is Saxon, Chauncey, Lafayette, Phineas." He gestured to each of his cronies as he spoke their names. Then he turned his attention on Ben. "And they call me Buxley."

"Pleasure to join your company, gentlemen."

"The biggest building on the docks is the Langston warehouse. If you have cargo going there, I'm afraid you'll have to wait till tomorrow. The earl has it locked up tight for the duke's wedding."

The man called Chauncey lifted his mug. "We're celebrating."

"The Duke of Nethersall is getting leg shackled this very eve."

Kit narrowed his gaze on the man speaking. An ache formed in his chest for Alex. He'd tarried in coming after the duke. Hoping to give Alex time to accept the man's leaving, he had planned a journey to France on business. Of course, that was before the Cape Verde Islands debacle. Seemingly, it would have made little difference if he had come straightaway. The duke had wasted no time in acquiring a wife.

So, the man was to marry. How in the world could he break the news to Alex? First, he would make sure of the truth of the matter. Apparently, Ben had the same idea.

"You are speaking of Giles, the Duke of Nethersall?" Ben asked.

"Giles Heathcliff Montague Litscomb, sixth Duke of Nethersall." The man stood and swayed before setting his mug on the table.

Clearly the gents had been celebrating for quite a while. Ben steadied the wobbly man on his feet. His brother was not one to hold his temper. At the moment, Ben did a fine job of doing just that. His back muscles bunched, his voice low and hoarse with anger, Kit recognized all the signs of fury.

"The last time I saw Nethersall, he was as free as the birds flying out to sea," Ben ground out in a controlled voice.

"My good man, he is a duke. His nobility requires him to carry on his line. Can't have a bastard claiming the title."

"Is there a bastard?" Only Kit noticed the rage lacing Ben's words. The possibility of Giles begetting a bastard had the hair standing on his own neck.

Buxley scratched his head. "Don't think so."

"Ain't heard a flicker of gossip regarding anything of the sort," the man called Saxon added. "He's clean as a mate's whistle."

"Aye. Not a shadow of scandal on his family title. He is above reproach." Heads around the table nodded in agreement.

"This very night, you say?" Ben asked.

Kit had to admire his brother's restraint.

One man dug in his pocket for a gold watch, then flipped the top open. "At the church right now, in fact."

"A toast." Ben held his mug toward the others. "To the Duke of Nethersall."

May he rot in hell.

If Kit had his guess, Ben toasted Giles to the flaming pit as well.

"Hatheridge looks a bit green around the gills."

At Carstairs' nod, Morgan glanced at his friend, standing just inside the church doors. Hatheridge pulled at his cravat, stuck his finger inside the starched white collar, and tugged. With the sweat rolling down his temple, one would think he was the intended groom.

Catching his attention, Morgan motioned him forward. The poor devil looked ready to bolt the next instant the doors opened. The younger man came forward.

"Your cravat is askew. Shall I lend you my valet?" Carstairs poked fun while he managed to look bored.

"Carstairs, you have the starchiest cravats of any gentleman I know," Hatheridge retorted bitingly.

"My good man, if you are to be seen in my presence, you must be properly attired. I have a reputation to maintain."

"Buck up, my boy." Morgan could not help but jab at Hatheridge. The younger man made it too easy. "Your time is coming."

"You simply had to go and post that bet in White's book. Have you any idea of the mockery I have endured? I've been scoffed at, poked fun at, and made a laughingstock, all around. If Roxborough was not a Viscount . . ."

"Yes?" Morgan taunted.

"Well, I cannot do anything to him."

"And me?" Morgan shifted his feet.

Hatheridge glanced up. "A man would be a fool to tackle someone of your size."

"Come now, Hatheridge, I know you. We have shared more than one round of fisticuffs."

"Excuse me," Carstairs interrupted. "Who is that chap in the back with thunder on his face?"

Morgan turned his gaze to the church entryway.

Hatheridge piped up, "Certainly not dressed for the occasion."

"One scorned by the look of him. Did Harriet have a lover?"

"Good God, Carstairs," Morgan admonished. "Curb your tongue, or you will have the girl's father challenging you to a duel at dawn."

A look of horror crossed Carstairs' face. "Mayhap the fellow lost his way."

"A pair of them, I see. By their clothing, looks like they just got off a ship," Hatheridge acknowledged.

"Any ships dock today you know of?" Morgan studied the two men standing in the back of the room. Blonde hair, tall, but not as tall as he. Their stance reminded him of his wife's brother. Definitely seamen. Both looked angry, but the slightly bulkier one appeared threatening, as if he were ready to pummel any man within striking distance.

"Maybe you should do something."

Morgan raised his brow to Carstairs. "And what would you have me do?"

"We cannot have rabble at the duke's wedding. If Pendorgrass gets a good look at them, he and his wife will both have the vapors."

Morgan smiled, thinking the wedding might not be a bloody bore after all.

Witherspoon joined their circle. He held his flute of champagne in front of his mouth. "Did you see the new arrivals?"

"We were just discussing the pair." Carstairs nodded in that direction.

"Could not help noticing the foreboding looks they are sending the groom."

Morgan studied the two men. Their glares definitely aimed at Giles.

"Bloody bore, weddings," Witherspoon complained. "By the by, Carstairs. You hate wedded bliss. Why the devil are you here?"

"I am here to show my face because I must. Appearances, my good man."

"And you are not about to let the occasion to gloat a bit go by, I'd say."

"He deserves every agonizing second of it."

Witherspoon chuckled. "And what of you, Hatheridge? You have a case of the blue devils."

Carstairs clapped his friend on the shoulder. "He would rather be at a bordello than a wedding."

"Who wouldn't? Deuced miserable business, a wedding."

"I need some air." Hatheridge turned, getting his first glimpse at the two newcomers glaring at Giles. "Who are those brazen devils?"

"I believe I shall mosey over and see if I can hear their conversation, find out who they are." Carstairs intermingled through the crowd.

"We may have some entertainment at this dullard wedding after all." Witherspoon patted the cigar tucked in his pocket. "Since we cannot smoke in here, how about a glass of champagne while we watch?"

"None for me," Morgan declined. "The wedding should be about to start."

"Not from the expressions on those two." Witherspoon nodded t the pair.

"I agree," Hatheridge said. "Looks like we are about to have a battle-*royale*."

Swarming in greetings, Giles had not seen the newcomers enter the church. Morgan thought he best apprise Giles of the arrows aimed at his back. Morgan tapped him on the shoulder. Stiff and somber as driftwood, he looked askance to Morgan.

"I remember being a mite happier on my wedding day."

"You interrupted me to discuss your nuptials?" Giles droned.

"Do you know those two?" Morgan angled a thumb over his shoulder.

The tightening of Giles' muscles registered his surprise. "Good God, it's Alex's brothers."

"Blood and the devil. What are they doing here?"

"Either to congratulate me or kill me." Giles straightened to his full height. With unfaltering steps, he strode to the back of the church, straight for the two brothers. The first one's expression never changed. The second one gave a menacing smile while butting a clenched fist against the palm of the opposite hand. He presented an eagerness for a thrashing.

"What are you going to do?" Hatheridge asked.

Morgan glanced at the younger man. "Me? Nothing."

"But they look ready to kill him." Hatheridge took a step forward. Morgan grabbed his arm.

"Do you think Giles needs our help?"

His voice lowered. "Normally I would say no. Those two would need more help to tip the scales in their favor."

Since Wesley had been a member in a few of their past exploits as well as a trusted friend, and he noted Giles' peculiar behavior, Morgan decided to give Wesley the reason. "I am not one to spread gossip, so keep this to yourself. While Giles was in America, he met a girl. They are her brothers."

"Girl? Or Woman?

"He fell in love."

"Holy hell. Blood is blood. Nothing good can come of this."

"Her brothers' appearance might actually be a good thing."

Wesley whipped about. "A good thing? How can you say that?"

"They just might save Giles from himself."

Chapter 26

Giles led Kit and Ben to a private room at the side of the church. He had barely closed the door and turned when a blur came hurdling at his eye. A blinding pain collided with his jaw. He staggered, thrusting a hand against the wall to keep from falling.

"You whoreson!" Ben shouted.

Another blur, a fist to his gut. Giles doubled over.

"By sweet holy Christ." He gasped for air.

"Hold, Brother. Leave some for me."

Recognizing Kit's voice, Giles braced himself for another blow.

"Stand up, you English scum. I want you to see it coming."

Kit was no match for his skills, yet Giles held back. He deserved an older brother's scorn. He steadied his legs, and straightened. Kit's rage blazed in his eyes and flamed like thunder on his face.

"Not much of a fighter, Brit." Ben stood beside his brother.

"Have you nothing to say for yourself?" Arms raised, Kit was ready for battle.

"What are the two of you doing here?" Giles gasped.

"Showing our soreness 'cause we didn't get an invitation to your wedding." Kit's sarcasm was not lost on Giles.

"You bastard." Ben took a threatening step and hurled another punch.

Giles' stomach rolled at the sound of a snap.

"Is this why you jilted our sister?"

Giles scuffed a hand over his heated face. Meeting Kit, glare for glare, he snarled, "I did not jilt Alex."

"Why you—"

Kit's arm shot out to stop Ben. "Go on."

"I would never hurt your sister."

"Yet you did."

After a tense silence, Giles decided to reveal the secret he had held close to his chest. What did it matter if Kit and Ben knew? "Alex is young. Your father convinced me her infatuation would fade, and she needed to remain with her family."

"So, you did speak with my father," Kit murmured. He seemed to digest that bit of news. "Did you care for her?"

"What's wrong with you, Brother?" Ben bellowed. "If he cared for Alex, he would not be marrying another."

"Answer the question."

"Yes." Giles gaze never wavered from Kit. "I cared. She is a lovely girl. But she is too young for me."

"Then why the hell did you lead her on?" Ben shouted.

"I have no excuse."

Ben threw a punch his way. Even though he saw it coming, Giles didn't duck. Maybe if the two pounded him, he could get through the ceremony without seeing Alex's face. Without regretting every tear he had caused to leak from her agonizing eyes.

A few more punches and he fell to the floor. *Ballocks.* He hurt. How degrading, curled up on the rug. He might need to rethink his strategy of retaliation. He stretched, and new twinges made themselves known. He struggled to open his eyes.

Kit tugged Ben's arm. "That's enough."

"Not nearly." Ben jerked his arm free.

"The man needs to be in one piece for his *bride*." Kit growled the word in disgust.

"Who says?" Ben glared at his brother. "She can have what's left."

"I promised my sister that I would give you a message. The message is this." Kit's venom bearing voice snarled as deadly as his dark expression. "If you ever come to New Orleans, do not step foot on Carmichael Plantation."

The threat rang loud and clear.

Giles would be a dead man if he did.

Hatheridge watched as the two sailors vacated the chapel. The doors slammed behind them. Gasps and loud whispers flooded the chapel.

"What was all that about?" Carstairs asked as he strolled up to Witherspoon.

"Appears the two sailors turned out to be the brothers of a girl Nethersall trifled with in America."

"The devil you say."

"Trifle is not a word I would use within Nethersall's hearing," Sedgewick stressed. "He is likely to strangle your ballocks."

"Or put lead through your gullet." Hatheridge added.

The side door opened again. Giles emerged, looking a bit ruffled. Morgan's large frame appeared next.

"Good God. Nethersall's cravat is off-center."

"You and your bloody cravats. Can't you see the man has a mark on his jaw?"

Seeing Morgan's discreet motion, Hatheridge excused himself and hurried to see what Morgan needed.

"Seems we have a bit of a pickle."

"You want me to go after those two?" Hatheridge glanced to the church doors Alex's brothers had just exited.

"No. We have a bigger problem. There is not going to be a wedding."

A wave of relief washed over him. Before he could give a whoop, Morgan grabbed him by his bloody cravat.

"Discretion, my good man. Giles is on his way to inform the bride. I will gather Pendorgrass. I need you to have Sedgewick relay to the guests the bride has a case of the jitters, and the wedding will commence as soon as her mother deems the girl ready."

"But you just said—"

Morgan yanked on his neck cloth. "Did I not mention discretion?"

Hatheridge nodded, and breathed easier once Morgan released him. He smoothed his cravat with an unsteady hand.

"As soon as you inform Sedgewick of his duty, join me in the bride's chamber."

"'Tis positively scandalous!" Lady Pendorgrass whined as she held the back of her hand to her brow.

"This is an outrage!" Pendorgrass roared. "You will not leave my daughter at the altar."

His handkerchief clutched in his fingers, Giles wiped a smear of blood from his lip. This was not going well. Attempting to reason with Harriett's father was akin to communicating with a raging bull. The similarities were endless. Including smoke flaring from both nostrils.

But then, he did just cast-off the man's daughter.

A fist came storming at his face. Giles landed on his backside.

Bloody hell.

Few people mustered the courage for a confrontation with a duke. He'd not considered Pendorgrass a fool. After the confrontation with Alex's brothers, he could barely stand. And here he was on his arse again. But he'd had enough.

There was a certain thrill in knowing one had his opponent at a disadvantage. Old money and nobility empowered him with a notable amount of forbearance, and if he so chose, clemency. Morgan stepped between the two and thrust out a hand to Giles. Leave it to the blasted Earl of Whetherford to find this amusing. God knew he wished he could.

"Stay out of this."

"I am merely a bystander." Morgan gave a smirk. "Allow me to pull you up?"

Giles accepted the extended hand and heaved to his feet. Pendorgrass, still in a tirade, took a threatening step forward.

"I suggest you think before you consider striking me again." Giles' voice rumbled with warning. He had allowed the man one punch. He would countenance no more.

Pendorgrass stuttered and shook. The man was no fool. Giles might be at fault, but he was a duke. Into the bargain, he was taller and carried extra muscle.

"You made a pledge. You signed documents." The man's jaws puffed out as words sputtered from his mouth. "I demand you honor your agreement."

Harriett sat on a chair beside her mother, not showing a smidgen of emotion. She stared straight ahead, her eyes empty. The porcelain doll devoid of any reaction—he'd expected crying, screaming, stomping her foot. But nothing. He suddenly realized that he had escaped a life of desolation.

Her mother, however, was the epitome of a body in torture. Her high-pitched wail echoed off the walls in mournful sounds, howling her grief.

God's blood, what utter gibberish.

"I am sorry, Pendorgrass. We do not suit."

"You are telling me this now? She will be ruined," the man shouted, and shook his fist. "I forbid it. Do you hear me? I forbid you to back out."

Giles never bowed to outward displays of fury, or extreme agitation. However, no man challenged him and lived to crow victory. His back teeth ground with indignation.

"*Forbid*?" Giles voice sounded calm, even to his own ears. Even as his temples throbbed anew in anger.

"The scandal. Tongues will wag. Harriett should not be shamed so. She deserves better."

"She deserves a good husband. It will not be me." He spoke each work slowly and distinctively so none would doubt his meaning.

"Scandal will not touch my daughter." Pendorgrass flailed his hands about. "Duke or no, you will not shame her. I challenge you to a duel."

The room stilled in deafening silence. Giles' jaw locked, his muscles stretched taut. His chest rose and fell in controlled fury.

"If you are stupid enough to entertain such a thought, have the good sense to keep your challenge behind your tongue." His voice ground out cold as frozen ice. The impulse to pummel the man so strong, he nearly accepted the idiot's challenge. Any man with half a brain knew he would kill Pendorgrass with little effort.

Pendorgrass' bluster sizzled like a punctured air balloon.

A bystander no longer, Morgan stepped forward in the role of peacemaker, correctly sensing Giles' tight control, defusing a powder keg ready to explode. "Come now, Lord Pendorgrass. There is no need for a duel."

No need a 'tall. Except the man had already demanded satisfaction. Morgan helped to calm the situation by allowing Pendorgrass a way out of his absurd circumstance.

Pendorgrass seemed to hesitate. Think things over. He must realize he had made a foolish error. One that could cost him his life. But his pride demanded bluster. "This will leave my good name hanging in the balance. The gossip."

"All will be well once the rumormongers have had time to forget. Or a new disaster takes this one's place."

Keeping his extended fighting skills under wraps had given the misconception that Giles was not a dangerous man. However, Morgan knew different. His interference to placate the man gave Giles the time he needed to calm his own fury. He maintained his even breathing, but when he spoke, the tone of his deadly voice commanded submission.

"A duke's influence will go a long way in fulfilling your political dreams. Most beneficial to you." Giles offered the man a bone to soothe his ruffled feathers. "You will agree, Pendorgrass, I am more valuable as an ally, rather than an adversary."

...Pendorgrass gasped. He understood well, the significance of Giles' words.

"I am a duke. The *ton* will follow my direction." A considerable amount of power came with the title he held. His dukedom more than most, due to his father's lordly life. Of course, substantial wealth aided their supremacy. Giles never used his lofty might. But now he wielded his influence like a bold banner. Pendorgrass' political ambition—and preserving his wellbeing—would have the man falling over his feet to accept Giles' bidding.

"Let us retire to another chamber where we can discuss this as gentlemen. Give the ladies their privacy." Morgan nodded toward Harriett and her mother. Morgan's wife held the old dragon's hand and tried to shush her to a reasonable volume. Harriett did not appear troubled in the least. He planned to apologize personally to the girl—if Pendorgrass allowed him near her after their *discussion*.

Alex's brothers showing up when they did merely gave Giles the sting he needed. Of course, he did not want to marry Harriett. Depriving himself of the one he truly desired only festered and made him more bad-tempered. Morgan's words had taken residence in Giles' mind, and the bloody wretchedness of his decision had been feeding on him all day.

The fact the brothers arrived at all was a favorable sign. Hotheads meant to protect their sister, or perhaps, take their pound of flesh from the man who broke her heart. Did he dare hope Alex still had feelings for him?

I promised my sister that I would give you a message.

Had Alex sent a message?

He would wager her message had been quite different than the one Kit gave him.

He'd been a sod of an ass.

Pendorgrass was deliberating his options. To continue in this vein, he would commit social suicide. Not to mention the wrath of a highly esteemed duke. After a moment, he gave a sharp nod.

Scandal must never be associated with the Duke of Nethersall, nor the Litscomb family.

Roll over in your grave, Father.

If he had a chance of Alex forgiving him, the imminent scandal would be worth it.

Chapter 27

Gulf Coast, 128

When Giles caught his first sight of New Orleans, more than the *Sea Sorceress* rocked beneath his feet. He was momentarily staggered. Unmindful of the waves lapping at the ship's hull, the heavy weight on his chest grew more burdensome. With a slight jerk, he shook back his hair into the gently stirring wind. His arm muscles tensed as he rested them on the rail, gazing out at the blue-black sea.

Feet braced on the swaying deck, he stood alone while men scurried around, preparing for mooring. In the encroaching darkness, miniature lights speckled the looming dock. After weeks of relentless soul searching and revisiting his priorities—the ravings of his mind assessing his life's values—he contemplated his decision. Allowing the ton to believe she had been the one to cry off was an easy pill to swallow. And the cash settlement helped to sooth Pendorgrass's wife. None of that mattered. Perhaps he was a tad annoyed for the months it took of setting the damning actions into motion. But his frustration was worth putting the matter to rest.

There was only one woman for him. But how to reach her?

If you ever come to New Orleans, do not step foot on Carmichael Plantation.

Would the threat be tangible after all this time? Whether he brought pandemonium down upon himself was yet to be known. But see Alex, he would.

He would curse himself for a fool, but he was beyond foolishness. His cronies thought him stark raving mad. Except for his friend, Morgan. Comrades for years, each had faced their demons and conquered their fears. Fortunately, Morgan reminded him that he had but one life to live. His life was no life at all without Alex.

His, for a lifetime.

Determination gave him strength. Love gave him purpose. He could not muddle his chance of a reunion.

Alex's galling brothers had warned him off, yet he had the intense urge to dive into the skirmish and get the fracas over with. His more reasonable side advised a ruse. A stratagem. If her brothers were determined to stop him, he should contemplate a plan of infiltration. God knew he'd had plenty of experience during his emissary years.

His entire countenance felt energized in a way he had not experienced since his spying days. He missed the thrill. The thought of thwarting her brothers sent his blood thrumming. Excitement bubbled in his chest.

Anxious to see Alex, his mind drifted down a path of conjecture. It would seem he was as stubborn as his father. Giles could only blame his acceptance of a nobleman's duties drilled into him since birth. Following society's dictates, like a horse with blinders, he had unconsciously followed the rules expected of him by the aristocracy. Months of performing his role as a duke, accepting his place among the *ton*, and then the preparation for a wedding. Thank God he escaped his blunder.

Then more months passed, allowing Pendorgrass his moment of pomp and glory while Giles fulfilled promises. Giving the man his backing was no problem. The hardship was in the waiting.

Nearly three years since he had seen her. He wondered if Alex would look the same. She had been so young. Surely, she has matured. Filled out. Blossomed. More beautiful than he could imagine. A spirited girl, he wondered if her blood still ran wild, if her tempestuous nature endured.

God Almighty, he wanted to see her. Smell her. Hold her. *Soon.*

Shouts from the first mate jerked him back to the present. Sailors rushed to carry out their orders. With a great whoosh, the wind-filled sails dropped from the swaying masts high overhead.

While residing at Morgan's shipping residence, he would hire runners—or whatever they were called in the colonies—to snoop around the Carmichael plantation. Spy on Alex and her bothersome brothers. Investigate her movements. God forbid she had a beau, or anyone of interest. Joe should have knowledge of some spies, or investigators, who would gather information. To meet his end goal, Giles could settle in Morgan's Colonial home for a few days.

As if his thinking had conjured up the man, Joe stood proudly waiting at the Langston Shipping dock. Hair blowing in the rousing wind, feet braced apart, he had the appearance of any ship's captain. Men scurried with large ropes securing the *Sea Sorceress* to the widely spread pillars. The ship lurched as she bumped against the oak wood supports.

Giles took a position at the ship's rail as the plank lowered. Joe scurried around the sailors, a huge grin on his wide lips.

"Welcome, Mister Giles."

"Hello, Joe." Giles shook the extended hand and slapped Joe on the back with his other. "Excellent to see you."

"Good sailing?"

"No difficulties." Although he did wish the sea to hell a few times in his hurry to reach New Orleans. Impatience was not a virtue associated with his hunger to see Alex.

"Soon as I got word you were coming, I notified Morgan's staff. For now, there's a cook, a maid, and a butler all awaiting your arrival."

"Thanks, Joe. My plans are indefinite. May hap I will not be occupying his dwelling for long."

As long as it takes.

"I hired a carriage and the driver is yours 'til you're done with him." Joe waved a thumb over his shoulder. "He's over there. I'll help with your luggage."

"No need, Joe. I travel light. Since this is my ship, anything I require will be within shouting distance."

"That's mighty fine. Just let me know if I can help you with anything else, and I'll take care of it."

The driver held the carriage door while Giles climbed inside. Peddlers shouting their wares echoed through the open window. Arms crossed, he leaned back against the squabs. Once again, his mind filled with visions of Alex; the way she looked when he left. He refused to dwell on her tears and concentrated instead on her beauty. Her large brown eyes with their tiny gold flecks. Her long blonde hair streaked with the sun's glint. Her full, ripe lips desiring to be kissed. Before long, he lost himself to a world of fantasy.

The coach rocked and the door jerked open, alerting him that he had reached his destination. At the first stone step, the hulking oak door creaked. The servant, in full uniform, stiffened to attention.

"No need for formality, Charles. Glad to see you are still here."

"Welcome back, sir."

"Thank you."

"We have a new cook, sir. She likes for folks to call her Tilly."

"As long as the woman can cook, I will gladly call her anything she likes." His stomach grumbled at the mention of food.

"I will let her know you are here, Your Grace."

"Now Charles. None of that. We are in America."

"Yes, Your Grace."

"As soon as I change, I will come down for dinner. It has been some time since I've had any palatable food in my belly."

"Very good, uh, my lord. You will find a bath waiting in your room."

"God love you, Charles."

Giles took the stairs two at a time in his hurry to change. He jerked his coat from his shoulders and tore the shirt from his back. Opening his trousers, he let them hang on his hips as he stepped to the boot jack to remove his boots. Once done, he strode to the large tub and tested the water.

Perfect.

He wondered if Charles could read minds. Perhaps he just knew how to please his lord. A nice hot bath pleased him, indeed. Anxious to plan his next move, thoughts raced in his head on how to approach Alex. He glanced at the steam rising from the claw-footed tub. He supposed there was no hurry. One more day would not make a difference in a three-year separation. He prayed his heart's desire was still within his grasp.

Anticipation swirled through him. Trepidation followed close behind. Giles knew what he wanted. And he wanted Alex greatly. But did she want him? How much had she changed over the last few years? Did she still care for him? Would she turn him away?

He never intended for things to advance so far. One kiss to set the little minx back on her heels. But the urchin stirred to life a sensuality that startled him. And brought him out of a void in which he had lived entirely too long. Alex had given him her trust, her innocence. In return, he not only rejected her, but scraped her raw. Regret burned like acid. He would never forget the look of betrayal flaming in her eyes the last time he saw her.

By God. This was not helping at all, dwelling on dreams of what might have been.

After a night of tossing and turning, unable to come up with a plan that did not involve him losing his neck, he had thrown the covers aside, ready to confront the day. Anxious to secure a horse, he found he could wait no longer. Now he tooled down the road at a fine clip, seated on a magnificent gray.

With every hour that passed, he grew more unsure. Nerves raced up and down his backbone.

For God's sake.

For years, he'd lived his life so close to the edge that he loomed on the verge of never coming back to a society of culture and elegance. The decisions he made, the cataclysmic life he chose—his comrades would never recognize the man who lacked confidence in his mission. They would laugh to find the sole cause of his shortcoming could be blamed on a mere woman.

Discarding those thoughts, Giles focused on the landscape, and recognized the familiar signs indicating the Carmichael Plantation.

Excitement pumped his blood.

Yet once again, doubt crept in to dampen his exhilaration. Naturally, he had been discreet in his questioning. Joe assured him Alex had not married. Giles considered many scenarios on how he would approach Alex without her interfering brothers pounding him into the ground. The threat at his supposed wedding did not go unheeded. He knew Kit meant his warning. Giles only hoped he found Alex before her brothers found him.

He was as anxious as a convicted man facing eternity in gaol. Imprisoned in a hell of his own making. He had no wish to be incarcerated, and even less to be shot. Need and instincts drove him. He had to find Alex.

As he rode on, he spotted a particular tree. Behind it lay the course to Alex's hidden lagoon

What were the chances she would be there?

On impulse, he followed the remembered signs of a trail. Expectation stirred his pulse. Most likely, he was gelling himself up for disappointment. He called on every ounce of his endurance not to kick his heels into the gelding's sides and race like a madman to his quest.

Before long, he spied a single horse standing in a memorable copse of trees. His heart raced. He would recognize that black anywhere. Emotions threatened to overwhelm him. At long last he would see Alex. He wondered if her hair was still as pale as the sun's rays, or had darkened to golden wheat. If her molasses eyes would glow in passion, or flash in fury when she saw him.

If she were here, he had to make certain—before she left the lagoon—that she was his forever.

Stardust reared his head and snorted, settling down once the horse remembered him.

Giles greeted Stardust, then tied his steed to a branch next to the black. He quietly slipped through the brush to the paradise branded in his mind long ago. Water cascaded over slate shingles of gray rock, forming large ripples in the pool below. A colorful rainbow arched on one side, drawing his attention to the flowers blooming in full force at this time of the year. He recognized daffodils and gardenias, a kaleidoscope of flora. Spotting honeysuckle vines along the mossy bank, he inhaled their sweet fragrance. The hidden alcove's splendor astounded him, as breathtaking as the first time he had seen its magnificence.

A vision sprang to mind of his golden nymph, sunlight dancing through the trees, silken hair lying across his chest.

At a tiny movement just at the edge of his vision, the hair on the back of his neck tingled. Suddenly, a splash of water assured him that he had found his prize.

Arms raised, Alex surfaced, appearing as an enchanting mermaid luring a soon-to-be-shipwrecked sailor in a magical paradise. Golden hair clung to her jawline, curving over a bare shoulder. Breasts jiggled as she secured her footing.

Giles swallowed, his gaze greedily devouring the stunning creature before him.

He thought he had armed himself. He thought he had prepared for the sight of her. But no amount of forethought could calm his thundering heart. He had not envisaged the slam of emotions finally seeing her caused. His eyes greedily caressed every luscious naked inch of her body.

Her head flung back, she smoothed golden tresses from her radiant face. Translucent beads shining like diamonds sluiced over creamy skin and sultry curves. His body heated with longing. Crystal beads lingered on the slope of her breast. His hungry gaze followed the trail of aquatic silver to the nip of her waist and a hint of a well-toned, satin buttock before disappearing into the lapping pool.

His wild American had blossomed into a beautiful woman. Too many years since he had encountered such perfection.

How he yearned to touch her exquisite skin. Feel her hands on his body. Of its own accord, his hand lifted, reaching for the buttons on his shirt. Keeping his gaze on the precious treasure, he slid each one through its slot. Slowly he pulled the confining material from his back.

The movement caught her notice.

Chestnut eyes, dark and alluring, shot up to meet his.

Awareness hummed between them.

Beyond the gold of the sun, the green of the grass, the blue of the sky reflecting over the ripples of water . . . her gaze was only for him.

His pulse pounded.

Several emotions crossed her face. Surprise. Hope. Awareness. The same forceful magnetism which held him enthralled seemed to have captured her as well.

He stood there, unabashedly marveling at her beauty; a goddess nymph, luring him to her side. His gaze riveted on hers, he removed his clothing, fearing any moment this alluring vision might disappear.

She stayed.

Her covetous gaze, drinking him in, gave him a surge of hope.

A gentle breeze wafted. Not enough to cool his skin, and certainly not enough to cool his ardor.

With honed stealth, he moved forward.

Chapter 28

The past three years blew away like ashes in the wind.

Giles' dark, magnetic eyes drew her, held her in a trance-like grip. Alex couldn't look away. The haunting image of her dreams stood proudly before her. She stood mute. Dazed. Soaking up every detail. Her breath constricted as sensations swirled through her. She did not need to study him to remember how his gaze hungered—or how his mouth crinkled at the corners—or how his nostrils flared in the heat of his passion. He looked . . . God help her . . . he looked divine.

A world of memories and emotions swirled through her. A face she had once trusted completely. She wanted to blink, but her eyes refused to close for fear he would vanish. Many times she imagined him with her—in her dreams.

He didn't look like the scoundrel who had shattered her heart. She had vowed no man would ever hurt her again. Yet she could not resist Giles. A part of her she'd sworn never to acknowledge again, reared with excitement.

A shock of hair, black as night, hung over his brow. His eyes smoldered like charcoal embers, making her skin burn where his searing gaze touched. Thick curls covered a broad, muscular chest. She followed the trail of raven silk tapering downward.

Oh, dear Lord.

With every long, unhurried step, he drew nearer. Like a sleek panther stalking his prey, he held her immobile with his hypnotic stare.

Then he was there. So close. Within a hair's breadth. The world faded away. Nothing else existed but the two of them.

His scorching gaze lacked the confidence she remembered. His eyes apprehensive. Was he as unsecure as she? It was as if he could not believe she was real. The very same speculation she'd had.

His hand lifted and she held her breath. One finger grazed her cheek, then slid along her jaw to the corner of her mouth. An all-consuming sensation began just under her skin. Ripples streamed through every nerve in her body. His eyes seemed to glow, his touch lingering only a moment before he stroked down the side of her neck.

Her pulse throbbed.

Giles closed his eyes and inhaled deeply. He reminded her of a sleek animal, enjoying the anticipation of devouring its prey.

As though it were only yesterday, the longing he created in her could not be denied. Her impatience reminded her of when she had wanted him to kiss her so badly, that she pursued him until he did.

But, she was no longer a child. Even so, she recognized the same desperation. He slipped his hands into her hair with such tenderness, a delicious shudder swept over her. She nearly cried at the raw yearning she read in his expression. Ever so slowly, he lowered his lips to brush her lids, her brow, the indentation at the side of her mouth, with kisses as light as the fireflies frolicking at night.

When his lips finally pressed to hers, he took her mouth in a kiss that was as slow as it was deep. Liquid desire flowed in every cell of her body, robbing her of breath.

"You've grown more devastatingly beautiful than I imagined." The words rumbled against her mouth.

Dear God in Heaven.

Despite how he had wronged her, Giles' touch ravaged her pride. She desired him. Only him. She twined her arms around his neck, melting into the kiss, liquefying into his body. She curled her fingers through his hair, craving everything he was willing to give. Oh, how she had missed him, wanted him for so long. Desire ached in her belly.

His lips caressed hers in a lazy rhythm, as soul entrancing as their very first kiss. When she could no longer breathe, his mouth followed the same path as his thumb, over her cheek, her ear, and down the pulsing vein at her throat.

Blood pounded with each beat of her pounding heart. Every nerve flamed with desire.

She sucked in a breath, overwhelmed with his essence; leather and the scent of Giles.

He bent, catching her thighs and lifting her high against his chest. Blazing eyes seared her, burned her with his yearning. She held on, thrilled that she would experience passion again. Gentle arms cradled her as she curled into his warmth. With long strides, he carried her from the rippling pool to the solid earth where he lowered her to the soft bed of green grass. She prayed she wasn't dreaming, for she would surely die if he disappeared.

His warmth encircled her in a protective cocoon, confirming he was most definitely real.She was no longer virginal, yet she remained innocent. The only man she had given herself to was Giles. Time had mended her despair, but love still lived in her heart. She willed the demon of doubt back into the shadows. She needed his touch, his strength.

"You are so damned beautiful." He cupped her cheek, one finger traced her jaw. "I've hungered for you for three long and lonely years. I have dreamed countless nights of holding you in my arms."

"Do not speak. Do not mention the past." She stretched upward, tangling her fingers in his thick hair, stroking his nape. "We are here. There is only now."

He sucked in a harsh breath, then claimed her lips with the voraciousness of a man who'd been denied far too long. A storm of ragged desire breeched the years they lost. This was an altered Giles. A man starved, possessed. The passion she had craved was hers. He held nothing back. The glorious fervor swamped her. Filled her. A roaring flame fired her blood. She ached. She arched. Devine flesh. Giles flesh. How wonderous the hunger. She had never craved anything so deeply as his touch at this moment.

He trailed fiery kisses down her throat, across her fevered skin, licking droplets of water from the sensitive flesh at her collarbone. Her head fell back, giving his tongue access to the pulsing vein in her throat.

He placed a hand on each side of her face, and once again stared into her eyes. Asking, begging . . .

"Yes, my love, yes."

Then their mouths crushed together again, their kisses flaming hotter. He gave her what her starving soul craved.

His knuckles grazed her ribs. The joining of their tongues halted her gasp. His hand shifted upward, caressing the underside of her breasts.

More. More.

He weighed their fullness, caressing, kneading, his thumb brushing her nipple to an aching peak. A quivering shudder ripped through her.

His head lowered.

Wet, hot heat lanced her rigid bud. Her lashes fluttered closed as she moaned and arched against him. He kissed and stroked with his tongue, then his lips closed over her nipple.

When he took the pebble between his teeth, desire coiled in her belly, and a soft cry tore from her lips. He laved her with his tongue, soothing the bite, only making her ache more.

"God's blood, Alex." His hands spanned her waist while he nestled his face in the fullness of her breasts. Warm hands massaged and caressed her breasts urgently, then gently fondled as indescribable sensations swamped her. She pulled at his hair until he raised his head for another scorching kiss. His tongue probed and danced madly with hers. *More*, she kept thinking. *I have missed you. I want you. I want more.*

Tantalizing fingers drew circles over her bare hip, then twirled across her belly and down to her curls. Amazing, how his stimulating touch set her body on fire. Oh, he knew how to caress her. Where to stroke her. How to kindle her simmering fire into a roaring blaze.

When he cupped her, pressing his hand over her pulsing center, she sucked in a quick breath. His fingertips brushed against her warm female flesh, then flicked.

She jerked as pure awareness seared her center. She held her breath, waiting for him to do it again. Thinking she would die if he did not. "Please."

"Yes, my darling. I will give you what you want." His hand against her tender opening, he speared a finger into her tight sheath. "So wet. So wet. God, Alex, I have missed you fiercely."

Arching upward, she seated his finger more firmly. Heaven above, the aching sensation made her quiver with need. Another finger joined the first and he worked his magic, drawing gasps from her throat. His kiss hot and possessive, his tongue matched the rhythm of his thrusting fingers.

She clamped her legs together, a tightening of crazed need claiming her body. "Giles," she begged him shamelessly.

He plundered, taking everything she had to give. Her pulse pounded in a wild rhythm. She gasped, clutched, and buried her teeth in his shoulder. Her body hummed, convulsing in a burst of pleasure.

When the earth stopped spinning, Alex opened her eyes. Giles gazed down at her with adoration. His hand skimmed lightly over her collarbone.

"Perfection," He murmured.

Happiness swamped her. Giles was here. He must love her. His eyes said he loved her. She wanted to shout her joy. This wonderful man, so adoring, so vehement in his attentions. She wanted to create a fierce need in him, as ferocious as the avid yearning he created in her.

She pressed her body against his, feeling the thick evidence of his need—proof of how much he wanted her. She smiled, twirling her fingers in the fine black silk spread across his chest. She ran her hands over granite muscles, teased a sensual path downward, finding velvet-soft skin over hard steel.

His breathing turned to a hiss, pleasing her more than he knew.

She explored his hardness. A ragged moan broke from his lips. Oh how delightful, the power she held over him. His fingers skimmed over her breast and strummed the hard bud, causing her to grip his iron flesh firmly.

He wrapped his arms around her, hugging her tightly against him. With a will of its own, her body moved in gentle undulation, as she stroked his length faster. Suddenly, he jerked her hand away, bringing her fingers to his lips. His eyes were closed, his hand trembling.

A taut moment passed before his eyes opened. His hungry gaze seared her.

"With every pore of my body, I want to ravish you. Make you completely mine."

"Then do it," Alex whispered.

With a predatory growl, Giles crushed her against him and ground his lips on hers. Simmering embers kindled and a new fire burned to life as a heady sensation overtook her.

He slid a knee between her thighs, then his large hand gripped her hair and gently tugged her head back, arching her neck up to him. Hot, open-mouthed kisses blazed down her throat. The scorching head of his passion brushed the quivering opening of her woman's core. She descended into a red haze of desire. She arched against him, willing him on in her need for completion.

At last, he buried himself in her.

She sobbed Giles' name. She felt his heart pounding a wild rhythm. Big, brown eyes latched on to hers. She could not look away from the rousing heat blazing in their depths.

"Ah, Alexandria. The way you say my name when I am deep inside you."

The words falling from his lips made her purr with longing.

Shifting his hips, he pulled out and slid in again. His hot, pulsing fullness sent a shock of raw pleasure zipping to every cell in her blood.

"Joined to you so fully, we are one." His dark eyes bore into hers, making it difficult to breathe. He stared at her. Somehow, they communicated their need, their hunger, their fulfillment ... their love. Holding her gaze, he lifted, then thrust forward. Strong, yet gentle fingers kneaded her bottom, squeezing, gripping. She grabbed his hair and pulled him down to meet her lips. She must kiss him again. And again.

She submitted to him with complete abandon as he plunged deep inside her. Oh God, so deep. Desire clawed at her. With murmurs of pleasure she arched, her hips moving instinctively with his. He groaned his approval, then quickened the pace. Shamelessly, she met each thrust. She only knew it felt good and delicious and she wanted more.

Reason deserted her.

Only need remained.

In his arms Alex became a sultry siren.

Her well-defined curves, the sweet bow of her lips, her honeyed moans—Sweet, sensuous Alexandria stirred his blood. He tried, he truly did try to dampen his raging possession.

Easier said than accomplished. Her drenched flesh sucked his manhood, stole his breath. All he wanted was to love her. Ravish her.

He tried to hold back, but he had been denied his heart's desire for far too long. And God Almighty, she was so wet, her curves fuller–she had blossomed. She burned with the same flaming hunger.

His hands hooked firmly on her hips, but she still arched against him. With him. He seized one breast with his mouth. His lovely vixen quaked with straining tension. Beads of perspiration slid down his temple as he thrust harder, giving her everything he had.

Together they fueled an out-of-control rhythm. Riding a tide of sensual longing, he took her higher, and higher, until she tumbled over the peak. He ground against her, wringing from her every drop of sensation.

Blood thundered in his temples. He closed his eyes as blinding pressure rose from the base of his spine, then shot through him erupting in his loins. *God's blood*, she trembled. His mind black, he went hurtling after her. He threw back his head and howled like a madman.

When he could breathe again, he dropped his head to her brow. The feeling was like no other. He had been lost in the woman he loved. *Christ,* she was so receptive. Nothing could have prepared him for the onslaught of emotions she aroused in him. A sensual creature with no barriers, no control over the power of his possession. She had drained every ounce of energy, every gut-wrenching breath from his limp body. He yearned to keep her just this way in her paradise cove forever.

Lulled by the sound of gentle rolling water, he stretched out beside her. She curled into him. So tender, so erotic, her palm over his pounding heart, her fingers combing the thick hair on his chest. The sun glinted in the wheat gold strands of her hair, nestled against his shoulder. He cherished this moment. She could have turned him away. But, he was exactly where he wanted to be. She was heaven in his arms.

He lifted a forefinger to twine about a wet strand. Softer than silk, she smelled of sunshine, springtime, and the flowers around them. Her skin had flushed from his loving. God, it felt so bloody good to have her beneath him, warm and eager. A prize he finally had the common sense to claim. He would never again bear the agony of living without her.

A shudder tore through him. He grimaced and held her tighter, thanking his lucky stars. Alex was his. He would prove it to her father, and her irksome brothers.

But first, he needed to prove it to her.

Chapter 29

Lord help her, she had succumbed to his advances once again.

Alex closed her eyes tight. She refused to open them for fear of reality crashing in. Let her dwell in the land of fantasies for a while longer.

He had invaded her retreat. Her private lagoon. Where she came to hide from the outside world. From him. But she never escaped her memories.

Giles was back. Why should she care what his reasons were?

"For three lonely years, I have dreamed of doing this. Holding you in my arms again."

Merciful heavens, so had she. The years seemed like centuries.

He played with a curl lying on her breast. "Thank God you cannot deny me, what we have between us, what we are to each other."

She had grown empty. So empty. One glimpse, one touch, and she'd fallen longingly into his arms again.

A whirlwind raged in her mind. What had she done?

She chewed on her bottom lip as the world dared to intrude. Reality slapped her in the face, and it was not pleasant.

Made love, was what she'd done. Without any resistance. Without any thought of accountability. She had wanted her lover's touch. He burned her anew just as he'd devastated her years ago.

"You cannot imagine what the past three years have been like for me," Giles murmured.

Sorrow lodged in her chest. "Pity. Empathy. Tolerance. Encouragement," she said softly. "Whatever my family could think of to lift my spirits. I felt so guilty. And it was not my guilt to bear." Remembering fueled her anger.

She jerked from him. Her breasts swayed, reminding her of her state of undress.

"I love you."

She froze.

Three years she had waited. Three years she hoped, prayed, and dreamed of his return. Knowing he never would. But he was here. Stirring desires that should remained buried.

"Did you hear me, Alex?"

Snapping out of the fantasy she'd succumbed to, she crossed her arms over her chest and faced him. "Why did you come here?"

"I had to see you."

"Why?" She wanted to scream, shout, take her hurt and anger out on him. She bit her inner cheek instead.

He leaned close, speaking softly in her ear, "Even though I do not deserve an ounce of your precious time, even though I know you can never forgive me, I had to try." His chest warmed her back, his breath—so close to her ear—sent butterflies frolicking down her neck.

She moved to stand.

"Please do not rush away." He stayed her with a hand, his eyes pleading.

She looked to the pool of rippling water.

"I love you. You just proved you still love me."

Of course, she loved him. Why else had she surrendered so easily to her desires?

"My foolish mistake."

Her harsh words shocked him. *Good*. Why had she allowed herself to surrender? She should have learned the lesson last time. Her regret claimed a moan.

"Your body tells me otherwise."

Yes, her traitorous body. She still wanted him. Foolishly loved him, still. Now she would have to heal her heart all over again. "You are mistaken."

"I did not mistake your legs wrapped around me. I need only touch you for you to melt."

How dare he throw her vulnerability in her face. She shoved to her feet and scurried to gather her clothes. She refused to admit he still had so much control over her. Holding the bundle of clothing as a shield, she faced him. "The intimacy between us is nothing. It will not happen again."

"I beg to differ."

"Do you think you can make love to me and all is forgiven?" She called on her waning courage to slight his lovemaking, as though it meant little. Her voice came out cold. "You took me by surprise. Consider this a moment of weakness, and nothing more."

Giles stood. "Alex, you don't mean that." Oh, he was a beautiful sight. Her mouth watered seeing him the way she had dreamed. His gaze had narrowed, and his eyes filled with concern.

"I am not the naïve girl I was three years ago."

"Believe me, I've noticed." His gaze traveled down her body.

She spun around and slipped behind a bush to dress.

"Darling, I am here to stay."

How she wanted to believe that. She didn't know what to say. In the quiet, she heard the rustling of his clothes. Thank God he was getting dressed. She tugged on her boots and stepped to the spot where she had carelessly thrown all caution aside.

"Wait." Giles called. His strong voice held a note of anxiousness.

"I'm not going anywhere. At least, not until I get some answers."

"Ask me anything." His voice came from just behind her.

She whirled around. "All right, then. Why are you here?"

"I can no longer bear the agony of living without you."

"Agony? You want to talk about agony?" She gripped her hands into fists. "I prayed for your return. Right up until the day Kit told me of your marriage. I descended into a well of anguish. Heartache I could never have imagined. Grief . . ." She choked on a sob.

When he reached for her, she took a step back.

"The pain of your leaving years ago is not gone. I had to live on. I had to build a life for myself without you in it. I will not bore you with details of the days and months that followed. How bitterness nearly destroyed me." Why was she blubbering like a fool? Once the words came forth, she blurted all.

"Alex, I wish I could erase the sordid past."

"We both know you cannot." Tears threatened.

Oh no. Not now.

Her anger saved her. "I did forgive you, you know. I knew whatever reason forced you to leave, tore at you. I saw it in your face that day."

"I listened to others," he protested. "I did what I thought best for you, squashing down my own wants."

What did you want? Fearing his answer, she didn't ask. He still left. Obviously, he had not wanted her.

Alex took a deep breath, pushing back the pain that threatened to choke her. She turned to the waterfall, needing its picturesque beauty to quell her anxiety, its soothing sound to calm her racing heart. "How could I hate a man who loved me? At least, I told myself you did love me. You were honest with me regarding your heritage. But I swore I would never allow another man to hurt me the way you did."

"As God is my witness, I'm sorry, Alex. So sorry."

I won't let the vulnerability of his voice deter me. Yet if his tone was anything to go by, he too suffered.

He left me.

She could not be weak. With steel in her backbone, she spun, and let fortitude empower her. "What about your wife?"

"What?"

"Even when Kit told me, I did not want to believe him. Did you love me when you married another?"

"I married no other."

Hope sparked to life so quickly, she quashed the alarming reaction. *Impossible.* After months of being numb, she had finally learned that she could function again. Thanks to her brothers, she even managed a smile now and then. Ironic, since their initial reaction to the duke's marriage had been ferocious. Their eyes brimming with storm clouds and murder, her brothers threatened to tie him to a boulder and sink him to the bottom of the ocean. At that time she'd been filled with pain, and too paralyzed to care.

"Alex, I have no wife," he insisted with sincerity.

"Kit said he saw you. In the church. On your wedding day. You yourself told me of your responsibility as a duke."

He took a step closer. "I am not married. I called it off."

Relief swamped her. He had not married. On the heels of her relief came the crashing reality, that he had every intention of marrying another.

"But you would have. You almost did. You planned to marry another. Tell me true." Rage replaced her despair. "I can't believe I defended you. I thought you loved me. You threw me away. Did you love her?"

"No! I loved none other. It would have been a marriage of convenience. My title demands I continue the line."

"Procuring an heir is not a marriage of convenience."

"I could not go through with it."

Why?

She did not ask. "You abandoned your bride?"

Giles thrust his hands through his hair. "God's teeth."

"When? When did you change your mind? And why? My brother was there. In the church."

"He made me see reason."

Her heart plummeted. "If not for my brother, you would have married the woman."

"Good God, no! I would not have married her regardless."

"Then why were you in a church?" Her hands fisted at her hips. "Why was your bride in the church? Did Kit stop the wedding only minutes before the vows?"

Again, he shoved his hands through his hair and pulled at the ends as if he would yank it out by the roots. "I waited too long to tell her. I thought I could not have you. So, I resigned myself to my fate. Still, I could not do it." He came toward her with his hands out. "I was miserable. I could not make her life miserable as well."

Miserable? She would not feel sorry for him.

"And now your wants have changed?"

"I deserve your scorn."

Several emotions crossed his features. But when his face softened and he took another step closer, she found she could not move.

"A man searches for a long time to find the right woman for him. At my age, I consider myself fortunate to have a young woman's love."

She could not deny it.

"I am here to make things right."

"Right? What you consider *right* does not mean your ideas are suitable to me. What's done is done. You cannot change what happened. I no longer care for you." She held her breath, desperately trying to maintain her composer, thankful she had actually gotten the lie past her lips.

"We have settled the issue of whether or not you care for me." His lips turned up into a dangerous smile. His eyes filled with intent and desire, reminded her only moments ago they had been flesh to naked flesh.

She hated her weakness, her attraction. But he could not be allowed to take advantage of her vulnerability. She aimed her nose in the air, hoping he would see the gesture as confidence. Thank goodness he could not see the quivering in her belly. She forced her voice to come out strong. "I have come to terms with our past. We have no future."

She spun on her heel and headed for Stardust. Enough of this insane torture. God help her, she needed his love. But she could not travel down that path again. She would not survive another heartbreak.

"This is your pride talking," he called after her.

She refused to turn. "You think my pride is speaking? I lost all sense of pride when your ship sailed away."

"Wait!" He followed her step for torturous step. "Deuced hell, if you will just listen."

Her fury saved her. She whirled around to him. "I listened to you three years ago. I don't care that you changed your mind. I have not. You are a duke. Your life is in England. Mine is here."

"I swore I would never let you go again." He raised hands clenched inti fists. She glanced at his whitened knuckles, then back to his pain-filled eyes.

"That is no longer your choice." If only his words were true. She quickly shook those thoughts away. How foolish to even be thinking of hope. Soon he would be gone. "What of your precious heritage? Your dukedom?"

"I want you for my wife. The *ton* can go to hell." His face resembled storm clouds, his voice like thunder.

I can't trust myself.

"Tell me, Giles. Will you make promises and then leave me again?"

His frown softened and his eyes grieved with such sorrow, her heart ached. She nearly damned her soul and threw herself at him. Only the sheerest force of will held her immobile.

"I will never be so foolish to repeat my past mistakes."

"Good," she heard herself say, and was proud she had not broken. "I'm glad you were miserable. I hope you rot in hell."

Unshed tears blinded her as she ran through the bush, leaves and stems scuffing her hands.

This time he did not stop her.

Of all the ways Giles had envisioned their meeting, having her in his arms and then seconds later, being told to sod off, had never entered his mind. While his tongue was in danger of being bitten clear off, he swallowed the frustration lodged in his throat.

How ludicrous. For most of his years he had confronted danger without a care for his person, faced life-threatening situations without fear, yet this urchin—who was an infant no more—scared him witless.

He wanted to grab her shoulders and shake some sense into her. Make her admit what happened between them was everything. Anger choked him, until he reasoned out her pride was speaking. She denied it, but he knew her.

He'd been unable to take his eyes off her.

Alex had changed a lot over the last three years. Her face had lost its girlish youth, to be replaced with the stunning beauty of a woman. Alex was tall, he liked that. All her curves fit him perfect. He swallowed just thinking of how she filled his hands. The young woman he'd once known now moved with seemingly effortless grace, no longer the carefree sprite on the verge of blossoming. He smiled. She still housed a mountain of spirit.

It was glorious to finally be with Alex once again. Smoothing her gold-wheat hair back from her forehead, twining the silken strands through his fingertips. Watching her lower lip quiver as he brushed his thumb over its fullness. The feel of her heart beating so close to his. Her eyes burned in passion, yet her vulnerability tore his heart.

To watch her run away, dismiss him as though he was a moment's pleasure and nothing more, chafed him raw. Maybe they could not go back to the way things were, but hell and damnation, he would not permit her to throw away what they could be. Mayhap, he should have given her a better explanation before he made love to her. How could he tell her that he had allowed her father to persuade him her age was an issue?

No matter now. He left. And in her eyes, he had deserted her. The caring creature he'd craved but threw away. He damned his soul for wasted years. Yearning ate so much of his life. Devil him for the cad he'd been, for his actions in the name of honor and family customs. No matter the time or distance, they both had suffered.

These past years had taught Giles regret. He would live with sorrow no more. He had been a complete sod of an ass. He would be denied no longer.

He loved her. He would find a way to breach her walls. He must convince her that he would never hurt her again.

Shaking off his guilt, he stood there, debating long after she fled. What to do? Allow her to cool down, or follow on her heels? He could still see the look in her eyes, how they'd stared into his with a mixture of outrage and longing while she'd shouted at him.

I have come to terms with our past. We have no future.

"We shall see, my love. No bloody way in hell I will let you go again."

Chapter 30

C armichael stables hummed with activity, which came to a halt as men recognized the rider galloping toward them. His mind set on the woman who had just left his arms, Giles ignored them, and cantered around the west-end fence behind the stables. Lady Luck was not with him.

Kit and Ben blocked the middle of the path, standing like two raging bulls.

Giles came to a dumbfounded halt.

One look at Kit's angry face and he feared Alex's brother had seen her return—and correctly jumped to the dreaded conclusion. Ben crossed his arms over a chest which had grown massive in size. Both men glared at him.

"Could have sworn I gave you fair warning." Kit drew his lips into a thin, hard line.

"Looks like the Brit didn't take your advice."

"Years without a word," Kit continued. "Never thought you'd be dumb enough to come back here."

"Ain't too bright, are ya, Brit?" Ben spat a stream of tobacco juice on the ground.

"I'm here to see Alex."

"You're not going anywhere near my sister," Ben growled.

Sam strode from the stables, a curry and brush in his hand. "Alex came tearing in here like a bat out of hell. Running from you. I had to take care of Stardust. What did you do?"

Three sets of angry, determined eyes glared at him. If looks were ammunition, he would be a dead man. Which from their threatening stance, annihilation could still be a possibility.

"The best thing for you to do is turn around and get the hell out of here." Ben's low warning throbbed intimidation.

Giles understood their desire to protect their sister, but he was just as determined to see her. "Under the circumstances, I do not think Alex would appreciate me beating up on her brothers."

"I'll tear your heart out." Ben took a menacing step.

Kit's arm shot out. "Stand in line, Brother. He is mine."

"I have no quarrel with you." Giles spoke to all three, but his gaze remained on Kit. "I don't want to fight. I only want to talk with Alex."

"But that's just the thing." Kit took his hat off, and shoved his fingers through his hair, and slapped it back on. "She don't want nothing to do with you."

Ben charged, ready to yank Giles from his horse. Sam hurried forward, grabbing Ben's arm. Which seemed an insane move on Sam's part, because with Ben's massive arms, he could easily swat off his brother like a pesky fly.

"We're too close to the house." Sam gave a nod over his shoulder. "She can see."

Ben seemed to consider. Then he glanced up to Giles with a smile that held no warmth. "Let's take the duke somewhere and explain his mistake in coming here."

"The south end." Kit's jaw clenched and his lip curled up in fury.

If her brothers wanted to fight, that was ripping fine with him. God knew he would love to get this over with, but by the looks of these three, he was in for one hell of a battle. With Sam and Ben riding along on each side, he followed Kit to an open field.

"We won't gang up on you, Brit," Ben said as he dismounted. "We'll give you a sporting chance."

"We'll take turns," Sam added. "And I get first crack."

"You'll get your shot, youngling." Kit slapped his brother on the back. "But Ben here is a pugilist. He's had more practice boxing with his fists."

Bloody hellfire. That explained the broader width of Ben's chest.

Giles dismounted from his horse. "Let's get this over with."

"A mite anxious, ain't ya, Brit?"

"I want this business done so I can be with Alex." Relying on skills he'd perfected during his spying days, Giles deemed the odds were just about even.

"You will not be with Alex!" Ben shouted.

"You will not be dishonoring Alex with your disgraceful sordidness. Where is the little wife?" Kit asked. "Leave her in your castle in England?"

"I will rip you apart with my bare hands." Ben threw his first punch, which Giles easily sidestepped.

"I do not have a wife."

"Never took you for a liar." Kit stared, disgust evident in his accusing eyes.

"You forget we were at the wedding." Ben sneered and threw another punch. Giles dodged again.

"You don't care a fig about our sister," Sam accused.

"I am here to dispel that idea." Giles raised his fists, sharpening his guard.

"Old attitudes die hard." Kit's lips tightened with resentment. Two blurred fists came at him from the side while his attention remained on Kit. Giles ducked and spun about.

"She has built a life without you. Why don't you just go about your blasted business and stay away from her?"

"You broke her heart." Sam's voice grew louder as he stepped nearer. The brothers were closing in.

Yes, he broke her heart. He did not survive unscathed. "Just so you know, I have been miserable for three long years."

"Not good enough." Ben threw another punch.

Giles' head whipped back with a snap. He could blame his distraction on the other brothers, but even his reflexes were swayed by his obsession with Alex. He shook the hair out of his face.

"Didn't look miserable in your black tails at the church."

"I assure you—"

"Your assurance means nothing." A fist to the side of his head. Bloody hell. Stars exploded in front of his eyes. Then, intense pain shot to his ribs. Damn, Ben was fast for his bulk. Fighting her brothers would not be a good way of gaining back the woman he loved. But he needed to live long enough to convince her of his intentions.

"She cares for me still." In the lagoon she showed him how much. Her brothers could beat him to a bloody pulp, but he threw the gauntlet. "I tasted it on her lips only moments ago."

"Let me at him," Sam cried.

"Why, you bastard—" Ben hit him again.

Giles threw his arms up to block and sidestepped. Ben hurtled by so fast he lost his balance and nearly ended up in the dirt. An arm grabbed Giles from behind, spinning him around.

"I want you to see it coming."

He saw Sam's fist. Felt it, too. Bugger packed a wallop of a punch. Still, Giles did not hit him back. Next thing he knew, Ben slammed him in the gut. He doubled over.

Holy hell.

"What's the matter, Brit? I expected more of a challenge." Ben lunged with his right. Giles felt the ground bounce off his head.

Kit intervened. "Give me one reason I should not kill you."

Good God, if Kit thought he had to protect his sister's honor, he would fight like a man possessed. Now was the time for Giles to defend himself.

Kit circled three steps, then lunged forward. Giles' intuition had never let him down, so he 'was ready for attack. But Kit did not let up. After several punches to his face and gut, Kit spun around on his boot heel and kicked. Much to Giles' chagrin, he landed in the dirt. The last man to plant him on his arse was Morgan. Damn if Kit didn't fight like his friend.

Pain sliced his side. He crawled from the ground ready to pounce on his opponent.

"Admit you lie. Alex would never . . ." In mid-sentence, Sam swung a fist.

Giles easily avoided the blow. Furious and red with humiliation, Sam tried again.

"You deserve to have your teeth knocked down your throat for defaming our sister." Ben swung the same instant as Sam.

With fists coming from two directions, Giles meant to block Sam and punch Ben. Instead, he struck Sam. Kit shoved into the mix and the three pummeled until all he saw was a blur.

How could he proclaim his love to Alex if her brothers killed him? He had already wasted too much time. Three blasted years for him to come to what little sense he had left. If he could not convince them, or her . . . he refused to even consider the possibility.

No retreat. No surrender.

The motto of his spying days spurred him on. He would have Alex, by God. Nothing less. But, even with his skills, three experienced fighters—two of them nearly equaling his abilities—gave him a pounding.

Gasping with pain, and holding his ribs, Giles climbed onto his knees. Ignoring the jarring pain in his leg, he stood. Every bone in his body ached. He elevated his arms and held out his unsteady fists.

"You got muck for brains, Brit." Ben glared and raised bloody knuckles. At least the man had his share of injury, although Giles figured most of the blood was more than likely his own.

"I love her." He tried again to convince them his intentions were most honorable. "I want to make Alex my wife."

"You already got a wife." Ben threw a fist. Giles heard his bone cheek crunch.

Lying on the ground, he stared at Ben through swollen eyes. "I told you," he gasped. "No vows were spoken."

"Are you going to leave willingly?" Kit ground out. "Or do you need more convincing?"

Seeing the bruise beginning on Kit's face, Giles grinned. A few of his punches had hit their mark. Then he groaned as his split lip screamed in protest.

"Throw the bastard off our land." Veins stood out on Sam's neck.

Giles braced both hands on the ground, palms down, preparing to stand. Maybe his legs would cooperate.

"You're a stubborn cuss, I'll give you that," Kit said with deep breaths. "She is doing just fine without you."

But I am nothing without her.

"I made a mistake." He barely recognized his own voice. Laced with pain, his lungs close to failing, he gasped his next breath.

"Mistake?" Kit repeated. "The only mistake I see is you coming here after I warned you to stay away."

Giles wiped the blood from his eyes. "I will not beg. And I will not go away."

"That's where you're wrong, Brit." Ben growled and raised his fists.

"You left years ago. Too late to change your mind," Sam yelled.

"I never stopped loving her. I will move heaven and earth to make things right." Giles glared from one man to the other, determined to get his meaning across. He would not back down. He would not leave without seeing her.

Kit peered into his eyes as if he could extract the truth from Giles' brain. Long moments passed in stony silence. Good God, would they beat him to a bloody pulp? He feared he had very little left. Ben and Sam seemed to be waiting on Kit. For what, only God knew. Was this to be his end? They had better kill him. For if they left him alive, he would return. Alex was worth every drop he bled.

"Do you know how much time passed before she even laughed again?"

"Kit, damn it." Ben whirled to his brother in surprise. "What are you thinking? Are you insane?"

Ignoring Ben, Kit added, "I will not allow you to inflict more pain."

"You can't be serious," Sam spat.

"The girl hates him. And if she has forgotten what happened three years ago," Ben turned his scowl on Giles, "I will gladly remind her."

Kit appeared deep in thought, wavering, undecided.

Giles shoved to one knee. Burning pain lanced his side.

"I told you to stay down," Ben growled.

He raised his head, focusing on Kit. "I am as good as my word."

"What of your word when you gave it to our sister?" Sam asked.

"I tried to explain." Giles grunted. He might have a broken rib or two. "I never meant to hurt her."

"Well, you did."

"Enough of this. Let's haul his carcass out of here."

Chapter 31

Every day for three years, Alex had prayed to forget. To rip him from her memory. To make the pain a little less. After months of being numb, she finally learned she could function again. After months of her mother's sad eyes and Papa's fierce scowl, she realized what she had put her family through. Her brothers stomped around in their normal huff like bulls in a pasture. They'd roused her from her doldrums and even succeeded in making her laugh. Kit convinced her to put the past behind her.

Life was for the living and one could not live in the past.

Now her past had risen to haunt her.

Only Kit knew how deeply she had suffered when he told her of Giles' wedding. He knew what the information had cost her, understood what Mama and Papa could not. If Giles could not love her, the way she had loved him, it was better to have an ocean between them.

How many times had she wondered if he was happy? If he loved his new wife? The man deserved her ridicule. After three years, the pain had lessened to a dull ache.

And the moment she saw him? All past injustices were forgotten.

She flung open a window in an attempt to cool her flaming cheeks. Her duke was here. Her body warmed at the unwelcome images of his naked flesh. At this rate, she would never be relieved of the oppressive heat. Had she really just left Giles' embrace? Three blasted years and she still craved him. She clutched her arms about her waist. Months ago, she decided to put the whole business behind her. At least her mind had finally accepted what was not meant to be.

Her heart was another matter altogether. Her heart just refused to let go.

She loved Giles as much today, if not more, than when he left. The shiny black curl over his brow made her heart remember too much. Such as how heated his lips were on her skin. How his tongue twined with hers in a dance made only for lovers. How being in his embrace made her safe and warm like no amount of heat from any blazing fire. The fire in his eyes melted her bones.

Appalled, she fell across her bed and grabbed her pillow, burying her nose in the clean smell. His scent drifted into her mind. Sandalwood and leather. And a tang of something which could only be Giles. His heat. His smell. Oh, how she had missed him. Broad shoulders, trim waist, standing so strong and bold like a lean, ravenous beast . . .

Her heart galloped, fast and pounding, the way it did when she raced Stardust hell for leather across the open fields.

She pressed her face into the cushioned pillow, trying to squash his image. Silken and rigid and hot. The yearning in his dark eyes mirrored the longing in her heart. How could she resist when her body cried out for his?

She would have died had he not touched her. Made love with her. Her face flamed at how eagerly she returned his caresses. She'd acted the harlot. Was she scampering down the road to self-destruction?

Their lovemaking had been so intense. Not the joining with an innocent as their first time, but more earth shattering. Souls connecting.

God, would this pain ever go away? Just when she thought she could endure, he had to enter her life again. Foreboding oozed an icy path down her backbone. She could not bear the heartache again.

Guilt cracked the wall she tried to put between them. She had succumbed to him. Surrendered too quickly. How could she have lain with him? Her traitorous body had bent to his will. Oh, but how could a girl take on blame, when such a magnificent creature stood before her in all his naked glory? Of course, she had never seen a demi god. But Giles' perfection surpassed any being in the human world. The powerful magnetism of his devastatingly good looks worked against any resistance. His heated gaze lured her, making the empty years dissolve like ashes to dust.

The heart wanted what the heart wanted.

How cruel to make her ache so.

She shivered. If only she could think clearly. She must be strong and not succumb to triggers of hope. Kill any notion of 'maybe' before those notions grew to real wants and desires.

A part of her she had sworn never to acknowledge again, reared its ugly head. Agony pierced her breast. Pain—as fierce as the day Giles left—stabbed her center. Tears pooled and blurred her vision. She viciously swiped them away.

At twenty-one, she had finally outgrown her fantasy. She had matured, grown stronger. And, she thought, wiser. Her actions of this afternoon were reckless. At least she left with some of her dignity still intact.

She punched the pillow, venting her frustration. *Guilt.* She'd had enough of the blasted compunction controlling her life over the past several years. Nothing seemed so clear-cut anymore. She should have learned her lesson long ago. Today proved that she had lost track of any well intentions.

The knock came a second time before she realized someone was at her door.

"Alex. It's Papa."

Dear Lord. Did he know she had seen Giles? Papa believed his only daughter hated the man who broke her heart.

"Just a minute, please."

She hurried to her vanity to check her appearance. Grabbing a kerchief, she dabbed at her nose. The blasted thing was red. Oh well. She could never fool him anyway. Sitting in her niche by the window, she called, "You can come in now."

He glanced her way, knowing she had not been idly sitting on the window seat. He cleared his throat. "I saw you when you returned. You were riding hard. Left Stardust to care for himself?"

"Sam is cooling him down for me."

"Hmmm."

What did that mean?

"I know you taught me to take care of my horse, but . . . I . . ."

"There is no need to make excuses. If Sam's taking care of Stardust, you must have come to an understanding. I'm just surprised Stardust would let anyone other than you care for him."

What could she say? The duke made her crazy?

"I thought we might have a little talk."

Oh, Lord. She must be in for a lecture. After the lagoon and her disillusionment, she didn't know if she could stomach Papa's displeasure. He sat in a chair and laced his hands between his knees.

"The past three years have not been easy for you. I've watched you, seen the sorrow in your eyes. You changed after Giles left. You were sad, distant. Your spirit was gone."

Uneasiness crept under her skin. Why in the world would he bring this up now?

"I am honest enough to admit I thought you were too young. I accepted what you imagined you felt for the duke as a young girl's infatuation. But more than that, I knew you would not adapt to the English aristocratic way of life."

He pierced her eyes with his stare. "I knew it just as surely as I know the sun is going to come up each morning. I knew one day you would wake up and want to come home." He shook his head. "I wanted to spare you any controversy."

"Papa. That was a long time ago."

"I know, girl. I'm telling you what I felt. I wanted to banish Giles from your mind. I wanted to banish him from your heart. I shouldered the responsibility, and denied my guilt."

Guilt?

What was he trying to tell her? The answer flashed in her mind.

It could not be true.

"Papa?" She swallowed, and forced the words, she intently hoped he would deny. "Did you send Giles away?"

He looked to the window, and back. "Three years ago, I did not want to lose you. I still don't."

"Why are you telling me this *now*?"

He cleared his throat. She had never seen her father as anything but strong. His apprehension baffled her. Whatever he had done, could not be bad. Papa was a good man.

"I've not seen you this excited in three years."

She frowned in confusion. What in the world was he talking about? She thought back to her actions of how she rode home as if her tail was on fire, and jumped off Stardust and left him standing. She probably looked like a madcap when she thundered down the lane to the corral. Surely Kit and Sam didn't say anything. She said not a word to Ben. He knew her temper. He took her horse without asking questions. No one saw her barrel into the house. But her father could have heard her pounding up the stairs, and most likely heard her door slam.

Is that what he calls excitement?

"For a long time, you went through each day as if it was a chore. You moved around here in drudgery. Dull, uninspiring. Stardust was the only thing you seemed to take pleasure in. Even your conduct seemed monotonous. You've not shown any enthusiastic emotion for quite a while. Your spirit is back."

She probably had a dumb expression on her face. Had she been that dreadful? He was right, though. She did feel alive. More than she had in these past three years.

"Something has built a fire in you. And I'm guessing it's the Duke of Nethersall."

Her breath caught in her throat. Her hair stood on the back of her neck.

"If this is a result of what he means to you, then ... I approve."

Approve?

This conversation astounded her. Why in the world—

"Does he make your heart leap?"

In all her born years, her father had never mentioned anything concerning her private feelings. His question stunned her. She wasn't sure if she was more shocked because he asked, or because he knew of her feelings for Giles.

"I guess you love that young man."

A huge weight lifted from her chest. "Oh, Papa. I do."

"Well, then." He slapped his hands together and stood. "What are you waiting for, girl? Go save your man."

Had her father lost his mind?

"What?"

"Those boys have your beau cornered down at the stables. Before I interfere, I wanted to know from you if I should. Do I let your brothers have at him, or do you want me to save his hide?"

Giles was here?

Her brothers ...

Alex charged down the stairs, threw open the front door and ran as fast as her legs would carry her. When she arrived at the stables, no one was there. Then, she heard the shouting. She took off in another direction. She found him in a heap on the ground surrounded by her exasperating brothers. Strong arms grabbed her before she could reach him.

"Giles." Her heart in her throat, she cringed at the bloody mess. "What are you doing here?" Her chest rose and fell at the horror of what her brothers had done. Furious, she tried to jerk free. "Let me go." She stomped the heel of her boot on Sam's shin. He howled and jumped, releasing her. But Kit grabbed her before she took two steps.

She glanced to Giles, desperate in her struggle.

"Stop it," Kit yelled. "You're going to hurt yourself."

She shouted right back. "What is wrong with you three? You've wounded him. Leave him alone!" She was so mad she could spit. Giles looked plumb awful. Blood covered his face, his clothes tattered and dirty. She couldn't believe he had followed her home.

"What are you doing here?" she asked him again as tears filled her eyes.

"I tried to find you," he gasped. "But I got a little side-tracked," he sucked in a breath, "by your brothers." A smile stretched his split lip. He winced.

How could he smile after what they had done to him? She jerked her arm free and dropped to Giles' side.

"Damn it, Alex, get out of the way," Ben roared.

She glared up at her brother. "How could you? You are a beast. Look what you've done."

Ben's face screwed up in guilt. "We did it for you."

"Go away."

"We're not going anywhere." Sam flexed his fists and stepped to Ben's side.

"And we sure as hell are not leaving you with him." Ben pointed a finger at Giles.

"Not happening, little sister." And Kit, supposedly the level-headed one of the bunch. All in on the same assault.

Lord save her, but she wanted to kill her brothers right now.

"Boys."

Three heads whirled around to find Papa at their backs. An angry Papa, by his brooding expression.

"Look what we found, Pap. Sneaking around our property." Ben sounded pleased with himself. The baboon.

If she were bigger, she'd wallop him good.

"You sneaking, Giles?" Papa asked.

"No, sir. Just came to see Alex."

Papa gave a nod of acceptance. "Come on, boys."

"But Pap . . ." At Ben's outburst, Papa turned with a glare. One that said he would take Ben to the woodshed if he talked back.

She brushed the hair away from Giles' face. "Are you all right?"

"I'll live." He wiped at the blood running into his eyes.

"It wasn't very smart to let my brothers get a hold of you." Alex used the bottom of her shirt to clean up his face.

"I concede to your wisdom."

"Oh Giles," she sighed. "What are you doing here?"

He took her hand, caressing the back. "I cannot let you go." His eyes glowed with affection.

Dare she believe? She wanted to believe. But, her heart hurt.

"You desire me." She glanced down at the stroking of his warm fingers over her hand.

He placed a knuckle under her chin and lifted her gaze to meet his. "I love you."

Those three words were all she wanted to hear. His intense gaze made her accept them as true. If she doubted before, only certainty filled her now. Love filled his eyes, promising her deepest desires.

"When you have something as important as love, anything is possible." He squeezed her hand. "I loathed my father. I thought I was free of his bondage. Yet he detained me from the grave with duty and honor. For years I lived by a motto. 'Never give up. Never surrender.'" His thumb brushed her lips, making them tingle. "The one time I needed to remember, the most important thing in the world slipped through my fingers. I gave up. The one person who mattered to me, the only one I ever loved, I let her go."

He lifted her fingers to his lips. He gripped them so tightly, her heart filled to bursting. Tears clogged her throat. His mouth pressed against her knuckles for several minutes. Then, he lifted his head, and what she saw in his eyes struck her heart.

"I ripped my own guts out the day I disavowed my love to you. I thought you were too young, that our love would never last."

"You . . . you didn't trust me."

"You have matured into a woman now. We both are stronger."

"You have to be able to stand up to my brothers. We cannot live in the past." Her voice quivered. "I won't allow you into my heart again."

His hand curved along her jaw. "What words will convince you how sorry I am for my actions years ago? Although I think my leaving may have been the right thing. You were so young."

She stiffened. "Papa told me—"

"I will never leave you again. Even if you send me away, I will not go. I hungered for you every day of the past three years. My love for you clouded my reason. I listened to others. I did what I thought was best for you. Ah, sweetheart. Seeing the pain in your eyes, knowing I destroyed your glow, replacing your love and trust with pain and grief . . ." His hand shook as he cupped her face. "I have walked the corridors of hell, aware of what I did to you."

Lifting her hand, she covered his as it pressed against her cheek. Leaning into his palm, Alex soaked in his warmth along with his words.

"Then today, I saw your eyes, your look of yearning desire, your look of ecstasy. Our coming together only proves you still love me. Let me spend the rest of my life showing you how much I love you."

"I've never stopped."

Whether or not Alex meant to speak aloud, Giles heard her. Words to sooth his ravaged soul. Head still spinning from the last blow, one eye swollen shut, blood running into the other, still he felt no pain. For his adorable nymph loved him. No amount of pain could diminish the warmth of happiness in his thudding heart. He wrapped his arm around her and ignored the twinge in his ribs as he drew her close.

"God, how I've missed you," he whispered, his lips against her temple. "I feel like I have waited forever to hear those words again." His heart soaked up the love she gave him. Her slightest touch gave him the greatest pleasure. He would never tire of holding her. And now, with her admission of what he'd most wanted to hear, by all that's holy he would never leave her again.

"My life had been laid out for me. I have been trained since childhood, destined to live as a nobleman, with strict rules. After my mother died, I became a shell. Empty, allowing no emotion. I need your enthusiasm, your energy, your liveliness." He leaned back and stared deep into her eyes. One finger pushed a strand of hair behind her ear. He gently caressed the fleshy lobe between his thumb and forefinger.

"My love. I love you. Only you. I have never loved another." He pulled her close for a kiss, but her hand lifted to his chest giving slight resistance.

"What if you change your mind . . . again?"

"For God's sake, Alex. I need you like I need my next breath. You are my every wish." He cupped her face with both hands, searing her with the intensity of his longing. "I want to live with you every day. I want you to be the one I fall asleep with at night and wake up to each morning. Together, I want to watch our children grow. I adore you. Everything about you. Even your damn breeches, which I will allow you to wear only for me."

Her fingers lovingly traced over the stubble on his cheek. He leaned his forehead against hers.

"I want you for my wife. For always. Whatever we had before, know from this day forward you are the only woman I will ever love. The only one I will ever need. I am the man for you, the only one to know you and to love you. I want you always by my side." He kissed the end of her nose, then leaned back so she could see his eyes. His gaze pierced hers, letting her know the depth of his devotion. He spoke from his heart.

"I'll give it up, Alex. I will give up my dukedom for you."

A long moment passed before he sensed she comprehended the impact of his words. She gasped.

"You . . . you can't. You are a duke!"

"From this moment forward, all I ask is that I may love you. The aristocracy and nobility and the *ton* can go to hell. You are the only one I care about."

A tear spilled over and slid down one cheek. He caught it with his thumb. She cupped his face, her gaze boring into his. "Will you marry me?"

A grin crossed his puffy lips. "If you will have me."

With a squeak, she gave him a hard kiss. He flinched. "Oh, my poor love. I'm sorry."

"Don't you dare pull away. Come back here." He tugged her onto his lap and cuddled her against his chest, again disregarding the twinge in his ribs.

"Does this mean you will not leave me again?"

While one hand caressed her back, the other massaged her nape. His harsh breathing rumbled and vibrated just below her ear. "Never."

She purred with contentment. Her fingers slipped along the plane of his face, and into the thick strands of his hair. God, he loved her fingers on his scalp.

"Where will we live?"

"Anywhere you want." His heart swelled with happiness.

"Will I be a duchess?"

"My love, you may be the wife of a duke, if that is what you want. We will live in England if you but say so. If you wish to stay in America, close to your family, I will grant you your heart's desire. I have already made a mess of things. I want only you. We will make our home wherever you want. The choice is yours."

"Oh, how I love you." She spread kisses on every cut and swollen wound, mindful of his injuries. With this kind of attention, he could learn to pout a bit.

"Can we stay part of the year in England and part of it here?"

"Of course." He wondered if one's heart could burst with gladness.

Her chest rose and fell in a sigh.

"A duchess. I think I would like that."

Thank You

Thank you for reading my story. I hope you enjoyed reading it as much as I loved writing it.
And, if you did, would you consider leaving a review online? It really would mean the world to me.▢

Thank you!
Samanthya

Book 1 in The Brothers Greystoke Series

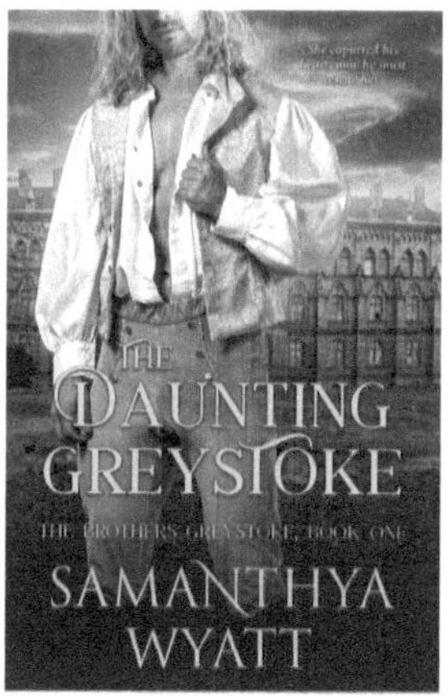

At his brother's insistence, **Nathanial** has returned to
Greystoke Manor; his ancestral home—the prison of his youth.
It is time for him to accept the inheritance he tried to escape
and face the ghosts of his past. Thinking the manse dwelling
deserted, he finds a female hiding in the stables. And so their
unexpected love story begins...

**Order your copy of *The Daunting Greystoke,*
Scan the QR code below!**

Acknowledgements

My deepest gratitude goes to everyone who has helped me along the way to getting my books published, which includes the writing process.

Beginning with my husband, who has been my main support.

I'd like to thank my editors, my publishers and those who helped in marketing my books. A special thank you to the art designers, for my covers are lovely and express the theme in my books.

Thanks to my friends' encouragement, the authors I have met, and every person who bought my books. Thank you for the emails, messages, reviews, words of praise, and likes on Facebook. All were a great source of inspiration.

Keep the Spirit!

Samanthya

About the Author

S amanthya Wyatt writes sizzling hot romance with suspense. Intensely emotional characters with a deep passionate love for friends, family, and most importantly—between the hero and heroine. Although her first love is historical romance, this award-winning author also writes contemporary romance under the pen name S. R. Wyatt. Additionally, she has written a book of one family's struggle based on true life events.

Samanthya left her accounting career and married a military man traveling and making her home in the United States and abroad. She now lives in the Shenandoah Valley. On a sunny day, you can find her and her husband driving on the Blue Ridge Parkway or going to car shows in their 1969 Mustang convertible. She loves long walks, and a book to read on a sandy beach. Starbucks is her favorite drink and she likes hearing from her fans.

She invites you to lay the worries of the world off your shoulders and get lost in the pages of a romance, where you embark on a journey with the hero and heroine, become involved in a dream, plunge into a world of fantasy, and live an adventure your heart can share.

To find out more about Samanthya Wyatt and her books, please visit her website: https://samanthyawyattauthor.com/